Endangered Species

VIKING
Mystery
Suspense

Endangered Species

A Gabe Wager Mystery

REX BURNS

VIKING

M

VIKING
Published by the Penguin Group
Viking Penguin, a division of Penguin Books USA Inc.,
375 Hudson Street, New York, New York 10014, U.S.A.
Penguin Books Ltd, 27 Wrights Lane,
London W8 5TZ, England
Penguin Books Australia Ltd, Ringwood,
Victoria, Australia
Penguin Books Canada Ltd, 10 Alcorn Avenue, Suite 300,
Toronto, Ontario, Canada M4V 3B2
Penguin Books (N.Z.) Ltd, 182–190 Wairau Road,
Auckland 10, New Zealand

Penguin Books Ltd, Registered Offices:
Harmondsworth, Middlesex, England

First published in 1993 by Viking Penguin,
a division of Penguin Books USA Inc.

1 3 5 7 9 10 8 6 4 2

PUBLISHER'S NOTE
This is a work of fiction. Names, characters, places, and incidents
either are the product of the author's imagination or are used
fictitiously, and any resemblance to actual persons, living or
dead, events, or locales is entirely coincidental.

LIBRARY OF CONGRESS CATALOGING IN PUBLICATION DATA
Burns, Rex.
Endangered species / Rex Burns.
p. cm.
ISBN 0-670-84601-5
I. Title.
PS3552.U7325E5 1993
813'.54—dc20 92-50397

Printed in the United States of America
Set in Times Roman
Designed by Brian Mulligan

To Bob and Pepa
Two good reasons why the species
should not be endangered . . .

Endangered Species

"**The fire fighters found it. After cooldown they could go through**
the rooms." Rodríguez, a barrel-shaped man, wore a slicker
striped with silver reflective tape that made him look even
broader through the chest. He wore a large helmet and flash
mask too, and all the equipment added authority to a posture
that said the firemen had done their job right, and it wasn't
their fault somebody died. Homicide Detective Gabriel Wager
nodded and added to his notes. The pumper crew had received
the call at 0312. By the time they arrived, less than eight minutes
later, the small frame house on Wyandot Street was a flare of
orange and red, and every window belched fire. None of the
wide-eyed and disheveled neighbors, awed by the roar and
heat, could tell the fire fighters if anyone was in the building.
"It wouldn't have made any difference anyway," said Rodríguez. "The place was gone." They set up containment and
began pouring water over the roof and walls. There was no
possible way to get through the searing flame that spiraled out
of every doorway, and little hope for finding anything alive if
they could.

"Look like a homicide?" Wager followed the glare of Rodríguez's flashlight and stepped where the fire fighter's boots

smeared ash and mud into the soggy carpet. The floor, like the rest of the structure, was wood, and in places it had burned through. Under his feet, the weakened joists were quivering beneath the weight of bulky firemen, their equipment, and the first wave of official investigators.

"Can't tell. But it was found curled up in a closet."

Which was probably the sign of a futile attempt to escape the flames. But whether accident, suicide, or murder, it was an unnatural death, and unnatural death meant a police report. Wager was the homicide detective on call when the body was found. "Male or female?"

"Can't tell."

The smell of wet, charred wood and burned cloth mingled with the heat of still-smoking embers and fire-blued metal. And another smell too: that of newly burned flesh, a greasy, sweet-fried odor that made Wager breathe shallowly through pinched nostrils. They crowded into a bedroom where the remnant of a door hung open to the black and glistening insides of a gutted closet. Huddled against the indignity of the flashlight's beam, and at the foot of one of the wet and steaming walls, was a cramped shape. In the pitiless circle of pale glare, it was mostly black, like the charred studs surrounding. But here and there splits of pink and white erupted through the baked crust. Wager could see, a darker circle against the flaking ash of the cheek, the socket of one eye. "The medical examiner been called?"

"Yeah." Rodríguez looked up from the tangle of heat-twisted wire hangers and the fallen clothes bar that lay atop the figure. "There's not much to work with."

He nodded agreement. The closet had been a trap rather than a refuge. Disoriented, blinded, choking, the victim could have groped for the bedroom door in the other wall, stumbled across the closet door instead, and, overcome, collapsed to smother in the heavy smoke instead of finding his way out. "How'd the fire start?"

"Don't know yet. Arson won't get here until morning." The

fire fighter glanced at the heavy wristwatch under the cuff of his glove. "Which won't be too goddamn long. You can't see that much at night anyway."

Wager gazed around the once-private room, now invaded by disorder and by figures lumpy with protective gear and bulky equipment. A platform of scorched slats held a futon that had charred and split to spill wads of water-soaked cotton. A broken lamp and a burned and overturned end table had been kicked into a corner. The sheathing had burned off two of the walls, to show fire-blackened two-by-fours that glittered and dripped as if a summer shower had passed over. Through glassless windows and ragged gaps in the outside wall, floodlights from the fire trucks threw streaks and patches of light. He could hear a thunk and creak as fire axes dug for hot spots in the smoldering debris somewhere in the back rooms. There wasn't much he could do in the dark, except to tell Rodríguez to keep everyone away from the closet until the forensics team arrived, which should be soon. He followed the high boots that mashed their way back through the small living room cluttered with fragments of plasterboard from the ceiling and a soggy, half-burned sofa that had been ripped apart in the search for remaining sparks.

Wager crossed the small wooden porch and went down the three steps to the cramped front yard. A clutch of neighbors huddled against the night's chill in robes and blankets and watched in silence. Wager used his GE radio pack to ask the dispatcher for a deputy DA to bring a warrant—the body was on private property, and any possible evidence gathered there had to be legally covered. Then he went over to the knot of silent people.

"Does anyone know who lived here?"

A man whose beard stubble looked like a dark smear of ash on his pale skin glanced at the woman standing beside him. Then he cleared his throat. "Told me his name's John."

Wager had his small green notebook out. "John? Did he give you a last name?"

"No. Hasn't been here long—rented maybe a month ago. John."

That was a problem: Wager wouldn't be able to notify the next of kin until he could identify the victim. "Can I have your name, sir?"

"I guess." The man told him and gave Wager his address. It was the house next door, a small frame building like the burned one, and the rounded eyes of the man and woman said they were staring at the sudden nightmare vision of their own home. The curtained windows behind them reflected the erratic flash of emergency lights as an unmarked official car pulled up. Probably forensics. "My wife saw the fire. Got up to go to the bathroom and saw it and called me. I called the fire engines." His voice dropped. "Seemed like they took a hell of a long time to get here."

The woman, brightly flowered robe gripped tightly at her throat, nodded and spoke in a puff of frosty breath. "Virgil got the garden hose out of the shed and started wetting down our roof. He had time to do all that before they got here."

"Yes, ma'am. Is this John the only person living there?"

This time the woman answered first. "He has some people stay with him now and then. Young people, you know. Visiting him, I think."

"Some? How many?"

"Sometimes one, sometimes two or three—wouldn't you say, Virgil?"

Virgil nodded. "Hard to say for sure. They come and go, and they're quiet. I mean, it's not like one of these party houses or crack houses or whatever you call them. But there's been maybe half a dozen people there one time or another." He added, "A lot of times from out of state. Arizona plates, and Oregon, I remember. Some others too."

Wager glanced up at Virgil. "You go out and look at their license plates?"

The man got defensive. "Sometimes they park their cars in

front of our house. You got to park on the street in this neighborhood, and sometimes parking's hard to find."

"Were the cars there this evening?"

The man's fingernails scratched in his whiskers. "Not when the fire was going. Didn't look like nobody was home." He glanced at the curb where the pumper truck made a steady clatter with its auxiliary engines. Another unmarked automobile was waved past the orange police tape by a uniformed officer. This would be the medical examiner, to say the corpse was a corpse. "There's no cars parked now. Maybe earlier. I can't remember, tell you the truth."

"What about John's car? Do you see it?"

Another squint. "No. Might be down the block—dark car, blue, I think. Like I say, parking's hard to find." The man looked again at the smoking hulk whose roof was half-eaten away. "You telling me he was in there?"

"Someone was."

One of the woman's hands went to her mouth. "Oh, Lord. Oh, Lord, that poor man!"

Virgil cleared his throat. "I—ah—I yelled 'fire.' I couldn't get near the place—it was too hot, and the sparks was coming down on my place. But if I'd of known somebody was in there . . ."

"He was probably dead by the time you saw the fire. Do you know the name of the realtor who rented the house?"

Virgil looked at his wife again. "Miller? Milton? Red-and-blue sign—Milltown Realty?"

"McMillan," said his wife. "McMillan—that was it. Had the sign up for the longest time. Big red 'McMillan Realty.' "

The post office could give Wager a name to go with the address, but most rental agreements also listed the name and address of the nearest relative. Wager elicited enough description of John to help verify the corpse—white male, about six one, maybe one hundred eighty pounds, in his mid-thirties—and went to the next group of staring figures. They lived on the other side of the burned house and told him pretty much the same thing, except that they didn't even know the occupant's first name. But they had heard a fireman say someone had been found inside, and no one wanted to say anything bad about the dead. "He was friendly and all; he waved whenever we saw each other. But we didn't have any reason to talk much."

Wager was finishing with the last of the neighbors when the ambulance team brought the body bag across the small wooden porch and down the steps to lay it on a gurney for the short ride to the vehicle. A few minutes later, one of the forensics people, Archy Douglas, followed. He paused to blow his nose into a wad of handkerchief and glance at the sooty results. Then he stuffed it back in his hip pocket. "Only one thing worse than bloaters or floaters: crispy critters."

"What's it look like to you?"

Douglas shook his head; his strip of balding scalp caught the red and blue of the flashers as the ambulance pulled out for Denver General. "Can't tell. I just had Lincoln take some pictures, and I marked the scene. If we have to, we'll come back tomorrow when there's better light."

The tall, lanky photographer—Lincoln Jones—came down the steps and rubbed wearily at bloodshot eyes. A still camera hung over one shoulder; on the other he balanced a video camera. Nodding to Wager, he told Douglas, "I'm done. Anytime you're ready . . ."

"See you later, Gabe."

Wager, too, was done—for a while. The search for identity and next of kin could start in a few hours, when the various offices and bureaus opened. Now there was only an hour or so left of the night, not enough for sleep, maybe, but at least enough for a shave and a long, hot shower to wash his skin and hair clean of the clinging smell of smoke and other odors.

He could have gone back to Elizabeth's to clean up. After their first three or four months of going together, she had bought him a toothbrush and a razor as an indication that he was welcome to stay at her place. But there was no sense waking her up again by clattering around in her house. Besides, he should check the telephone recorder and yesterday's mail at his apartment. He didn't expect anything—the dispatcher had Elizabeth's number for emergencies, and the mail was never anything but bills and ads. Still, it was his habit to look.

The red light of the answerer gleamed for message waiting, and as he stripped off the smoke-tinged shirt and dropped it into the wicker hamper, he played back the tape. Elizabeth's sleepy voice said, "Hi. If you get this before you go to work, I'll be in meetings all day. If it's after work, give me a call. I don't know what my schedule is for tonight."

That's what he got for shacking up with a city councilperson: someone whose days were as busy and unpredictable as his own. But the warm, slightly husky voice brought an image of her face looking up at him through the half-light, dark hair curling out on the pillow, and the pale glimmer of her teeth between lips slightly swollen from kissing. The image tightened his groin with sudden yearning, and he had that hunger to cling to a living body, a feeling that often came after he'd seen death. Maybe he should go over there. . . . No, not stinking with the odor of smoke and burned flesh. And by the time he showered and shaved, it would be morning anyway.

They had talked about his moving into her home. It was a hell of a lot larger than his apartment, and he spent a lot of time there. But so far it was only talk, and casual at that; they had each lived alone so long that it was difficult to think of sharing all their space and time with someone else. And given the chaos of days that each of them faced, periods of isolation were a necessity.

His trousers had a black smear from brushing against something in the burned house; he set them aside for the cleaners. His sport coat he placed on a hanger, which he looped over the towel rack before stepping into the hot shower. The steam would loosen the smoky odor from the wool, and in a day or so he could wear it again without clamping his lips against the smell. It was a trick he'd learned while he was still in uniform and the cleaning bills ate deeply into his patrolman's pay. The maintenance allowance never had been enough to cover shoe repair and the various rips and stains from cleaning up others' messes. Now he made enough so the steam trick wasn't necessary, but old habits have long life, and that—in a roundabout way—was another reason why he and Elizabeth had decided to keep separate homes and why they steered away from any talk of marriage.

He washed his hair three times before trusting that the smell was gone, then boiled up a cup of coffee as he dressed. Twenty minutes across town, and he would walk in the door of the homicide offices, bright-eyed and bushy-tailed.

Max Axton greeted Wager when he checked in for the regular shift. "Christ, Gabe, you look almost as good as dog puke." A wide finger tapped the brief notice of the unidentified body found in the fire. "You catch this one?"

Wager nodded and sipped at a mug of sour-smelling coffee. No matter how often the coffeemaker was washed out or what brand they changed to, it always smelled and tasted the same. And started each day with the same vicious bite. "Anything from the morgue yet?"

Axton shook his head. His heavy shoulders pushed his collar up a thick neck. "Homicide?"

"Don't know. Doesn't look like it."

"Let's hope not—I've got an interview lined up on Moralez this morning. I could use your help, partner."

Ray Moralez was the latest teenaged victim of the increasing gang violence over on the west side of town. Not too long ago, neighborhood gangs were just bunches of kids who hung around together, drank a little illegal beer, maybe had a few fights to show how tough they were. But west Denver's gangs were becoming big business, with cheap labor and high, tax-free profits from dope. Now there were ties between gangs in L.A. and Denver, Chicago, and Kansas City. There was a viciousness now that spread to younger and younger kids, along with a carelessness about life that, more and more, erupted in quick and deadly violence. The line had become thinner between a bunch of kids hanging out and acting tough and a criminal gang, and as a consequence the room for those kids to bend a few laws had become smaller, the results harsher. Wager didn't know the causes of it—maybe the feeling that the country is crumbling away and nobody gives a shit, maybe throwaway kids whose mothers had them when they were thirteen or fourteen years old, maybe so many people out of work or sweating their *talangos* off for nothing while they see people with connections and power steal millions with the blessings of Congress. Maybe it was from the river of drugs our own government had allowed in to pay for its illegal wars in Central America. Maybe it was the still-echoing effects of that decades-old turmoil called Vietnam. Whatever it was, a feeling of resentment and anger and frustration filled the streets like an evil odor and affected the kids who lived there.

With the Moralez shooting, no witnesses had been found, as usual, and no one wanted to talk to cops. Or at least to Anglos like Axton, and that was where Wager, with his roots in the barrio, came in. "Let me make a couple calls first."

Axton glanced at his watch. "Sure—take your time," he lied.

The first call was to the fire department's headquarters; the arson investigator hadn't reported in yet, but the woman who answered the telephone took Wager's name and number and told him the investigator would get in touch with Wager as soon as he had any conclusions about the fire's origins. The second call was to Denver General and the morgue. The secretary said the pathologist hadn't started yet on that case number. "Dr. Hefley will get to it as soon as he can, Detective Wager. It's the best I can tell you."

Wager tried to keep the impatience out of his voice. "I need to know as soon as possible if it's a homicide or not."

"I understand that, Detective Wager. And I'll tell the doctor."

He thanked her and hung up.

"No luck?" Axton was shrugging into his jacket.

"He's in no rush. Victim's health insurance ran out." Wager drained the bitter coffee, rinsed his mug in the break room's small sink, and hung it on its peg to dry. "Let's go talk to your snitch."

They parked the unmarked cruiser in front of a two-story brick building that filled a busy corner on Tejon Street. Here and there, in the rows of windows that punctured the blank walls, potted plants—geraniums of the same bright-red shade—sat on the whitestone sills. They were probably all cloned from a single plant; Wager could remember his mother's kitchen window and the jars of cloudy water that held cuttings from a friend's geranium she'd admired. As a kid, he used to watch for the first tiny wisp of root at the ragged tip of the pale twig, and when the water was filled with a swirl of white roots, like coarse, bleached hair, he and his mother would gingerly transplant the fragile plants into wax-paper cups filled with rich, black earth. Then, when the scalloped leaves grew wide and dark with health, the plants would be set out in the warm sun of late spring to form an avenue along the entry walk. Here, where there were no walks, the red flowers perched in the windows like bright targets in a shooting gallery.

The desk was vacant, the lobby almost bare. It had a tired, worn feeling, but it was reasonably clean; Wager had seen much worse. High in a corner, a silent black-and-white television with an ill-adjusted horizontal hold slowly rolled its image frame by frame over the screen. A couple of Naugahyde chairs, sagging and wrinkled from too much use, faced the grainy screen. On the stained plaster beside an old-fashioned mirror was a large poster of a Hispanic youth in a black beret wearing some kind of olive-drab uniform. He clenched his fist against a threatening red glow, and under the figure, raw brush strokes spelled a black "Vinceremos!"

"Everybody's on a crusade," said Wager.

"Yeah. Well, some of these people, that's all they have, Gabe. They're alienated from society's normal avenues of change, and their traditional family values are breaking down."

Wager never liked it when Axton talked like a goddamned sociologist—one of those people who made up labels for everything and understood nothing. "Sure, man—tha's why we off the peegs when we're deprived of offing each other, man."

Max's large head wagged, but he didn't push it. He'd been Wager's partner long enough to know that the smaller man didn't like to hear excuses for criminal behavior. And to Wager, the word "family" meant only the Denver Police Department.

"What room's she in?" asked Wager.

"Two-oh-three." His partner had never said much about it, but Axton knew Wager's divorce had put a lot of distance between him and his own family, especially his mother, who had liked Wager's wife. And the death years later of Wager's longtime girlfriend, Jo Fabrizio, hadn't left many people in Wager's world. Maybe this new woman—City Councilperson Elizabeth Voss—was helping. His partner had been dating her for half a year now, and what little Max had seen of the woman, he liked. And apparently Wager did too; he wasn't the kind of man to spend any time with anyone he didn't like. Wager had met her on the Councilman Green homicide, and at the time, Max had thought they didn't like each other. But then, Max had to admit, Wager wasn't the easiest guy to get close to; you had to understand his compulsion to do the job better than anyone else—a textbook case of overcompensation for the insecurity Gabe felt at growing up half Anglo, half Hispanic. You just had to understand those things, and when you did, you could see Gabe was good people. And there was no one at all that Max would rather have back him up in a tight spot—you could trust the man, and that's what Max told his wife whenever she got going about his partner.

Well, Wager and Elizabeth might have started out rubbing each other wrong, but that, Max figured, was because they were alike in a lot of ways. Which, he also figured, was why that dislike had turned to mutual respect and maybe even something more.

A span of scarred and uncarpeted stairs lifted to the dimly lit landing. At the top, they turned left. Wager found the number and rapped on the door. From an apartment down the hall came the mumble and the long, music-filled pauses of a soap opera. From somewhere else, the squawk and loud laughter of a game show. But Vickie Salazar's apartment remained so quiet they heard the cautious squeak of a floorboard. Wager had the feeling someone was peering through the peephole. Finally, a dead bolt grated, and the heavy door opened to a length of security chain above a brown eye. "Who're you people?"

"You're Miss Salazar?"

"Yes. What you want?"

Axton showed his badge. "I'm the one you talked to on the phone."

The door closed and then opened just quickly enough to let them in. Wager and Axton crowded into the narrow entry that led past a doorless closet to a sunlit room divided by a breakfast bar into a kitchen and a living area. A foldaway bed had not yet been made up into the couch. Cigarette smoke spread from a wavering column that rose out of an ashtray on a magazine-littered coffee table and layered the closed room with haze. In a corner, the small television set had its volume turned down to a whisper so the woman could listen to the sounds of the hallway.

"This is Detective Wager. Miss Salazar."

They touched fingers like a couple of boxers.

"I heard of you," she said. "You're Charlene Quintero's cousin, right?"

The name was familiar to Wager. Second or third cousin, maybe—his grandmother's sister married a Quintero, so it was likely. His mother kept book on all that family stuff. Wager figured he had marriage or blood ties to half of Hispanic Denver. But the only time it meant anything was when he used to get an occasional call from some relative who needed something from the police. Then Wager had had to put two of his cousins in the Canon City prison, which didn't do much for his relationship with the family, and even those calls had stopped.

Max sat on one of the wooden stools at the tiny breakfast shelf, and it gave a startled groan as the heavy man settled. "You told me you had something on the Moralez shooting."

"Yeah, I got something—Flaco Martínez. He's the one did it."

"How do you know, Vickie?"

"Everybody knows. The whole barrio. You ask anybody." Ignoring the smoldering butt in the ashtray, she rattled another cigarette from the pack and lit it with a match, striking the head toward her like a man.

"We have," said Wager. The woman was somewhere in her mid-twenties, though the dark circles under her eyes made her look older and Wager thought she was a little on the scrawny side too, which added a few years. "All the people we talked to didn't know anything. Now all of a sudden you do."

"You go find Flaco. You ask him where he was at when Raimundo got hit."

"He was your man?" asked Wager.

Her shoulders under the baggy sweatshirt sagged, and she stared for a long moment at the large patch of naked weave that showed where the carpet took the most wear. "Was. Yeah."

Max cleared his throat. "Did you actually see Flaco shoot Ray?"

"Nobody saw it. You know that."

Wager corrected her. "Nobody's told us they saw it." He strolled to the window and lifted a side of the gauzy white curtain to peer down at the traffic on Tejon. The threads felt stiff, more like plastic mesh than cloth. "That's why you're dropping the dime on Flaco?"

She shrugged and then said angrily, "I don't owe that *pendejo* nothing! I heard it from my *compañera*—she asked me did I know Flaco killed Raimundo. She says she heard it from her man."

"Names?"

"No. No names."

Wager had seen the woman's hand and the dark-blue gang symbol tattooed on the smooth flesh between thumb and forefinger. She was taking a big chance to tell them anything, especially here in the neighborhood, where every kid over the age of eight would recognize the unmarked police car at the curb. He could understand why she didn't want to name her best friend and the boyfriend, but the case would need corroboration and—if possible—an eyewitness. "All this Flaco will have to do is say he wasn't there."

"But he killed Raimundo. I'm telling you, he's the one killed him!"

"You may know it, and I may know it," said Wager. "But we got to prove it in front of a judge and jury who won't know it. We need a witness for that."

"Goddamn it, you bust our people all the time and you got no goddamn witnesses! What is this shit?"

"Murder," said Wager. "Premeditated and first degree."

"Miss Salazar," said Axton soothingly, "we'll arrest Martínez—we can bring him in and ask him questions. But without some kind of evidence to justify a charge, we can't even serve papers on him, let alone take him to trial."

Her stiff jab broke another cigarette in the ashtray. "I don't know who saw him do it! I just heard it was him, that's all!"

Wager walked away from the window and looked down at her. "So find out who saw him. Find out who heard Flaco brag about it."

"What the hell you supposed to be doing? You're the goddamn cops—you want me to do your fucking job for you, that it?"

Axton pulled out his notebook and clicked a ballpoint pen. The tiny mechanical noise punctuated the tenseness of the woman's silence. "What can you tell us about this Martínez, Miss Salazar? Where he lives, who he runs around with, where he hangs out?" Wager and Axton needed the information, but equally important, the questions turned her anger away from them and back on her boyfriend's killer.

From what she said, Wager guessed that Flaco Martínez was another of those criminals whose careers were just getting under way; most likely, a police computer—the contact file—would hold a little more information on him: aliases used, criminal convictions, time served, any instance where Martínez's name had turned up in conjunction with other investigations. But there were a lot of things the computer wouldn't know that people in the barrio would, and if Vickie Salazar really wanted to nail Flaco Martínez, she'd find out those things.

All that she could or would tell them now was the kind of information that drifted through the barrio on whispers and boozy gossip at corner tables or behind pulled blinds. It would be overheard by the women, either because the men were drunk enough to talk loudly or because they wanted this or that one to be impressed without bragging openly in front of her. And the women passed it on to one another for the same reasons: "My man was there, *chica;* here's what he saw go down . . ." "That *cabrón* Flaco, he told my man . . ."

Flaco Martínez had been in Denver a few years, but no one seemed to know much about him. He'd come up from Albuquerque, claiming to be a member of Los Puñales, one of that city's smaller gangs, which claimed some territory on the north side. Something about running from a murder charge, but nobody knew for sure. Flaco didn't deny it; the whisper helped his image. He said he had contacts down there who could bring up stuff for the local market: weed, Mexican brown, a little ice, maybe, and even peyote from off the reservation. It's a good market, Denver, and he wanted to expand, and that's where he started stepping in shit with the locals, who had their own ideas about whose territory it was. So what he did was make some promises to the Gallos, and that started trouble with the Tapatíos, Ray Moralez's gang. Vickie Salazar spoke only in general terms about the causes of the war, and neither Wager nor Axton pushed her on that; if she was forced to choose between giving the cops information on her own people and letting Flaco walk, it would be the latter. She finally told them what neighborhood Flaco lived in—but she didn't know the address—and the bar where he liked to hang out, La Taverna Chihuahua. "Him and three, four others. They pretend they got colors, you know? Hang around a lot with some of the Gallos. Bunch of *bobos!*"

Max asked, "Names?"

She thought a moment. "Sol. I don't know the others."

"Does he have a *chunda?*" Wager asked.

The thin shoulders rose and fell under a sweatshirt stenciled with a sunny palm tree and the name Venice Beach. "I don't know. *Maricón* like that don't have enough to have a *chunda* with."

Max didn't ask until they were on the sidewalk and getting into the car. "What's a *chunda?*"

"Girlfriend. Lover."

The big man glanced over his shoulder at the traffic as he pulled out. "Think any of this is reliable?"

"Only one way to find out." Besides, it was the only lead they had.

• • • • • • ;

The Chihuahua tavern was in the southwest corner of Denver, just across the line of District Four. On the way, they called in Flaco's name for anything the computer might have. The report came back as Axton pulled their drab white vehicle into the bar's parking lot, a small square of muddy gravel. As Wager suspected, the information didn't add up to much: a few rumors and whispers of a tie-in with a couple of drug dealers, an investigation for assault that was dropped at the victim's request, a reference to the Albuquerque PD for further information.

Max made a note to himself to call New Mexico when they got back to the office, then they picked their way across the parking lot to the bar. It was flat-roofed and stuccoed with grimy tan plaster and looked vaguely southwestern. The door was sunk in the corner and stood open to a stale-smelling interior. A long mirror, smeared with a wipe or two, reflected a row of bottles behind the counter. This early in the morning, the place was almost empty. A pair of men sat hunched at one end of the bar. An old man bent over a short broom to dig out last night's detritus from a corner and sweep it toward the door. In the glow of a small desk lamp set near the cash register, the bartender leaned to check figures in an account book. He looked up, baggy eyes going flat as he smelled cop.

Axton flipped his badge case over a forefinger and snapped it closed again. "We're looking for Flaco Martínez. Seen him around?"

"Who?"

"Flaco Martínez. He hangs out here with Sol and a couple other buddies."

The man frowned and scratched at his ledger with a ballpoint pen. Nobody wanted a snitch label—they were easy to get and never went away.

Wager eyed the line of bottles. Many held varieties of tequila and mescal, complete with pickled worm. The bar's license was posted on the wall under the mirror. He leaned over to read it. "You're George Urbano?"

He looked up from the page. "Yeah."

"Don't make us hassle you, George. We don't want to go to the trouble. And you don't want that kind of trouble."

"I don't make no trouble, man."

"You don't make no answers, either." Wager glanced at his watch: half after nine. The various offices would be open now, and he could start the process of identifying last night's corpse. "You tell us where Flaco lives, we're out of here. You don't tell us, we keep coming back." He nodded down the bar toward two men who tended their own business in careful silence. "Your customers won't be comfortable with that."

Urbano, too, glanced down the bar. Then he made up his mind. "A guy they call Flaco comes in sometimes. I don't know his last name. I don't know where he lives."

"Who's he drink with?"

A shrug. "I don't know their last names, either. Sol and Dave, that's all I heard."

"They belong to a gang?"

"Not in here they don't." He jerked a crooked thumb toward

a sign above the long mirror: NO COLORS SERVED. "What they do outside is up to them."

It was the way a lot of neighborhood taverns tried to stay neutral in the turf wars. Sometimes it worked; a number of the gangs were mostly made up of kids below legal drinking age anyway. But a number weren't, and a lot depended on how tough the bartender was and how tough the gang wanted to act.

"He drinks with the Gallos?"

"If you say so."

"All right. When Flaco comes in, you tell him we were here asking about him."

Max handed the baggy-eyed man a business card. "You tell him we said he better come down and talk with us."

Urbano glanced at the name. "If I see him."

In the car, Max sighed. "I guess we have to go talk to Fullerton."

Wager felt his cheek twitch in a tiny smile. Fullerton, the Gang Unit's sergeant, was like flypaper. When you had to see the man about something, you got stuck there. "What's this 'we' stuff, honkie? It's your case."

Another sigh. "I figured you'd say that."

Back at the Crimes Against Persons offices, Axton checked his box for messages and then headed upstairs to Intelligence and Fullerton's desk. Wager settled down at the telephone.

The forensic pathologist still hadn't gotten to last night's victim. The secretary said he would probably be in around ten. She'd be happy to call Wager when Dr. Hefley was finished. Another secretarial voice said the arson squad was on the scene now. They should have some preliminary information by this afternoon. Wager was looking up the McMillan Realty number when his telephone rang. "Homicide. Detective Wager."

"This is your favorite *Denver Post* reporter, Wager. I understand you were on duty last night. How about filling me in on that fire victim."

The only thing Wager wanted to fill in for Gargan was his grave. But just last week Chief Sullivan had sent a memo to all personnel reminding them to cooperate as much as possible with the press. Improved public relations, the memo said, would be a departmental priority. Wager figured the brass hadn't been getting enough favorable newspaper clippings lately. "No identification yet, Gargan."

"Was it a homicide? Arson? What?"

"I don't know yet. All I have so far is a fire and a body—still unidentified, cause of death unknown."

"And of course you'll call me as soon as you know something more." He didn't wait for the answer. "What about the Moralez gang shooting? Any more on that?"

"I don't know a thing about it."

"Come on, Wager. Goddamn it! I know you and Max are working that one. It's news, and the public's got a right to know!"

Wager reasoned sweetly. "I'm not working it, Gargan. It's not my case. But we do have a public information officer, who will be overjoyed to give you whatever facts the investigating officer is free to reveal."

"You're a real bastard, Wager."

"I think highly of you too, Gargan."

As soon as he hung up, the telephone rang again, and he answered with disgust still in his voice, "Detective Wager, homicide."

"Gabe? That you?"

Well, yeah, it was; nobody else in the division was named Wager. "What do you need, sir?"

"It's me, Gabe!"

The voice was kind of familiar, but he couldn't place it. "Fine, 'me.' What do you need?"

A brief, hurt silence. "It's me: Stovepipe. You know—Henry Stover?"

"Stovepipe! It has been a while, Henry." Almost three years, in fact, since the man went to Canon City on a burglary charge.

"Yeah! Tell me about it. Look, man, I just got out. I'm in a halfway house, you know? But I wanted to thank you, you know, for helping out with my mother."

Stover was a burglar who claimed to be reformed, and a good thing. One more conviction, and he faced a long time in a small space. He had given Wager a key tip on a knifing four years back. He didn't do dope, he hated violence, and, except for an overwhelming curiosity about locked doors and other people's goodies, was—given the circumstances—a fairly reliable citizen. At least that's what Wager told the judge at sentencing. But Stovepipe also had a spotty record—a string of juvenile stuff, mostly car snatching—and already one stretch for B and E. He could have been hit with ten years on this arrest, but he got off with six, less good time. This was his last bust, he'd promised Wager; when he got out, he was going straight. He had some money saved up that the IRS didn't know about— "I earned it, Gabe. I've paid for it, man!"—and his mother was getting pretty old and weak. He didn't want to cause her any more hurt. So when he got out, he was going to get a job; he was going to buy a little house in the country for him and his mother. "She grew up on a farm, Gabe. And Denver's getting too big, you know? It's dangerous, too, especially for somebody getting old like that. I want to get her and me a little place where we can raise some chickens and I don't have to see any goddamn walls." He was going to be a genuinely righteous citizen; prison just wasn't worth it.

Now he was out on early release.

"Anyway, Mother said you called a couple times to see how she was getting on, and I just wanted to say I appreciate it, Gabe. It meant a lot to her. And to me too, man."

A lot of cops went out of their way for the families of prisoners. It didn't show up on the fitness reports, and it didn't count in the public-service column of the official-activities sheets. But it answered an urge that was one of the reasons many people went into law enforcement in the first place: to help people in trouble. Besides, sometimes the perps' families had been ripped off as much their victims. And Wager had another reason too—the care and training of a good snitch. "No problem, Stovepipe. How's her health?"

"It's OK—it's basically fine. She's just getting old. There's all sorts of crap when you get old." He cleared his throat. "I wanted to tell you, too, I think I got a job lined up. The counselor here says he can get me work as a janitor in a electronics plant up around Brighton. It's a start, man."

"That's fine. Just don't use it for casing hits."

"No way, man. I'm not even thinking like that anymore. That kind of shit does not even cross my mind!"

"Glad to hear it. Anything I can do to help out?"

"No—I don't think so. I mean, maybe, you know, if somebody wants a character witness for me . . . You know, like you did with the judge."

"I'll be glad to. Just let me know who to write or who to talk with when the time comes."

"Thanks, Gabe—come on around sometime. Be good seeing you, and Mother'd be real happy to meet you."

"I'll do that, Stovepipe. Welcome back." Wager hung up, certain that wasn't the last he'd hear from the man but hoping that when he did hear, it would be good news. With luck, Stovepipe would make it. Some ex-cons did. It was in the man's favor that he wasn't an addict, and maybe he could turn things around for himself. One of the few drawbacks of working homicide was that most of the people Wager was called on to help couldn't say thank you. And the people he ran across after their discharge from Canon City were usually on their way back to jail for another murder. It would be nice to know one ex-con who was changed for the better.

McMillan Realty's office secretary had a perky, friendly voice that made buying and selling houses sound like fun. She told him that the realtor who handled the property in that block of Wyandot was Sandy Ebert but she was out of the office right now. Would Detective Wager care to leave a message?

"I need to know who owns the house." He explained about the fire. "Is there any way I can get in touch with Miss Ebert?"

"Oh, that's awful! Just a moment, Officer. I can look at the file for you." Her voice came back to tell him that one Gail Weil had bought the house almost two months earlier.

"Do you know if she lived there or if she rented it?"

"No, sir. All I've got is a file copy of the sales contract."

"Can you tell me what bank she borrowed from?"

"Sure. Citizen's Bank of Denver. Their mortgage and loan office handled it."

He thanked the secretary and asked her to give his message to Sandy Ebert. Then he called the bank's mortgage and loan desk and headed for the elevator down to the garage.

The loan application not only listed references and a next of kin but also told him that Gail Weil's current home address wasn't where the fire had taken place.

"She told me she was buying it as an investment property, Detective Wager." The loan officer was a short woman in her late twenties or early thirties. Her long, dark hair made her seem even shorter. "It was a VA foreclosure and needed some work, but she thought it would make a good lease property."

"You don't know who she might have rented it to?"

"No. She makes the payments, and they've been on time." She added, "Of course, there've only been a couple."

"Have you called to tell her about the fire yet?"

"I called the insurance company right after I heard from you. I suppose they're the ones to call the property owner." A small, relieved smile. "The policy covers the market value of the property. We require that as a condition of the loan."

"Borrow your phone?" The dark-haired woman nodded, and Wager dialed the number on the loan application. After three rings, Gail Weil answered, and Wager mentally crossed her name off the list of possible victims. He told her about the fire and asked if he could come by.

"Fire? My property—it burned down?"

"I understand your insurance company's already been notified. Will you be at home in the next half hour, ma'am?"

"My new house? The one I just bought?"

"Yes, ma'am. Are you going to be at home?"

"My God! How did it start? Who did it?"

"I'll be over in a few minutes, ma'am."

"My God—that's my property! How—"

Wager hung up and thanked the loan officer. Gail Weil was waiting for him when he pulled to the curb in front of her house. On Ivanhoe a block north of busy Colfax, it was one of those English brick cottages with steeply pitched roof and arched front door that were supposed to remind people of a castle. What it reminded Wager of was a Sinclair gas station that used to be near his home when he was a kid. In fact, Ms. Weil looked like a pump jockey. She wore a tan jumpsuit with short sleeves, and her graying straight hair was combed back from the forehead and cropped at her neck. She didn't glance at Wager's badge case when he introduced himself.

"I called the insurance company. They told me it was a total loss!"

"Yes, ma'am. It looked that way."

"My God! I'll never get my investment back!"

"You'll want to talk to the insurance company and the bank about that, ma'am. Could you tell me—"

"I did! I told you that. All that man would tell me was that he'd get back to me. Wouldn't tell me anything, and I can't make heads or tails out of that policy, the way they put things in language a body can't read!"

"Can you tell me—"

"I didn't have a replacement clause. It was covered for the market value—I had to have market value when I used it for collateral. But I don't know if that's enough for replacement, and that insurance man wouldn't tell me. . . ."

"Ma'am—Ms. Weil—I need your help. Somebody was killed in that fire."

"Killed! Oh, my God! Killed? The insurance man didn't say anything about that!" She clapped both hands to her cheeks and stared at Wager with wide eyes. "I'm not responsible for that—you can't arrest me for that!"

"I'm not here to arrest you, lady. I just want to know who rented the place. I'm trying to identify the victim."

Her mouth snapped shut, lips making a hollow click. "Name? Of the renter?"

"Yes, ma'am. Can you tell me who you rented it to and who lived there?"

"Marshall. Just a minute." She left Wager standing on the small, unsheltered slab of concrete that served as a porch to the cottage. He heard drawers sliding and papers rustling. Then she came back and read from a legal-size sheet of paper marked with heavy type and a lot of blank spaces filled in by pen. "John Marshall. He rented it by himself, and as far as I know he lived there by himself too."

"Does he list a previous address?"

"Oceanside, California. North Tremont Street—951." She asked, "Is that who died? Mr. Marshall?"

Wager looked up from his notebook. "We're not sure yet. Any next of kin listed?"

"His mother. He put her down as a reference: Elizabeth Marshall. Same address in Oceanside."

"Can you tell me what he looks like?"

"Young, but not too young. Maybe thirty, more or less. Had kind of long brown hair but not real long. Not like a hippie, you know. He seemed nice enough, I guess."

Wager found himself using the past tense too. "Did he have any facial hair?"

"No."

"Wear glasses? Rings? Any jewelry?"

"Not that I recall. I didn't really notice that."

"Do you know the names of anyone who might have been living with him?"

"No. I told you, he rented it by himself."

"The neighbors said several other people stayed there from time to time. He never mentioned any names?"

"No. But it was his house. To use, I mean. If he wanted people staying with him, that was up to him. That don't break any laws, does it?"

"No, ma'am. Was he tall? Short? Fat? How would you describe him?"

"Taller than you. Maybe six feet. Kind of slender but not what you'd call skinny."

"Did he put down his work address?"

She looked at the blanks on the lease agreement. "Crystal Pure Chemical Corp., 11589 San Bernardino Boulevard, Los Angeles."

"Did he tell you anything about his work?"

"Said he was a salesman—an area rep, he called it." She added. "Said he traveled a lot."

"Did he pay by check or cash?"

"Cash. The damage deposit and three months' rent. The next month's not due yet."

"Three months? You require three months' rent up front?"

"No. That was the way he wanted it. Said he might be out of town when it was due and wanted to make sure it was covered."

Wager nodded. "Anything else you can tell me about him?"

"No. No complaints. He just looked around the place and said it was fine and he'd take it."

"Was it furnished?"

"Stove, refrigerator, washer and dryer. He said he'd get his own furniture." She thought about that. "I don't know if the appliances are covered in the insurance, either."

"Did he say if he'd rent the furniture?"

"No. I didn't ask."

"And you didn't go by the house to see how he was getting on?"

"No. His rent's paid, and the house is his to use. I was a renter for a long time, and I never did like landlords coming by all the time and snooping. And then when something went wrong, they couldn't be found."

Wager thanked her. As he turned to go, she said, "I don't have any liability for him. If anybody's liable, it's Marshall himself."

"Sounds fine to me, ma'am."

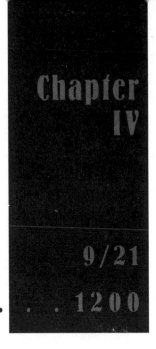

Doc Hefley had been expected at the morgue around ten, so he should have been working on the body by noon. Wager went south and took Eighth Avenue across town to Denver General. The usual crowd of limping, dragging, and halting figures clustered in the shade of the hospital's long covered walkway to wait for relatives or Handi-Vans to pick them up. Inside, the large echoing lobby always reminded Wager of a train station crowded with Denver's poor of all races. Just beyond the entry, Wager turned past the desk that provided both information and security. A bored guard surveyed people entering and kept an eye on the escalators leading up to the second level. The lobby noise was a steady shuffle on polished stone, worried voices in a variety of languages, the echoing wail of a crying baby. In a way, the building *was* a busy depot, except that the place a lot of the travelers were headed for wasn't on the map and they wouldn't be coming back.

The morgue was in the cool, windowless basement. A shortcut led through an unmarked door, down an ill-lit stairway, and along a maze of halls to the reception room. The secretary saw him through the glass and answered before Wager could ask the question. "He's working on it now, Detective Wager. I told him you were in a hurry."

"Thanks." He followed the dark-paneled L-shaped hall back past the pathologists' offices to a cramped lounge. There, morgue assistants waited between jobs to watch television and eat sandwiches. An open doorway on the far side led to the examining room. At the nearest end of the room, a ramp sloped to the ambulance bay, and a concrete-block wall half-hid a faintly hissing gas furnace, used to cremate bits and pieces. At the other end of the room was a narrow hallway to the viewing station. Making up part of the far wall, like a large built-in filing cabinet, stainless-steel cadaver drawers formed three long rows starting at the floor and reaching as high as two men could lift a body. On the end closest to the delivery ramp, two larger drawers were designed to hold awkwardly stiff or swollen bodies that wouldn't fit the normal space.

The rest of the wall was a narrow, waist-high workbench backed by a supply cabinet whose glass doors reached to the ceiling. In the center of the brightly lit room, three stainless-steel dissecting tables were anchored above floor drains whose chrome winked in the tile. Doc Hefley stood at the middle table, bending over a charred, stiffly contorted body. In the cold fluorescent glare, it looked like something left too long on the barbecue.

"Wager." Hefley turned from the microphone that dangled over the body. "I should have known who it was when Sharon said Homicide kept calling about this one."

"I need an ID, Doc. Somebody somewhere will have to be told."

"Somebody somewhere will have to wait. I'll do what I can to get fingerprints, but the hands are burned so badly, I don't think anything's left. My guess is it'll take a forensic dentist to establish a definite ID."

Wager nodded and tried not to notice the smell. An X-ray machine on an extension arm hovered above the corpse. Wager watched as Hefley, without touching the victim, scanned the remains carefully, muttering into the microphone. The torso and arms were clenched something like a boxer—the usual "pugilistic attitude" caused by heat-contracted muscles. "Did the forensics crew get photographs of the site?" Hefley asked.

"Archy Douglas said he'd have them back this morning."

"I ought to go look at the site, Wager. But goddamn it, I don't have time." He nodded at the rows of steel drawers. "There're four more jobs waiting in there, and everyone else is in a hurry too." He didn't add what Wager already knew: that Hefley was the only forensic pathologist currently available to the City and County of Denver. The latest spate of vicious politics and ineptitude among the hospital's managers was taking its toll. The mayor, of course, claimed nothing was wrong —the chief administrator was his appointee—but Elizabeth had told Wager that a real scandal was building in the mayor's office over the hospital administration's failures.

"The victim was found in a closet." Wager described the site as he remembered it.

"Any debris around the body?"

"Some hangers. The clothes bar. Hard to tell about anything else—ashes and muck, mostly."

"I'll look at Archy's photographs. That'll have to do."

A buzz interrupted the background silence, and Hefley fished wet X-ray plates from the developer. He pinned them in a row to the screen's white surface and began studying the hazy blobs and smears of white and gray. Wager could identify some of the larger bones in a couple of the negatives, but Hefley was busy peering at shadows and dark spots that meant little to the detective.

"Any foreign objects?"

"Don't see any."

"Fractures?"

"Yeah." He pointed to a crooked line in a long streak of white. "Ulnar fracture. But it might have been caused by sudden muscular contraction. Fires are a bitch that way, especially hot ones."

"Did it happen before or after death?"

"As tight as this body's clenched, it could easily be after." He moved to another plate. "Well, now . . ."

"Something?"

He tapped a pencil at another smear of shadow. "Bit of extradural hemorrhage here." The doctor muttered something into his microphone. "Fire this hot, Wager, you can get postmortem fracture of the vault of the skull, resulting from transudation of blood between the dura and calvarium." He glanced at the detective. "That means the brain steams and cracks the skull open. Ever cooked clams?"

Wager hadn't. Didn't want to, either. "But you say that's postmortem."

"Right. The victim would have died of smoke inhalation before the brain boiled. But here's something interesting." The pencil tip moved to another shadowy area, about the size of Wager's thumb. "A depression at the base of the skull. Now, that kind of fracture doesn't come from steaming."

"Antemortem or postmortem?"

"Where in hell'd you learn all your Latin, Wager? Parochial school?"

"Some. But a lot of it's like Spanish too."

"By God, you're not as dumb as you look, are you?" Hefley spoke while he studied the plate. "It could be antemortem. And it could be either the primary or a secondary injury—a falling beam, for example. Maybe that metal clothes bar you told me about. That's one of the reasons I should view the site. But we'll know better when I check the blood for carbon monoxide." The man made a note on the plate's margin with a red grease pencil and then began pulling on chain-mail gloves, whose tiny rings looked heavy and oiled. The steel gloves were supposed to keep a pathologist from nicking his hands with a scalpel and infecting himself with AIDS.

"Did you see any external wounds?"

"Christ, Wager, this cadaver's one big wound."

The doc knew what Wager meant, but like a lot of people who handled corpses—including cops—he had his tough act. Wager watched as the man made long slices into the torso's stomach and chest and then gingerly stuck a needle into the victim's heart. The syringe's tube filled with dark blood. "Good. Sometimes there's no blood left in a fire victim—cooks away, and you have to use bone marrow. But this is real nice." Hefley labeled it and placed it in a tray of still-empty vials. "The lab will tell us how much carbon monoxide's in the blood. More than forty-five percent, and we can blame death on the fire." He held up a pair of stubby snips and squeezed them a time or two. "Less than that, and we presume the victim stopped breathing before the smoke began. And that, Detective Wager, means that little trauma at the base of the skull becomes very important."

Hefley plunged the snips into the open cut and began clipping. "Now comes the weighing of organs. You want a little fried liver?"

"No. Can you estimate his height and weight?"

"Who says it's a he?"

Wager looked at the starkly illuminated figure with its contrast of black crust, spongy pink interior, and white bone. "It's a female?"

"Somewhere in her twenties, I'd guess. And a guess is all it is, so far. Good, healthy musculature, normal internal organs —if a bit well-done." He used a pair of tongs to lift something out and lay it in the pan scale. When the needle settled on a number, he stepped on the recorder pedal and muttered into the microphone. Then he took it out of the pan and placed it in a shallow stainless-steel bowl, to be sectioned for further tests.

"Can you look for evidence of rape?"

"I know my job, Wager."

"I mean, is there enough left to determine if the victim was sexually assaulted?"

"External evidence, no. Internal, probably." He peered toward the head area, at a part of the body Wager couldn't see. "Except the mouth—throat's pretty well burned through. Won't be able to tell until I get there."

Wager took his word for it. "The house was rented by a man. That's who I thought this was."

Hefley used the cuff of his chain-mail glove to scratch at his nose. "That adds to the possibility of a homicide."

It was finally Wager's turn. "That's pretty damned obvious, isn't it, Doc?"

Back at his desk, Wager first phoned Information in Oceanside, California. There was no listed number for a Marshall on Tremont, and the operator wouldn't take Wager's word that he was a cop and needed to know about a possible unlisted number. His next call was to the Oceanside PD. As he waited for that to be shunted to the right desk, Wager had vague memories of Camp Pendleton and the sun-washed beach city that was home to so many marines living off the base. Aside from the flat expanse of sea that stretched away from the sandy cliffs, the only part of the town he clearly recalled were the bars and dry cleaners outside the gate at Camp Del Mar. And even that, he'd been told, was nothing like it used to be.

Finally, a deep voice announced it was Detective Harwood, and Wager told the voice what he needed.

"This Marshall is the resident but not the victim?"

"Right. He listed the Oceanside address as his previous residence. His mother lives there too."

"Not there she don't, Detective Wager. Tremont Street don't run that far north."

"There's no such address?"

"I used to patrol that area. There's no such number."

Wager thought about that. "Maybe it was copied down wrong. Could you check for any Elizabeth Marshall? See if she has a son named John living in Denver?"

"I'll get back to you."

Wager gave the voice his number and thanked him, and then he dialed Information in Los Angeles. Another male voice confirmed what he was beginning to suspect; there was no listing for a company named Crystal Pure Chemical Corporation.

He sat staring at the wall for a time. Someone had taped up a Xerox sheet proclaiming "Lost Dog," and beneath the heavy print a one-eared, one-eyed fuzzy face stared out. Under that, a description: "3 legs, Blind in left Eye, Missing Right Ear, Tail broken, Recently Castrated. Answers to name of Lucky."

A renter who gave a false last address, a false work address. And possibly a false name. Who may have disappeared. Possible arson. And a victim. It added up to a possible homicide, and Wager felt that little increase of pulse that came when he had a suspect. He turned to his list of numbers and dialed the business office of the telephone company and left his request. A few minutes later, as he shuffled through the morning's stack of notices, announcements, and requests from other sections and departments, Mr. McClinton called back.

"Good morning, Detective Wager. I understand you need information from our files?"

In the decade Wager had known McClinton, the telephone company officer had never relaxed his vigilance where police inquiries were concerned. The procedure, when Wager or any other cop wanted information, was for McClinton's secretary to take the request and the requester's telephone number, verify it against the directory to be certain it was an official police number, and then McClinton would dial back to see who answered and to determine the officer's need to know. Wager told the man why he wanted Marshall's last telephone number.

"So this is for identification purposes only?"

"That's right, Mr. McClinton."

"Very well. The subscriber lists his last telephone number and address to be 494-9062, 951 North Tremont, Oceanside, California."

"That street address doesn't exist. Could you find out for me if that telephone number does?"

A brief silence. "Doesn't exist? What do you mean?"

Wager told him what he'd learned from the Oceanside PD.

A muted note of warmth entered the administrator's voice, and Wager had the feeling that McClinton would be as eager as he was to trap a malefactor. "I'll get back to you as soon as possible, Detective Wager."

Motor Vehicles cooperated without any hassle. They had eleven John or Johnny Marshalls in their file of automobile registrants. Five were twenty to thirty-five years old. None listed the address Wager looked for, but he took the information anyway and began calling. The four people who answered gave variations of the same reply: they had not rented a house on Wyandot Street, they had no knowledge of a fire, they had no knowledge of a female victim of a fire. The fifth John Marshall had a telephone answerer that filled the receiver with laughter, music, and the clink of glasses and said that John was too busy having fun to answer the phone right now—leave a message and he'd get back when the party was over.

"Gabe—you had lunch yet?" Max settled on the side of Wager's desk and wiped a handkerchief across his forehead. He frowned at the dark, oily smear it picked up: sludge that came from the air he breathed.

Wager looked with surprise at the wall clock. It was after two already. "Did you get anything from Fullerton?"

The big man sighed heavily. "That guy takes more time to say less than anybody I know. He ought to run for mayor. You know there's an estimated 3,200 gang members in Denver? Anyway, Flaco Martínez he's heard of. But as far as he's learned, Martínez doesn't belong to the Gallos or any other gang. He might belong to a 'collectivity.' That's not quite a gang and it—"

Wager interrupted him. " '—doesn't have a fixed leadership.' I've heard Fullerton before." He shrugged on his jacket and followed Axton. "What about Albuquerque? They have anything?"

"Don't know; their man wasn't available yet. He's supposed to call this afternoon." Axton slid his and Wager's name tags across the location board to the column headed OUT OF OFFICE. It told the civilian secretary that they were gone but on duty and she could contact them on the radio if necessary. "The Brothers?"

My Brother's Bar was across the river bottom from lower downtown; the noon crowd would be gone by now, and Wager thought the aching memories associated with it and Jo Fabrizio had finally gone too. Still, when they entered the cool dimness of the corner bar, he couldn't help a glance at the back tables, where he and Jo had spent a lot of time talking. It wasn't a place where he brought Elizabeth, not because it was some kind of shrine but because it was a different period of his life— different people in it and perhaps even a different self living it—and he did not feel right about mixing them. Jo was dead, having literally disappeared into that emptiness we all go into sooner or later, her body still not found. It was that, Wager had finally come to realize, which made things worse: without a grave, grief had no focus, and the tiny voice of unstifled hope that said "Maybe she is still alive" was more of a cruelty than a solace. That observation had been Elizabeth's, made when Wager had finally loosened up enough to tell her about Jo. Her words had been true, though they weren't things that Wager would have admitted aloud, even to himself. And in fact, he still remembered the effort it had been to admit to Elizabeth that she was right. After that, they had made love for the first time.

Max led the way into the adjoining larger room and the heavy wooden tables and benches that the big man liked because they could hold his weight. The large sandwich menus painted on the wall hadn't changed over the years, and neither had Max's order—two Moisheburgers.

"Fullerton did say there could be some trouble at the Holy Name Church fiesta." Max talked through a mouthful of sandwich.

"When's that?"

"Tonight. What are they celebrating?"

Wager was "ethnic"—that was the latest buzzword. He was supposed to know all the Hispanic festivals. Some people said his minority status was the only reason he'd made it to Homicide. Others said he was put on Homicide because he was too much of a pain in the butt to work with anyone but Axton.

"I don't know. Maybe they just feel like having a party." He caught Max's raised eyebrows. "Hey, I'm only half Hispanic. I only know half the fiesta days."

"Oh." The rest of Max's sandwich disappeared from his fingers and reappeared as a lump in his cheek. "Anyway, Fullerton thinks there might be gang trouble. The parish includes the turf of the Gallos on the north side and the Tapatíos on the east."

Gallos meant "roosters," and a lot of the neighborhood's graffiti featured a stylized crowing bird; a *tapatío* was someone from the Mexican state of Jalisco, though Wager didn't think any of the punks in that gang could even find Jalisco on the map, let alone claim to be from there. "The dance is going to be at the church, right?"

Max nodded.

"Then it's the priest's problem." Nothing new about that. For many of Denver's Latino immigrants and even a lot of the second-generation Chicanos, the church was their social as well as religious center. Which, of course, the priests did their best to further with dances, fiestas, and neighborhood celebrations. A small band, a keg of beer at a dollar a glass, a potluck table, and they were in business. And the priest always deputized a small cadre of hefty men—some of whom were ex–gang members—to keep things under control.

"Fullerton also said he heard Flaco was trying to make a deal with the Gallos. Which," Max added, "could explain why he shot Moralez."

"A dope deal?" The jostling between gangs for power was always restless, Wager knew, and if Flaco could offer the Gallos an edge over the Tapatíos, they might take it. Depending on what Flaco promised and what he wanted in return.

Max shrugged. "That's my guess. Fullerton didn't know anything more."

"It fits with what Salazar told us." He finished the sandwich. "So you want to go by the church?"

"Maybe we'll find somebody to talk to."

Maybe; maybe not. More likely, they'd end up wasting time. But if anybody was going to talk, it would be not to Max but to Wager, who, even if he was a cop, at least looked Hispanic.

Wager had two messages waiting at the office when he got back. The first, from the arson investigator, was terse officialese: "Traces of accelerant and origin of fire indicate arson." The second was from McClinton: "The telephone number in question does not belong to the subject under inquiry. No listed or unlisted number in that exchange area is subscribed to by the subject or subjects under inquiry." Wager took that to mean no on both counts: no number, no Elizabeth or John Marshall. He tried the morgue again, and the secretary, with excessive politeness, assured Wager that she would call him as soon as the final report was ready. She really would.

Then he called the forensics office to alert Archy Douglas. "Last night's fire, Archy—it's an arson. And as far as Doc Hefley's gotten, it looks like the victim could have been dead before the fire started."

"That's definite?"

"The arson is. I just heard from the investigator's office. Doc's still working, but the victim's not a man. It's a woman." He added, "The doc'll need copies of Lincoln's crime-scene photographs."

"I already sent them over." Wager heard that tiny whistle that Archy gave when he was thinking. "OK, the place is still sealed; I'll get over there. Thanks—I think."

Forensics didn't want to waste a lot of time on a scene if a crime hadn't been committed. But that reluctance had to be balanced against the need for speed if the death was a definite homicide. Wager guessed that Archy would spend the rest of the afternoon charting and measuring the room and the closet where the body had been found, and while that was going on, there wasn't much Wager could do at the scene except get in the way.

He scanned down the federal government listings in the telephone book for the postal station nearest the Wyandot Street address. The woman who answered his call said the carrier for that route was Alfred Morris and he should be back at the station by four-thirty. She would be happy to tell him Wager wanted to talk with him. That gave Wager time to catch up with the afternoon's paperwork and just beat the evening rush across town to the Highland Park Station.

There was no change of address card for a John Marshall at the Wyandot address. That didn't surprise Wager. What did surprise him was that the route carrier remembered the man.

"Yeah—I saw that this morning. A bad fire." The mailman was about Wager's height but thick around the middle. A fringe of whiskers about as long as the bristles on a toothbrush, and just about as wide, ran from ear to ear along his jaw. It merged with the stiff hair of his sideburns and head to frame a round, pockmarked face with a sharp, triangular nose. It was a dumb-looking beard, and Wager tried his best to ignore it. "Anybody get hurt?"

"We found a body. I'm trying to identify it. Maybe you can help." Morris nodded, and Wager asked the mailman if he could describe the people who lived there.

He thought for a moment. "Sure. Guy named Marshall. I remember because it's not a Mexican name, you know?" He glanced at Wager and smiled widely. "Most of the customers in that neighborhood are of Mexican descent, you know?"

Wager nodded.

"You get used to the Spanish names, so that's how I remember. He just moved in a couple weeks ago." Morris scratched at an inch or two of the line of whiskers. "The Florios lived there for a long time—years. Then came the"—he searched his memory—"the Colimas. They had it about a year. Then it was up for sale again for a long time, and then this guy Marshall moved in."

"Can you tell me what he looked like?"

He shrugged. "Brown hair, brown eyes. A lot taller than me—I'm five eight. Slender. Healthy-looking, you know. Not skinny. No beard or mustache."

"Did anyone else live there?"

"Sometimes—guests, maybe. I don't remember any mail for other names at that address, but I did see other people there sometimes."

"Can you describe them?"

He shook his head. "Not really. I saw a girl get the mail from the box a few days ago." He explained, "I deliver one side of the block and then go down the other. She was on the porch taking the letters from the mailbox when I came back down."

"Can you describe her at all?"

"Young. Nice legs. She was wearing these white shorts cut real high and had on a top that showed her middle. Light hair, light brown, maybe dark blond. Straight. Down past her shoulders in back."

"Did you see her face?"

"No." He gazed away toward the room's corner and smiled. "What I did see looked good. Nice tan all over."

If she was the same one, her tan was a lot darker now. "Do you remember anyone else who stayed there?"

"I didn't really see them. I'd come up on the porch and put the letters in the box, and I'd see some shadows on the other side of the screen door. Sometimes Marshall would come out and hand me a letter or take the mail. Most of the time I'd leave it in the box."

"Do you remember any of the addresses? Where Marshall's mail came from, where he was sending it to?"

Another shake of the head. "He got a few packages—small ones, you know. I think some of them were from L.A., but I couldn't swear to that. Some magazines. Where he sent stuff to, I can't remember. What I do is take the outgoing and put it all together until I get back here. Then I sort it. So I wouldn't know which was his unless I read the return addresses. And, man, I got too much work for that."

The mailman's pledge talked about rain and snow and dark of night; fire was another thing. "Did you have any deliveries for that address today?"

He looked through a small stack of undeliverable mail. "Just some third-class stuff to 'Occupant' and this catalogue." Morris handed over a magazine-size mailer for survival gear and war surplus equipment. "Nothing first class."

"Will you give me a call if anything comes in?"

"Sure. But if it's first class, I think you got to have a warrant to open it. You know, federal regulations."

Wager didn't know, but he could guess. He asked, "Would you be willing to come down to police headquarters and work with the artist?"

Morris wasn't all that willing. "When? And how long's it going to take?"

"It won't take long," Wager lied. "We could do it now. I'll drive you down and bring you right back."

The man glanced at the wall clock. "See what the super says."

The super said yes, and Wager escorted the man downtown. Like a lot of civilians, once he got settled in the car he started asking questions about police work and telling war stories about cops he'd known and crimes he'd heard about. He was still talking as they glided down the ramp and past the security gate.

"Jeez—you guys park right under the police building?"

"Yeah." Wager pulled into a slot near the elevators. In the dim light on the other side of the cavernous garage, a metal clanging drew the mailman's attention to a passageway fenced in heavy wire mesh. A pair of prisoners in county orange were being guided by a sheriff's officer to the lockup.

"That's the jail? Right over there?"

"That's one of them." He steered the man's elbow. "This way, Mr. Morris."

They rose up to the third floor, and Wager led the mailman down the gray carpet of the hallway past display cases holding homemade weapons, police badges from different eras of Denver history, photographs of past chiefs, samples of banned substances. "Here we are."

"Here" was a small, windowless interview room, slightly more comfortable than the ones used for prisoners. At least the table and chairs weren't bolted to the floor and there was no two-way mirror set into the wall. Larry Westover, the identikit specialist on duty, had already set up; a blank of ovals and a stack of transparencies sat on the gray table. Westover came in a few minutes later, wiping his mouth with a paper napkin. "Hi, Mr. Morris. You want some coffee? Gabe?"

Morris wanted some; Gabe didn't—he knew what it tasted like. Westover brought in a Styrofoam cup for the civilian and nodded Wager out of the room. The sketching had to be done without other faces for the witness to see; otherwise, the picture began to look like whoever was in the room. Westover positioned himself just behind Morris's shoulder and pulled a sheet of blank ovals toward the mailman. As Wager left, he heard Westover's familiar litany. "OK, Mr. Morris, now here's what we're going to do, and don't be afraid to make corrections as we go along. . . ."

Wager, back at his own desk until Westover was finished with the witness, added what little he had learned to the file of the unknown victim and started a summary report for Chief Doyle. A lot depended on what the pathologist found, and despite Doc Hefley's sharp tongue, Wager was grateful that he had Hefley instead of the part-timer the hospital used to bring in when business piled up. One of that guy's cases was being challenged in court for sloppy work, and a whole series of homicide convictions where his testimony had been used were suddenly very shaky. In fact, Wager bet lawyers' phones all over Denver began to ring when that story came out in the Canon City papers.

As he finished Bulldog Doyle's report, Wager had a hunch. He dialed Vice and Narcotics and Lieutenant O'Brien. The shift commander's secretary told him O'Brien was at a meeting but Sergeant Politzky was in.

"Fine. Let me talk to him, please." It wasn't fine. Anyone who called was a captive audience for Politzky's comedy routines. But Wager had no choice.

"Gabe! Is it true homicide detectives are called stiff dicks? Ha!"

The sergeant thought of himself as a comedian and was his own best laugh track. Wager thought of him as something else. He gave Politzky the Wyandot address and asked if there was any narcotics trafficking there.

"Narcotics trafficking! Do you mean someone might actually deal in banned substances? What is this world coming to?"

"If I knew, I'd step off."

"Hey, that's pretty good, Gabe—I like that. Naw, that address doesn't ring a jingle with me. There's some activity in that area, but it's not what we call a known address. But the dopers don't mail us a postcard when they change addresses, do they? Ha. Let me ask around when the people get here, OK? Our people work creeps while others sleep—ha."

Most of the V and N detectives worked nights and hadn't yet reported in. Wager thanked the sergeant and hung up before Politzky could try another joke. He made a note to call back if he didn't hear tomorrow; like his jokes, Politzky often promised more than he delivered.

His next call was to Elizabeth. She didn't answer her home number, so he tried her office and found her working late. "I have a reception for the Downtown Boosters, Gabe. I should be home by nine, if that's not too late for dinner."

Elizabeth was one of the most active council members and one of the most effective. She did a conscientious job and had the respect of a lot of staff members and citizens. Because of that, she was something of an outsider on the council. It was, Wager knew, not unusual for a person—a woman especially— who did good work to be a threat to those who gave less and took more from their office. But despite being the junior member, she hadn't been intimidated, and that was one of the things he admired about her. Another one was the fact that the pace of her official life made it impossible for her to complain about his. "I'll have to give you a call. Max wants a little help tonight."

"I understand, Gabe. By the way, was that another homicide this morning?" She took pride in and worried about her city and used the crime rate as an indicator of its health.

"It could be—homicide and arson. But all the reports aren't in yet."

A sigh. "Well, give me a call when you can."

He promised he would. "I'll come by if it's not too late." There were other things he liked about her too, but they had nothing to do with her official capabilities.

Such as that slightly husky note that appeared in her voice now and then. "It won't be too late whenever."

When Morris was brought back to Wager's desk, it was long after six and the Crimes Against Persons offices were relatively quiet.

"Mr. Morris did a fine job, Gabe!" Westover slapped down a Xerox of the composite drawing. "Good job, Mr. Morris— I mean that."

What Westover meant was that it took a hell of a lot more time than it should have and he didn't want the civilian to go away mad.

Wager, too, smiled. "This looks real fine, Mr. Morris."

"Well, I tried to remember everything about the guy. It sure looks like what I remember."

The face gazing from the page was a long oval with a high hairline and eyes whose tops seemed arched a bit more than usual. The ears were small and tucked against the skull; the lips were slightly puckered and the upper lip thin against an almost pouty lower one.

"No marks or scars?"

"Not that I remember. But this is what he looks like." Morris glanced at the wall clock over the notice board. "Can I use a phone? I got to let my wife know where I am."

Wager shoved his across the glass-topped desk. "Tell her I'm taking you back right now."

Max pulled their unmarked car to the curb, and he and Wager
sat for a couple of minutes, looking at the dim street. Behind
them, busy Sixth Avenue was a constant flicker of light and
noise. Ahead, Elati Street stretched almost empty in the darkness. On each side, one- and two-story houses sat behind silent
patches of lawn, heavily curtained windows making a faint glow.
Occasionally, a car cruised through the shadows of heavy trees
and under the pale orange glare of street lights. The call from
the Oceanside PD had come in: no Elizabeth Marshall there
who had a son in Colorado. But Max had had better luck with
the Albuquerque police. Flaco Martínez's local rap sheet listed
burglary, possession of a controlled substance, and receiving
stolen goods—the familiar pattern of a small-time druggie. He'd
had two falls, the last resulting in a couple of years in medium
security. "The guy said Flaco was a wannabe with the Puñales,
Gabe. He might have been in with them on some little crap
but never was a real member of the gang."

"Why's he up here?"

"Guy didn't know."

"Flaco's not wanted for anything down there?"

"Flaco's not wanted at all down there. Guy said we were welcome to him."

In the rearview mirror, they watched a car pull off Sixth Avenue and nose out a parking place along the dark curbs. Then shadows of men, women, and children wandered across the street toward the well-lit annex nestled against the tall darkness of the Catholic church.

"Gargan talk to you yet?" asked Wager.

"Yeah. Wasn't much I could tell him: 'We're working on a lead.' "

"He wants to make it into a goddamn gang war."

"He might get his wish if Flaco's working with the Gallos."

"Yeah."

Maybe Flaco had come up to Denver to expand the Puñales's trading territory. Gangs from L.A.—Crips, Bloods, 357 Crips—held the same idea and had been setting up in the mostly black northeast side of town. If Flaco was so hot to be tighter with the Puñales, that might be a way to do it: deliver a new market to them, especially if he could base it in the Gallos' newly expanded territory. It would also explain Flaco's bragging about contacts in New Mexico who could provide dope.

"Gabe—hey, Gabe!" Max jerked a thumb at a low-slung Chevrolet that rumbled slowly past in the far lane. "There goes Arnie Trujillo."

Trujillo, a longtime member of the Tapatíos, was now one of the gang's older leaders. A few years ago, his was a name familiar in the police department for being at the scene of various gang fights. Wager hadn't heard much lately about the man. "He's parking."

"Yeah. Let's go."

The two detectives watched the metallic-purple car glide to a halt down the street. A man and a woman got out, the woman holding a shawl-wrapped baby. They paused in the glare of passing headlights before crossing to the church. Max and

Wager stepped out of the gloom of a low-branched tree. "Hello, Arnie," said Max. "How's things?"

The man's face, a dim blur of dark eyes and mustache, scowled. His woman held the baby tighter and fell back a step or two. "Things was all right until I seen you."

Wager nodded to the woman. "*Buenas noches, señora. Queremos hablar con su marido, por favor.*"

The woman didn't answer but looked at Trujillo. He bobbed his head toward the church, and she left. Trujillo watched her for a moment, then glanced around the dim street and its scattering of closed doors, its windows glowing yellow behind pulled shades. With a rise and fall of shoulders, he asked, "What you people want?"

Wager said, "We hear Flaco Martínez was the one shot Ray Moralez. We're looking for him."

"What's that to me, man?"

"You're still with the Tapatíos, right?"

"Wrong. I retired. I got a family now. A job, a family— responsibilities, you know?"

It was a familiar pattern. As gang members got older, some moved up in the power structure, some retired to the straight life, and some retired to the penitentiaries. A lot of those came back with grander dreams than a neighborhood gang could serve. "But they still talk to you, right?"

Arnie, short and stocky, could have been Wager's cousin. Maybe, given the neighborhood's tangle of intermarriages and legal and illegal births, he was. The man shook his head. "Not about business, man. That's the rule: you leave it, you're out of it. *Fin.*"

"Where you work now, Arnie?"

"The city. For the street department." A glimmer of teeth beneath the dim line of his mustache. "I'm a civil servant. Like you."

"They know you got a record?"

"Hey, I got nothing heavy, man. All my shit's juvenile crap. They seen my jacket. I passed a test and everything, so don't hand me no shit, Wager."

"That a son or daughter you have?"

"Daughter. Why?"

"You need your job, Arnie. You don't want any cops talking to your supervisor—you know how bureaucrats are. Always worried about public image."

They heard another vehicle pull to the curb, followed by the slam of car doors and loud, excited voices. Trujillo stepped into the darker shadow of the tree. "What the fuck you want, man? I told you I don't wear colors no more."

"But they talk to you, Arnie. You're *un viejo*—they got a problem they want to talk over, they come see you, a few others. Pay attention to what you say. Just like an uncle."

Trujillo watched the carload of people head for the church annex, the stacked heels on the men's shoes cracking loud against the pavement. "So I maybe tell a couple people you're looking for Flaco Martínez. That all you want?"

"That, and they tell us where he is. We don't want any crap starting up between the Tapatíos and the Gallos."

"What's the Gallos got to do with it?"

"That's one of the things we want to know," Wager said. "We heard Flaco was trying to work some kind of deal with them."

"I don't know nothing about that."

"But somebody in Los Tapatíos would know."

"You're asking a lot, man."

"You got a daughter who lives here now. Four, five years, she's going to be riding her tricycle up and down these streets, Arnie. Another five, six years, she's going to be wearing lipstick. You want to think about what that means."

Trujillo didn't answer. Finally, he said, "We'll see," and started to turn away.

"One thing more, Arnie. . . ." The man paused. "That house over on Wyandot that burned down last night—you ever hear of any action there?"

Trujillo shook his head. "I didn't even know about a fire over there."

Wager told him the street number. "Ask around—see if any of your people know about anything going down at that address."

Back in the automobile, Max drummed large fingers on the steering wheel. "You know anybody in the Gallos, Gabe?"

"Just to talk at, not to talk with."

They pulled away from the lengthening lines of cars parked at the curbs. "If they didn't have a hand in it, they might help spot Flaco. He's not one of their boys."

Wager shook his head. "If they do have a deal going, they want him clear." Wager smiled. "I think you and Fullerton will have to work real close on this one."

Max sighed.

They had just turned off Colfax between the sprawling levels of the Rocky Mountain News building and the gray stone walls of the U.S. Mint when Max's radio popped with his number. "Homicide detective needed at the Blue Moon Bar and Grill, 2145 Larimer."

"On my way." Max replaced the handset in its car charger. "Crap." He was the homicide detective on duty tonight, and the Blue Moon was a familiar call. Both he and Wager had spent a lot of time there since it opened, five or six years before. "Want me to drop you at the parking lot?"

"No, I'll go along. I got nothing better to do." Elizabeth had said she'd be home by now, but Wager doubted that she was. Those committee meetings went on forever, because every mouth there believed it had to be heard at least twice.

Max didn't argue with Wager. If it was the usual stabbing,

there could be twenty or thirty witnesses to interview. Two of them could do the job faster, and perhaps he'd get home in time to shave before returning to work in the morning.

A familiar cluster of emergency lights flickered in front of the bar's blue neon sign. Across Larimer, a handful of street people, equally familiar, stared. In front of them, a uniformed arm waved traffic past. A television van had already arrived, and its camera lights hollowed out a spot of white glare for a reporter. She took a moment to run a comb through her hair before taking the microphone and speaking earnestly into the camera lens. Wager spotted Gargan talking to a patrolman and writing rapidly in a notebook.

The glow of street lights spread up the brick faces of the old nineteenth-century commercial buildings, making them seem to lean forward to watch the commotion below. But the tall, narrow windows were blank and empty at this time of night, and except for the officials and nonofficials standing around staring, so was the rest of upper Larimer Street. Max flipped down the car's visor to show its paper, and the traffic cop nodded and stepped aside to let their car pull to the curb. They parked between a blue-and-white and the high orange-and-white box of the ambulance. Wager went quickly into the entrance before Gargan could notice him. The responding officers had the building secured, and as Max and Wager entered, the forensic team's unmarked vehicle arrived behind them.

"Hello, Floyd." Wager nodded to the aproned man who leaned his elbows on the bar. "Don't tell me you didn't see this one, either?"

Only the balding man's eyes moved as he shifted them to Wager. "Too busy working."

A dozen or so customers had been herded to the far end of the long, narrow room. They sat around tables with that fuzzy wariness of people who had sobered too quickly. An impassive officer stood guard over them, rocking slightly from heel to toe.

Max talked to the patrolman who had answered the call; Wager walked around the body sprawled on its back in a large smear of blood that had spread across the wooden floor in clotted pools. The medical examiner was just finishing his work. He dropped the stethoscope into his bag and stripped off the rubber gloves. Then he carefully folded the square of oilcloth he liked to use for a kneeling pad to protect his trousers. Job done, he nodded busily to Wager—"All yours, Officer"—and hustled out past the uniform guarding the door.

The victim was Hispanic or Native American, possibly in his forties, though the dirt on his face and the lack of light made it hard to tell. Wager glanced at the bartender. "Turn up the lights, Floyd."

"They're up. That's as far as they go. You know that."

The old-fashioned pressed-tin ceiling was high, and a line of unshaded bulbs dangled down the center of it on a row of wires. Most of the room's light came from the pale neon running behind the bar, and Wager guessed that the dimness, with the help of booze, covered a lot of blemishes in the decor and the patrons, both. He reached under the dead man's hip and, with two fingers, lifted out a bent and shiny leather wallet that, like the man's clothes, had seen a lot of wear. Most of the scratched plastic windows were empty. One held the grinning face of a girl, about ten, whose black hair was parted like a curtain and tucked behind large ears. It looked like a school photograph. Behind that was a South Dakota driver's license whose picture identified the victim as James Littletree. His home address was a rural route number in Wanblee, S.D. Wager jotted down the information and then counted the bills in the money pocket— seven dollars. He stuffed the wallet back into the stiff cloth of the man's jeans and looked up to catch Floyd's eyes sliding away.

Wager started with the bartender and with the routine questions. "Do you know the victim?"

"No. He's been in here a couple times. But I don't know his name."

The answers, too, were routine. As he went through the litany, Wager tried to remember how many murders the bar had seen. Most had been closed out. Two, neither of which were Wager's, were still open—the suspects were Mexican nationals who apparently ran back across the border. "What's this make in three years, Floyd? Eight? Nine?"

"How the shit do I know, Wager? I don't keep count."

"I think this is nine, Floyd. Your bar's a hazard to the community's health."

The bartender rubbed a finger across a large mole on his cheek. "It ain't my whiskey kills them, Wager. And I can't do a goddamn thing about what they bring in from the street."

"Is that what this was? A fight from the street?"

The man's lips tightened. He'd let something slip. "I don't know."

A muffled clatter of equipment said tonight's forensics team was setting up. Wager glanced around to see Hawkins aim his video camera. A few moments later, a bright gleam pulled the sprawled victim out of the bar's dim light as the police photographer on duty began recording the body and its environment. The videotapes were expensive to make and bulky to store, but the DA preferred them to still shots; they were a hell of a lot more effective in jury trials. Hawkins's voice was a low murmur as he talked into the hooded microphone and identified each shot. Max had moved from the uniformed officer to one of the witnesses, who seemed eager to tell what he'd seen and downright pleased at being asked first. Max nodded as he took notes.

Wager turned back to the bartender. "Last week it was a brawl, week before that we had complaints about people getting beat up in the alley out back. Floyd, this bullshit has to come to a screeching halt, or you're going to lose your license."

"So talk to my lawyer."

They both knew it was an empty threat. One hearing had already been dismissed, and the liquor board wasn't about to start another one so soon; they weren't worried about a Larimer Street bar whose only neighbors were vacant or closed commercial buildings.

"Besides, I pay my taxes. Which pays your salary."

"And the city spends ten times your taxes investigating homicides in this place. Any idea who killed him?"

The answer didn't come from Floyd; he hated cops and didn't care if Wager saw it. Max put the story together from the other patrons in the bar. They knew the victim only as James; he'd started coming in regularly three, four weeks before, and they thought he crashed at the mission up on Thirty-fourth Street. Yesterday he had an argument with an Anglo kid. Fudd something or other—that's the only name anybody heard. Tonight this Fudd comes in really steamed, and he and James start shoving at each other. Money, said one of the women; she'd heard Fudd telling James he'd better pay back what he owed. James told him to fuck off, and Fudd cut him. Just like that. James swung at the kid and the kid came up under him with a knife and James went down. The kid ran out.

Max got a description of the suspect and relayed it to the dispatcher. A minute or two later, the description came over Max's radio pack on an APB to all districts. Now the task was to identify Fudd, his friends, his usual hangouts. And then to track him down.

"You never heard of this Fudd?" Wager asked the bartender.

"You got it, Wager."

On the way up to the mission, Wager said, "I'm getting sick and tired of Floyd and that place of his."

"Yeah." Max pulled into a no parking zone in front of the mission. Half a dozen men lounged against the old red brick of the converted warehouse. As the two men parked and got out, the loungers fell silent and looked away, not meeting the cops' eyes. "But he'll never lose his license. Even if he gets cited, his lawyer'll scream due process for the next ten years."

Wager nodded.

"Talk to your girlfriend about it, Gabe. See what city council can do."

"I don't tell her what to do, she doesn't tell me what to do."

"Hey, just a suggestion!" Max added, "I wish me and Francine had that arrangement."

If the bar had been in a residential area, there would be a chance to pull its license. But in an all-commercial district, the only complainants were the police who had a mess to clean up every few weeks. Besides, the citizens on the licensing board, reluctant to interfere with taxpaying businesses, also liked to keep the Larimer Street bums in their own zone.

The mission's night manager, a recovered alcoholic whose face showed a lot of old scars and breaks, nodded when Max asked about James Littletree.

"I just heard he got stabbed. You gentlemen are looking for Fudd now?"

"You also hear Fudd did it?"

The thin man nodded again. His voice had a kind of burned-out calmness to it. "That's what's on the street. Fudd stays here sometimes too. That's not his real name. I don't know what his real name is. It's just what he's called." He added, "He never caused any trouble here. He's just a kid—kind of slow in the head."

Wager grunted. "He was fast enough with a knife."

The manager picked at a callus under one of his twisted fingers. "Wasn't no need for it. Wasn't no need for any of it."

There was no need for a hell of a lot of the things Wager saw, but he wasn't going to get sentimental about it. He asked the man for a more complete description of the suspect and about the places where he might be. One was the Denargo market area, about a dozen blocks away. There, the Burlington Northern, Rio Grande, and Union Pacific tracks came together and led north into Adams County and points beyond. "He talked a lot about the trains. He knows the routes and all."

While Max interviewed the night manager, Wager borrowed his GE radio pack and alerted the District One patrols and neighboring police agencies. In his mind's eye, he saw the blue-and-whites swing into the dark river bottom where the tangle of steel tracks gleamed red and green in the railroad lights. Spotlights would flicker across the undercarriages of boxcars, transients nesting in cardboard shacks would be rousted, train crews questioned. Wager's guess was that they wouldn't find the kid before morning, but the call came as he and Max left the mission, headed for the Denargo area: a man matching the suspect's description had been picked up in the railroad yards north of the city line by an Adams County sheriff's officer and was being transported downtown. Max yawned widely and looked at his watch. "God, it's after one o'clock. I'll book him tonight and do the positive IDs tomorrow. Might even get a couple hours sleep."

Wager, too, yawned as the excitement of the hunt suddenly evaporated and the weariness caught up. It was far too late now to go by Elizabeth's, but it wasn't the first time it had happened. Probably wouldn't be the last. She would under-stand—long meetings and last-minute changes occurred in her line of work too. Yawning again, he made a half-hearted effort to add up the day's hours. He'd been called out on the Jane Doe at four this morning, and another three hours would see four A.M. again. He thought he remembered grabbing dinner somewhere, but he couldn't swear to it. Now this long day was ending with a routine bit of mayhem, a routine bust, a routine corpse waiting for a hole in potter's field. With tonight's book-ing, another, far longer routine would start: the legal grind that would give the guilty man his fair trial before locking him away. As he had read somewhere, "the wheels of justice grind slow but exceeding fine"—but even the wheels wear away, in time.

• • • • • • •

Elizabeth had left short a message on Wager's home telephone answerer, and it told him he didn't need to apologize for last night. "I saw the knifing on TV—call when you can." He did, the next morning before heading for the office.

"That bar is a real trouble spot." Her voice reflected Wager's disgust. "But Henderson doesn't seem to grasp that."

The bar was in Councilman Henderson's district, and as long as he wasn't worried about it, no one else on the council was going to raise the issue. And as Wager had told Max, he didn't try to tell Elizabeth how to do her job. "Want to meet for lunch?"

"Just a minute."

He could picture her opening the well-worn pocket calendar to read the cramped entries in the hourly slots. "I can't—the hospital budget hearing starts this morning. It'll run over—it always does."

"I'd rather work a homicide."

"If we don't get that place straightened out, that's just what you'll be doing. But try explaining that to the mayor!"

"You try, Councilperson—that's why you get all those free-bies. I'll see you tonight."

Wager's first chore when he reported in was to answer questions from Bulldog Doyle, chief of Crimes Against Persons.

"This apparent arson death, Wager, what's new on it?" Even this early in the morning, Doyle had a cigar smoldering on his desk. The column of smoke rose straight up to form a pool of blue haze just under the ceiling. The mayor, after jogging through one of his marathon races, had stood around in his running shorts and proclaimed that all city buildings were now no smoking areas; in reply, Doyle had placed a sign on his desk: THANK YOU FOR HOLDING YOUR BREATH WHILE I SMOKE. Wager brought the chief up to date and showed him a copy of the artist's composite of "John Marshall."

"Douglas and his people are going over the scene?"

That was one of the things Wager had just told the man. Maybe the mayor had something; maybe cigar smoke affected the hearing. "Yessir."

"OK. Keep me informed on it." Doyle's tone held Wager a moment longer as his finger tapped another folder. "This is Axton's report on that homicide last night."

Wager nodded. Officially, he hadn't been there, so his name didn't show in the report.

"Max did a fine job on this one. Suspect apprehended and booked within four hours of the incident report. Damn good job." Now, said the tone, with that gentle comparison, Wager could go and do likewise.

At least Doyle wasn't comparing him to Ross, Wager's favorite screw-up in Homicide. And Wager couldn't do worse than Ashcroft—he was on temporary assignment at the FBI school in Quantico.

Shoving those thoughts out of his mind, Wager sent a query to Missing Persons on the girl described by the letter carrier. It was a weak gesture—in the first place, Missing Persons didn't even take reports until a citizen had been gone for seventy-two hours; in the second place, somebody would have to complain that the girl was missing. Wager didn't think anyone would, not right away. Maybe in a month or so, after phone calls or letters were unanswered. But it was a loose thread, the kind that would irritate until Wager had done something about it, so he did.

Then he sat down to the morning's messages and queries, official notices of changes in procedure or personnel, requests from other police departments for information on this or that. Despite Doyle's needling, Wager was a hell of a lot more concerned about the fire victim than the chief was. But he took care of the queries first—somebody at the other end was waiting, just as, at this end, he was waiting for answers from somewhere. Then he sorted through the routine and time-wasting items quickly so he could get back to the Jane Doe. "Marshall" 's picture was sent out on local distribution for help identifying and locating the man. He listed him as a murder suspect, in the hopes that urgency would catch some cop's eye. Most likely, the picture would only end up on bulletin boards in the districts' squad rooms; Wager had only to lift his eyes and see his own department bulletin board with a half-dozen ID photos and artists' sketches of murder suspects possibly in the Denver region.

He tried again to telephone the final John Marshall on his list. Like last night, the tape recorder gave its jolly little party and asked him to leave a message. This time Wager did, identifying himself and asking Mr. Marshall to call as soon as possible and at any hour. Then he leaned back to stare at the ceiling and sift through aspects of the case. Among the other puzzling things was the dead end on the man's employment: none of the neighbors knew where he worked. But he had to get his money from somewhere. And, chances were, he had to spend it too. Wager checked his watch—a little after nine: too early to pester Doc Hefley again, and Archy Douglas wouldn't turn in his report until he finished mapping the crime scene. Lifting his radio pack from the charger on his desk, Wager shoved his name across the location board and headed for the garage.

His first stop was a Payless Drug on a busy street four blocks from the fire. Three young women tended cash registers at the front of the store. Two shook their head, but the one whose red plastic name tag said ANGELA studied the picture carefully. "I think I seen him, maybe." She tossed back a strand of long black hair from her face as she bent over the sketch. "He's been in a few times. What'd he do?"

"He may know something about a fire. Did he come in alone or with anyone?"

The girl thought back, her eyes a clear brown as she stared without seeing along the aisles of brightly packaged products. "Alone, mostly. Once he came in with a girl. Blond. Nice-looking."

Wager had her describe the girl as well as she could. "Do you remember what he bought?"

A slow shake of her head. "Some magazines—he always bought four or five magazines. That's why I remember him. But I can't remember what else. Stuff."

"Can you remember what kind of magazines?"

"Newsmagazines. *Time. Newsweek.* And these nature magazines. You know, save-the-elephants kinds of things."

"Did he pay by check or credit card?"

"I can't remember for sure. Cash, I think—I don't remember looking at his ID."

"Can I have your name?"

"What for?"

"In case I need to come back and talk to you again." Or in case she needed to spend a session with the police artist drawing a likeness of the victim. Wager smiled, "It just reminds me who to ask for."

"OK. Angela Cruz."

He thanked the girl and drove down the street to a Safeway, whose parking lot was already crowded with cars. No one in that busy store recognized the picture. Wager moved to the next block and a string of neighborhood shops divided by the walls of a long, flat-roofed brick building. Part of the wide sidewalk had been scooped away to make room for angle parking to serve the complex. The corner store, with iron bars welded over the display windows, sold liquor. The owner thought he remembered the face. "I try to know my customers, man. I been held up three times, and it helps to remember faces. Yeah, this dude comes in now and then. Beer and wine—but good stuff. The imported stuff. I don't carry much of it, but that's what he wants." He explained to Wager, "Not much call for fancy stuff—my customers want the most for the buck: Gallo jug wine, Pabst. This dude's a Sam Adams. I remember him."

"Did he pay by check or credit card?"

"Cash. Always cash." He elaborated. "A lot of times on payday I cash paychecks with a purchase. But never for this dude. That way I get to know my customers better. Learn their names, find out what they like to buy. Small businessman, these days he's got to be in the service business too. If he's not, he's in no business at all."

"Does he ever come in with anyone?"

"Yeah, once. Week or two ago. With this young guy. Never saw him before, though. Anglo. Maybe six one, good build—looked like a outdoors type. Talked with a accent."

"What kind?"

"I don't know. Out East, maybe. New York, something like that." He explained, "They were buying for a party or a celebration. I figured the tall kid just got in from somewhere and they were having a party for him."

"Anyone else?"

He lifted a pair of heavy glasses with thick lenses and rubbed at the red dents they left on the bridge of his nose. "Not that I remember. Mostly he comes in alone."

Wager got the store owner's name and jotted the information in his little green notebook. Marshall hadn't talked to the owner about anything—the weather, the price of beer, his job. Just picked up what he wanted, paid cash, said thank you, and left. But he left in a dark-colored Toyota sedan, Colorado license number BAC 881. "I kind of jot these things down, you know? Car pulls up out front late at night, I just automatically jot down the license number. I told you I been held up three times?"

"You remember this license number?"

"Yeah. Funny. 'BAC'—my name, Baca. Eight eight one—adds up to seventeen, my oldest daughter's age. It just clicked, you know?"

Wager radioed Motor Vehicles from his car and waited until the reply came back: "Registered to a Roger B. Taney, 3514 Wyandot Street, Denver. No warrants."

"I need a description of the vehicle and any previous owners."

"We'll have to get back to you on that, Officer."

"Anytime soon."

"Ten four."

The call from MVD hadn't come by the time he reached his office. But there was a short message from Doc Hefley: "Apparent cause of death on Jane Doe 9-21 a blow to skull." Wager dialed the morgue number; the secretary put him through to the pathologist. "She didn't die of smoke inhalation, Wager. The carboxyhemoglobin level was normal—lower than normal for downtown Denver, actually: three percent. No particulate matter of a carbonized nature in the bronchi, no blistering of the trachea or bronchi. It's strong presumptive evidence that she was dead before the fire started."

"Somebody dumped her in the closet and then torched the place?"

"All I can say is that she stopped breathing before the fire started. How she got in the closet is your problem."

"Did you find any trace of flammables on the skin or clothes?"

"That's the lab's job, not mine, and it'll take a while. You're goddamn lucky to get the blood results so soon. Wouldn't have if I hadn't pushed for them." He added, "That fracture at the base of the skull is the only trauma I've found. But the hyoid and thyroid cartilages are too charred to rule on strangulation, and I haven't yet examined all the internal organs, so I don't know about poisons or an overdose, so don't ask me."

"Thanks, Doc."

"Right. Now maybe you'll stop by God pestering me and my staff, and we can get our work done."

"Doc—"

"Jesus."

"That lower-than-normal carboxy-whatever. Does that mean she was new to Denver?"

"Right, Wager—that's good. She didn't breathe as much of our fine city air as someone who's been here a long time. But I can't tell you how long that is. Not much work's been done on that, and there're a lot of variables. Satisfied?"

"One more thing—"

"Jesus II. Christ."

"Identification. What can you help me with on that?"

"Not much. We'll need a forensic dentist. From what I could tell, the teeth were well cared for, and I suspect she had some damned expensive orthodonture work done. But it's not my field."

That meant more delay and expense. The nearest forensic dentist was in Kansas City, and Wager would have to get the DA's approval to bring him in. "Any way to tell the color of hair and eyes?"

"The lab's working on what hair samples I could find. There was nothing left of her eyes."

"Thanks, Doc."

"Right. Now don't call me—I'll call you."

And it's always a pleasure doing business with you too. Wager hung up the telephone and, on the Jane Doe file, whited out "Unknown" on the line headed "Cause of Death" and inked in a red "Homicide." He scribbled a note to Doyle and put it in the chief's box. Let him wheedle the DA for the forensic dentist—that's what administrators were for. Then he tried MVD again.

"Yes, Detective Wager. I just tried to call, but your line was busy."

"What do you have?"

"The tag belongs to a 1985 Toyota Corolla." The woman repeated the title number and VIN number slowly so Wager could copy them. "The previous owner was Vance's Used Cars, 15587 East Colfax. The vehicle was bought by the present owner on 12 July of this year."

"The title clear?"

"That's affirmative."

He thanked the woman and once more headed for the garage.

The 15000 block of East Colfax was beyond the Denver city-county line, in Aurora, and outside Wager's jurisdiction. But the salesman who looked up from the small desk to glance at his police ID didn't seem to know that. "In July?"

"The twelfth."

"I can look it up." The man was somewhere in his early thirties and had sideburns that came down below his ears. A large pimple made an angry red mark on one side of his chin, and he squeezed at it gently with his left hand as his right thumbed back through the pink sheets in a loose-leaf folder. "Yeah. Here it is." He read for a moment and then said with relief, "The paperwork's in order, Officer. As far as the paperwork shows, that vehicle wasn't stolen." He turned to the folder to show Wager. "See?"

Wager read the bills of sale. The car had been bought from one Rita Pace on July 6 by Vance Autos. It was sold for a quick profit on the twelfth to Roger B. Taney. "It didn't stay on the lot long."

"That's the idea, Officer. That's how I stay in business: low markup, fast turnover, volume sales. The finest used cars in the metro area, and warranted too, every one of them. Satisfaction guaranteed."

"Is this Taney?" Wager showed him a copy of the sketch.

"By golly, that looks like him. He had sunglasses on when I saw him, but the face sure looks like him."

"Did he pay cash or check?"

The man looked in another ledger. "Cash."

"That's a lot of cash. What was it, three thousand?"

"A little more. Forty-one. Four hundred off the original asking price—the customer got a good deal on that one. I remember that vehicle. A real cherry—low mileage, real good condition."

"What color was it?"

"Blue. Dark blue, with factory trim package. A real cherry."

"Did he come in alone or with someone?"

"Alone."

"What was he driving when he came in?"

The salesman stared at Wager, finger and thumb pausing on the pimple. "Good question!" He shook his head. "You know, I don't think he was driving anything—he paid his money and drove the car off the lot. So I guess he wasn't driving anything."

"Did you see anybody let him off?"

"No. I saw him looking at the car and went out. He checked it over and then bought it."

"And handed you forty-one hundred dollars in cash."

"Hey, it happens. Some people don't trust banks. Other people go shopping, they take their money with them. There's nothing illegal about doing cash business, is there?"

Wager had to admit there wasn't. "You didn't ask to see his ID when he signed the purchase papers?"

"Well, no. Why should I? I mean, if he paid by check, then, yeah, I want an ID. But cash . . ."

And the permanent car registration would be sent to the address on the sales slip—the Wyandot address—regardless of whose name was given as the new owner.

Wager thanked the man and started out the door.

"No problem, Officer. Say, if you're looking for a good deal on a good car, here's my card. I give a special discount to public servants. And hey, something else: if you bring in a friend who buys a car, I'll throw in a bonus discount for you on your own choice of fine vehicle. Here, take a couple more cards."

In his car, Wager requested a BOLO for the blue Toyota and its BAC 881 license, then for any arrest record on Roger B. Taney. He didn't expect any, and that's what he was told. A scan of the now-computerized contact file didn't bring up the name, which fulfilled another expectation. One or both of the man's names were aliases, and for some reason he'd gone to a lot of trouble to hide his identity even before the arson and homicide. False names, cash business, and a series of visitors. It fit what Wager had heard about safe houses for draft dodgers, or even a cell for the Panthers or Weathermen. But that had been the Vietnam era, and this was the nineties. A stash house for a narcotics ring? It didn't match any pattern Wager had run across during his stint in the Organized Crime Unit, but that didn't mean new patterns couldn't evolve. And dope dealing was a high-risk business—half the murders in Denver were related to dope. Look at Ray Moralez.

———

He could have waited for Archy Douglas to finish his report on the Wyandot crime scene, and Douglas would have preferred that. When he saw Wager, he nodded shortly and turned back to measuring the distance from the chalked outline of the body to something half buried in the black ash of a charred baseboard near the closet. Walt Adamo, drawing sketches and taking the notes, was a little friendlier. "Morning, Gabe."

Wager nodded hello. Forensics usually operated in teams, not only to check each other's work and save time, but so at least one officer would be available out of the work schedules to testify when the case was finally heard. "Did the arson squad give you a copy of their report?" Wager asked.

Adamo answered. "Yeah. Four points of origin: bedroom closet, here; the living room near the front door; small bedroom across the hall; the back porch. Accelerant trailers along the walls. Arson, no question."

"Gasoline?"

"Looks that way. The lab tests should be back tomorrow."

"Hefley says the victim probably died from a blow to the back of the head."

Douglas looked up from the measuring tape. Its other end was anchored at the left toe of the chalked outline by a colored tack. "Any idea what the weapon was?"

"Blunt instrument."

The technician's finger pointed at the object he measured, a small bed lamp whose metal shaft was bent by heat. "About this size?"

Wager, too, stared at its neck and heavy base. He would have to make another survey of the neighbors to ask about any loud arguments they may have heard, any indications that "Marshall" and his woman didn't have the most copacetic of domestic lives. "Can you people get fingerprints off that?"

Adamo wagged his head. "We can try, that's about all. Dust, ash—harder than hell to get anything with enough points for courtroom use."

A satisfactory courtroom identification usually called for ten points of similarity between a latent print and a suspect's fingerprint. The more the better; but the fire's ash, the flood of water, the traffic of fire fighters, all cut the chances of finding good prints. "It looks like the guy living here used an alias. And there was no identification on the victim."

Archy Douglas let out a long breath as he glanced around the gutted room. "You're saying this crap is the only evidence you've got."

"Hey." Wager smiled. "You're always telling me that physical evidence beats eyewitnesses."

"Yeah, well, that's still true." He told Adamo the measurement and tied a tag around the small lamp before reeling in the tape. Adamo penciled in the item number and recorded it on his clipboard. "But all I can do is give you the facts, Gabe," said Douglas. "You got to bring in the suspects."

Easier said than done. Wager began a slow tour of the broken and sagging house. The yellow police tape was still strung around the entry, and an occasional car would slow as it passed on Wyandot. But for most of the neighborhood, the excitement was over, and only a cluster of preschoolers chasing a ball next door paused to peer through the scorched and withered lilac bushes to see if anything interesting was going to happen.

Wager, hands in his pockets to avoid touching anything, stepped cautiously through the gaping rooms to look at things he had not been able to see in yesterday morning's darkness. The living room was a tumbled mess of fallen plasterboard, broken and burned studs, padded furniture that had been split and soaked to kill any sparks. The only surviving decoration was a scorched and curled poster taped to one of the inside walls; it showed a whale curving gracefully in the blue light of a clear ocean. Its caption read, SAVE THE EARTH FOR ALL OF US. In the silence and through the punctured walls, Wager could hear the murmur of voices from the bedroom. Scattered in the debris and muck of the carpet was a partially melted telephone and a handful of torn and fire-scarred newsmagazines—*Time, Newsweek*—and several copies of glossy nature publications: *Audubon Magazine, Greenpeace, Nature.* The small drawers in the living room end tables held nothing. The drawers of the bedrooms were also empty, and that's what Wager felt about the entire house—it was empty. A lot of rental properties had that feel. Even after more than a decade, his own apartment still had a temporary quality to it that upset Elizabeth. She said it seemed as if he were a guest in his own rooms. Which didn't bother Wager: a photograph or two and his Marine Corps NCO's sword on the wall, clean underwear in the rented bureau, his shoes and an extra sport coat in the closet, and he was home. But these rooms were even more stark than that. Aside from the cooking utensils—the usual hodgepodge of spatulas, rusty can openers, and dented spoons that a series of tenants had left behind—this house had been stripped. No television set or stereo, bathroom cabinets empty of both toiletries and cleaning gear, even the refrigerator and storage shelves missing everything except a few perishables. The only thing left behind in the closets was a body.

The more Wager wandered through the rooms, the more they had the look of a stash house, a place to store drugs and divvy shipments for further delivery to street sellers. He took a last look around the shattered kitchen with its scorched stove and refrigerator, doors gaping open to lightless and wet interiors, then he went back to Douglas and Adamo.

"Will you run some dope smears on the kitchen table and counters?"

Walt Adamo was tying another numbered tag to a piece of evidence before bagging it, a small brass belt buckle blued by heat and burned away from any belt. "You think that's what this place was?"

"Either somebody cleaned the apartment out before the fire or they never really moved in."

Archy Douglas nodded. "We'll get to it."

It would help if the department could spare another team from the crime lab. But that had been one of the places where the chief had decided to save money: support units weren't allowed to hire the replacements to fill retirements or transfers. Only the already overtaxed street divisions were allowed to keep their strength up. The patrol units, the chief liked to say, were the first line of defense. But as in a lot of other cities, Denver's population paid more and more in taxes and got less and less back for what it paid. It was Elizabeth's complaint that most of the local tax money now went to the state and especially to the federal government, where it was dumped by the truck-load into the bottomless pockets of the greedy, the crafty, the dishonest, and even some who weren't Congressmen. Mean-while, high prices went higher, low income went lower, and the city's ability to function began to stumble and fail. It was, she said, a hell of a tough time to be on the city council, but it was no time to quit.

Wager's job was to catch killers, and it was work he knew he was good at. But seeing the world more and more from Elizabeth's perspective lately, he had the feeling that many of the murders he faced were symptoms rather than causes—the results of crumbling neighborhoods, of city services that no longer worked, especially of inept or self-serving state and federal bureaucrats and of politicians who did not care, of the cynical flaunting of greater and greater wealth in the faces of more and more poor people. And so much of that wealth stolen from the neediest. The big crooks got away with it; the little ones got chased by Wager.

He wandered back through the remains of the kitchen and out into the musty, charred odor of what was left of a screened room that served as a back porch. A pair of iron cots and wet, half-burned mattresses showed where visitors had stayed. A washer and a dryer stood against one wall, their white enamel finishes blistered in large brown patches. But this area, like the rest, was void of signs of life. A few scattered and empty plastic containers, many half-melted, a small pile of soaked newspapers stacked against one wall. He lifted the top wad of charred and browned pages—the *Rocky Mountain News*—and looked at the date: September 20, two days earlier, the last paper delivered before the fire. Under that were copies of the *New York Times* and the *Christian Science Monitor* bearing the same date. The three papers alternated in the stack, starting with the twentieth and going back for about a week. All had that refolded look of having been thoroughly read before being stacked.

The backyard, too, had a little-used feel about it. Though the lilacs and honeysuckle bushes nearest the house were burned and withered, the remnants of a flower bed along the back fence blossomed with unkempt life and held a few scraps of windblown trash. The concrete sidewalk that led to the alley gate was tufted with grass and weeds. Someone had stretched yellow police tape across the outside of the board fence to seal the gate, and Wager looked over it into the narrow alley: trash cans, garage doors for those few houses that had garages, the power lines that served the neighborhood. If the scene had anything to tell him, Wager wasn't sure what it was.

A survey of the neighboring houses was just as informative. No, there were no loud parties or fights; no one had heard angry noises coming from the house prior to the fire; in fact, there was nothing to draw attention to the inhabitants. A young blond woman had recently been seen hanging laundry to dry out back, but nobody had a chance to talk to her and she didn't seem interested in anything outside her own yard.

Wager looked up from his little green notebook. "She hung out clothes to dry?"

The woman in the doorway was one of those he'd talked to the night of the fire. Today, however, instead of a tightly clutched robe, she wore a pair of denim pants and a faded T-shirt that read: WEST SIDE STREET FAIR. "Yes. They have that clothesline thing in the backyard. A lot of the houses around here have them."

Wager remembered. It was a galvanized pole set in an old concrete pad, with four braces to hold clotheslines in a series of squares. "Their dryer didn't work?"

"I don't know. I remember seeing clothes hanging out there, is all."

He thanked the woman and drove slowly over to Zuni Street and a telephone hood at the corner of a 7-Eleven store. A survey of the yellow pages gave him addresses for the area's newspaper dealers, distributors, and services. Local papers and the *New York Times* could be bought at hundreds of vending boxes all over town; the *Christian Science Monitor* was harder to find. Wager guessed that if they weren't delivered by mail —and that mailman hadn't mentioned carrying them—they must have been purchased at a newsstand. The closest one he found was downtown at Fifteenth and Stout.

"**Sure, I know him. Comes in almost every day.** *Times, Monitor,* and *News*. Sometimes a magazine or two." The man behind the glass counter handed the sketch back to Wager. "Don't know why he doesn't subscribe to the *News* or the *Post*, at least. Home delivery, you know. *Times* too, for that matter. But I'm not complaining if it's the way he wants to do it."

"When's the last time he came in?"

"Well, it has been a couple days—hasn't been here yet today, either. Wasn't yesterday. Maybe the day before."

"Ever talk to him?"

"Talk?" He ran a hand over some strands of lank hair raked across a balding spot on his crown. "Not much. He comes from California, I know that."

"How?"

"We got to talking once about the difference in traffic between here and L.A. I got a son lives out in L.A. Visit him sometimes."

"Does he ever come in with anyone?"

Another rub. "Yeah—last time, maybe time before that, he came in with a tall fella. Maybe six two, young-looking, but I think he was older than he looked."

"Any facial hair or jewelry?"

"No. Tinted sunglasses—you know the kind that shooters or aviators like? Gold rims."

"Do you know what kind of car he drives?"

"Doesn't. Bicycles. Locks it up on that No Parking sign out front. Says that's the way he gets his exercise, so I figure he lives near here somewhere."

The newsstand wasn't more than two miles from the Wyandot address, and he'd have his choice of three or four bridges over the South Platte into downtown. Probably the new Speer Bridge and then along the Cherry Creek bike path, which was only two blocks away from this corner of Fifteenth.

"Did he ever mention where he works?"

"No. He usually comes in midmorning, though, so I figure he works nights."

"Can you remember anything at all he's said? Even talking about the weather. Anything."

"Well, he doesn't really say much. He's friendly—says hello. But . . ." The man frowned at the cigars and pipes and brightly colored tobacco tins in the fluorescent light of the display case. "His friend said something about the arsenal—made some kind of comment about it when he saw a headline on it."

The Rocky Mountain Arsenal was a major army depot for chemical weapons. It was on Denver's northeast corner. "What kind of comment?"

He thought back. "Something about the government shutting it down but not really wanting to clean it up. It's been in the news a lot lately, you know—all the delays and the politics." He added, "The federal government wants to make a nature preserve out of it so they won't have to clean it up."

Wager knew, but he hadn't paid much attention. People had been screaming for years about closing the arsenal, with its stockpile of biological and chemical weapons, and the newspapers periodically ran scare stories about nerve gas leaks or water table contamination. It was supposed to be the worst—

and most expensive—Superfund site in the country. He handed the man a business card. "If he comes back, give me a call right away, OK? It's very important."

"What's he done?"

"There's been a death. He might know something about it."

"Holy cow, a murderer?"

Wager shook his head and lied. "Looks like an accidental death. But he's a possible witness. It's very important." A suspect was more likely to call if he thought it was safe enough to make him seem a good citizen.

The man read the cardboard and placed it next to the cash register. "I hear you, Detective Wager."

On his way back to the office, he swung by the Satire Lounge for enchiladas and green chili. As usual, a blue-and-white sat in the parking lot beside the building and a pair of uniforms were eating their cut-rate lunch at the window booth. Wager recognized one of the patrolmen, who slid closer to the wall to offer him a seat. The other officer was a new face, one of a growing number in the department, and he was very interested in the requirements for detective. Wager finished the eager young officer's questions and his own enchiladas at about the same time, and it was a little after two when he reached his desk. Before he turned to the small stack of messages from his box, he once more called Mr. McClinton's office. The man was in a meeting, but his secretary recognized Wager's voice and gave him the information from her reverse directory.

"The number at that Wyandot address, Detective Wager, is 629-2493, a Mr. John Marshall."

"Can I get a record of calls from that number?"

"Only any long-distance calls billed to that number. If it's a local call or direct dial from somewhere else, we won't be able to help you."

"I'd appreciate what you can get me."

"Yessir."

The first of his messages was from Henry Stover: Important, please call, followed by a number. Wager put that at the bottom of his list. The next was a copy of the arson investigator's report, and he scanned those pages but found nothing that Archy Douglas hadn't already told him. An interoffice memo from Sergeant Politzky told him that he and his people had heard no mention of any narcotics activity at the Wyandot address—"But we got plenty of other places if you need one, Gabe!" A copy of a memo from the coroner's laboratory to Dr. Hefley said that traces of gasoline or a gasoline-like substance had been found on pieces of the clothes and skin of the victim. A hard-to-read note scrawled at the bottom of the sheet added, "Dental X-rays and hands sent to FBI—Hefley." That meant that the doc couldn't get any decent fingerprints off the corpse with his equipment. Severing the hands and mailing them to the FBI was the last resort. It usually took a long time to get results, and occasionally there were no results at all. But it seemed the best Hefley could do.

Max stopped by Wager's desk to ask if he'd heard anything from Trujillo yet. The answer was no, and the big man grunted disappointment. "I'll be in court this afternoon." His finger tapped the radio on his hip. "Call me if you hear anything from him." Wager nodded; he guessed that Trujillo—if he did have any information—was holding it for a day or so as a way of showing the cops he wasn't anybody's snitch.

Wager was elbow deep in the day's reports and queries when the telephone rang and a hesitant voice asked for Detective Wager. "Yes, sir. What can I do for you?"

"My name's John Marshall—I got a message on my telephone answerer to call you."

"Yes, sir! Are you the John Marshall who lives at 3514 Wyandot?"

Relief in the man's voice. "No. I live on South Pearl—1574."

"Do you know the John Marshall who lives on Wyandot?"

"Sure don't. Sorry."

He didn't sound very sorry; just relieved. Wager thanked the man for returning his call and crossed that John Marshall off his list. Now the only one left was the missing one. Mildly disappointed but not surprised, Wager called the dispatcher to see if any reports had come in on the BAC license plate.

"Nothing yet, Detective Wager." She reminded him, "The APB just went out this morning."

"Yeah—I know. Thanks."

He turned back to the steady flow of paperwork. Most of it was time wasted, and the rest wasn't of much importance. The department was undergoing another of its periodic convulsions over efficiency. Long questionnaires had been handed out to all personnel, and they were supposed to break down the hours of the week into percentages spent doing various tasks: interviewing witnesses, crime scene analysis, telephoning, traveling, lunch breaks and other leisure time . . . The only category not listed was one for filling out stupid forms.

The telephone's ring was a welcome break from figuring the percent of the week he spent in conferences. The percentages were supposed to add up to one hundred, but the numbers wouldn't fall into place that neatly, and he was wondering which figures to cheat on. "Homicide. Detective Wager."

"Gabe—man, I been trying to reach you!"

"Hello, Stovepipe. I got your message; I just haven't had a chance to call back yet."

"OK, man, that's cool, no problem. But listen, I need some advice. Mother and I want to sell her house and move into a place up in Weld County. Remember I told you about her and me moving someplace out on the prairie where we can raise chickens and shit?"

He didn't, but he grunted something like a "yes."

"Well, I been looking around, and I found this place ain't too far from Brighton, so I won't have to drive too far when I get that janitor's job, you know?"

Another grunt as he tried to add up twelve and three quarters percent and seven and an eighth.

"I mean, when I get out of the halfway house. Anyway, we want to borrow against her house to make a down payment on this other place. Understand?"

Wager understood that, but he didn't understand what Stovepipe needed from him. "That's fine."

"No, man, it ain't. I tried talking to somebody in the bank. They don't want to lend us the money. Mother's not employed, and I'm, you know, an ex-con."

He wasn't even ex yet; Wager could see the bank's point of view. "Why don't you wait until you're off parole?"

"Aw, man, that'll be more'n a year! And this place we want ain't going to stay on the market that long. What I want to do, see, is borrow against our equity for a down payment on the other place and then sell this house and pay off the new one. It's not like I'm asking the bank to goddamn give me the money—this house is good collateral!"

"This is interesting and all, Stovepipe, but—"

"A character reference, Gabe! Maybe if you talk to this person at the bank—you know, you're a cop an' all. Tell her I'm good for it. Christ, they can't lose on this house—the loan would be a hundred percent secured."

Wager sighed. "All right. Give me her name."

Stovepipe did. "Thanks a lot, Gabe! Mother appreciates it too."

He dog-eared the page in his little green notebook with Stovepipe's name and a cryptic abbreviation for memory's sake, then turned to finish the time study. If he put in the actual hours he worked each week, he'd come out to damn near two hundred percent. But officially he only worked forty, so he scaled down the hours, balanced the percentages, said "Screw it," and initialed the form's signature line.

"Gabe—how's it going, *hombre!*" Golding strode in briskly, a sheaf of papers in his hand. He wore sharply creased gray slacks, a dark-blue blazer, a scarlet power tie. "Air conditioner's on the blink in the courtrooms again. Judge Zell's about to have a conniption—she threatened to dismiss all cases until the city fixes it."

"Too goddamn bad a judge has to be a little uncomfortable." Especially one whose findings kept getting overturned on appeal.

"Kolagny's about to shit his pants. He's got four cases scheduled in front of Zell this week."

"Too goddamn bad about the assistant district attorney too." Especially one who couldn't win a conviction against even Charles Manson.

"You're sure in a good mood, Gabe. Hey." He leaned on Wager's desk, breath a puff of some kind of mint. "You want to try some chamomile oil—just rub on enough so you can smell it. It'll calm you right down."

"Do what?"

"Chamomile oil. I been studying aroma therapy up in Boulder. Ancient Chinese wisdom. They been using herb and flower scents for thousands of years, Gabe. Specific aromas can relieve tension, cure depression, improve concentration, a lot of things."

"Golding—"

"I'm serious—it really works! I go home at night and before going to bed I rub on a little essence of mandarin orange. Right here on the inside of my wrists. Tension just floats away. Sleep like a baby."

"I don't want to smell like a goddamn fruit."

"Well, hey, they got flower aromas too. Lavender oil, that comes from a flower. 'Every perfume is a medicine.' That's what the ancient Chinese say."

"The ancient Chinese died too, right?"

"Hey, just trying to help, Gabe. In France and England, you want to practice aroma therapy, you have to be a certified doctor. That's how much they believe in it."

"We're in Denver, and I've got a case that stinks."

"That's a sign of unhealthiness. It's not just a metaphor, Gabe—you can diagnose a lot from a person's smell. The body chemistry gets out of whack, and you start getting these smells. Most people just ignore them or cover them up. But if you know your aroma therapy—"

Maybe Golding had something. A lot of homicide victims smelled, and all of them were unhealthy. "I got to make a phone call, Golding."

"Sure, Gabe." He moved on. "But you really ought to try the chamomile oil."

Wager nodded thanks as he escaped by dialing the bank number Stovepipe gave him. A secretary put him through to Mrs. Lindell, and Wager explained why he was calling.

"I understand what you're telling me, Detective Wager. But Mr. Stover's current—ah—situation doesn't inspire our confidence. Moreover, the home Mr. Stover wants to use as collateral is in the name of both his mother and father and would need the approval of both of them."

"His father's dead, I believe."

"Then we'd need proof of death and a copy of the will naming either Mrs. Stover or her son as his heir." She added reasonably, "If, however, you qualified and wanted to guarantee the loan, we'd be happy to process it."

Wager didn't want to do that.

"Then you can understand our caution too."

"All I was asked to do was be a character reference."

"We're happy to note that, Detective Wager."

He hung up with a vague feeling of insult and checked that little task off his list of chores. It wasn't much, and Stovepipe wouldn't like the outcome, but it was the best Wager could do. As Wager had told him, he would be better off waiting until he cleared probation and had a visible means of support before asking a bank or anyone else to give him money. After all, Stovepipe wasn't the son of a U.S. President.

The telephone rattled again, and this time it was Archy Douglas, telling Wager that he and Adamo had finished working the crime scene. "We found a couple possibilities for murder weapons but no clear prints. They're items one twenty-seven and one forty-one in the report. There were some fingerprints in the bathroom area, but I haven't had a chance to check them against the elimination prints yet. In fact, I haven't even got all the elimination prints—a couple firemen have been off duty."

"Did you find any dope traces?"

"No. And we looked too—not a thing."

It didn't necessarily negate Wager's theory about a stash house. Dope was sometimes measured and mixed on a plastic shower curtain, and if it wasn't taken away, it could easily have melted or burned in the fire. "I'll be down for a copy of the report."

He hauled the thick folder of papers back to his desk and started reading through it. There were a lot of entries, but they didn't make any kind of statement. As Archy said, that was Wager's job; all forensics did was record the facts at the crime scene.

Finishing the long list of items and their location in respect to the body, Wager rubbed his stinging eyes and stretched against the back of his chair. Identification—that was the problem. Of the victim, of "Marshall," of anyone else connected with the house. It was a dead end that so far said only one thing: the people in the house had been hiding something. Or someone. But what or who or why? It wasn't that there were too many loose strings—there just weren't any strings at all. That was what he was going to have to tell Doyle when the Bulldog called him in for another pep talk.

One by one the section's detectives checked out for the day. Ross, as usual, was the first. He was one of the detectives that chose to join the police union, and his rules didn't allow him to work overtime without compensation. But leaving early was something else. He ignored Wager just as Wager, who had never joined the union, ignored him. Ross's partner, Devereaux, said, "Call it a day, Gabe," and waved as he left. Golding started to tell him something more about aroma therapy but stopped when Wager stared at him. Max, thumbing the final report on the previous night's stabbing at the Blue Moon, paused by Wager's desk.

"Here it is—wrapped up. It's all Kolagny's now."

"He'll plea-bargain."

"You kidding? Three eyewitnesses saw Fudd knife the victim."

"Only three? Hell, Kolagny'll probably drop the charges for lack of evidence."

Max waved good night. "He's not that bad, Gabe."

Wager shrugged. Assistant DA Kolagny preferred guilty pleas, and if he couldn't get those, plea bargaining. Trial was a last resort, in order, he said, to save the taxpayers' money. Wager thought it was because the man knew he was a lousy trial lawyer.

The tweedle of his telephone drew his hand. "Homicide. Detective Wager."

"This is Elaine from Mr. McClinton's office. I have the print-out of all calls charged to that number on Wyandot, Detective Wager. There aren't many. You want me to read them to you?"

He did. The three outgoing calls were to a number in San Diego. Two incoming calls were charged from numbers in Portland, Oregon, and San Francisco. Other calls went to Steamboat Springs, Colorado, and Estes Park, Colorado. She had looked up the two Colorado numbers—the Estes Park number was a Holiday Inn. The one in Steamboat Springs belonged to a Charles Pipkin on Rural Route 7. Wager thanked the woman and asked her to fax him a copy of the printout.

West Coast offices were still open. Wager called the detective divisions in San Diego, San Francisco, and Portland to ask for names and addresses on the telephone numbers. That information might be waiting for him in the morning, if a couple of detectives out there felt like making phone calls. The Steamboat Springs number rang without answer, and Wager turned to the contact file, scanning the computer unsuccessfully for Pipkin's name. A call to the Routt County sheriff's office told him that the person who could help him was gone for the day, but she'd be in at eight A.M. tomorrow.

It was dinnertime; his stomach told him that. His burning eyes told him he'd been working long enough. The phone message from Elizabeth told him that she would meet him at Racine's. He was being told a lot of things, and most of it crap. He was shrugging on his coat when the phone rang again. Muffling a curse, he answered, "Homicide. Detective Wager."

Wager didn't recognize the voice at first. "I got something for you."

Then he knew who it was. "All right, Arnie. I'm listening."

The noises behind the voice were of traffic and the sporadic clang of a pneumatic bell; Wager guessed the man was calling from a public telephone at a gas station. "I heard the same thing you did—you know, about Flaco and Ray Moralez."

"Anybody witness it?"

"I don't know."

"Then where's the story coming from?"

Trujillo was silent a moment. Somewhere beyond the clang of the bell, a siren wailed thinly. "I don't know, man. And I don't know if I can find that out. It's just what the people are saying."

"I need something I can use in court." There was no answer. Wager asked, "Anybody saying where he is?"

"He's still in town. I heard that much. But he's keeping away from the Tapatíos—they want him bad. They're after his ass, man."

"What about the Gallos? He getting any help from them?"

"Maybe. I don't know. *Un broder* I talked to said the Gallos is laughing, man. If they are, it could turn into some bad shit between them and the Tapatíos."

"That's what we want to stop, Arnie. You read about that little girl who got hit with a stray bullet last week?"

"Yeah . . ."

"We want Flaco before anybody else gets hurt. And we'll need witnesses too."

"*Chale!* Nobody wants a snitch jacket, man."

"Nobody's going to get one—Flaco's a one-shot deal."

"That's for true?"

"I say it." Arnie was talking about himself as much as anyone else, and Wager wanted to reassure him. The proof of that reassurance might be somewhere in a hazy and unformed future; Wager might need to use the man again. But he wanted to do his best to make it voluntary on Arnie's part, because talking to cops about the gangs was a high-risk game.

"I'll call you back," Arnie said.

Wager hung up and dialed Max's number. Francine answered, and when she heard who it was, her voice got short and testy. "Just a minute, please."

A moment later, Max picked up an extension. "What's up, partner?"

"Francine's blood pressure, for one thing. She's not happy I called."

The big man's voice was embarrassed. "She's not mad, Gabe. It's just . . . well, I was on duty last night. She wants me home tonight."

Which was one of the reasons Wager shied at the word "marriage." "I heard from Arnie." He told Max what the man had said.

"All right, Gabe! I'll start shaking some people tomorrow. Thanks, man!"

"I promised Arnie nobody gets a snitch jacket on this one."

Max had the same reluctance about the promise that Wager

had felt. "Well, sure, I'll do what I can, Gabe. But if a witness turns up . . ."

"Then we have to figure a way to handle it, Max. I gave Arnie my word."

"All right, all right. I hear you."

Wager hung up the telephone and rubbed his eyes again. The rumble of his empty stomach was loud in the quiet office. He finally slid his name across the location board to OFF DUTY. The civilian night clerk at the Crimes Against Persons desk smiled good night and turned back to the television set mounted in a corner of the office.

It was almost eight o'clock when he finally met Elizabeth at the restaurant just off Speer. They both liked it for the same reasons: good food, fair prices, and a slim chance of seeing someone who wanted to talk business.

"Your hardworking councilperson has been rewarded with another of those famous freebies, Gabe. Interested?" She swirled the clear liquid in the martini glass just under her nose and smiled at him. In the dim light, her eyes and lips and hair formed a pattern of dark that contrasted with the clear gleam of her face, and Wager couldn't help thinking of the way she looked in the bedroom's faint light.

He sipped at the foam on his beer. "It's probably not the kind of freebie I'm thinking of. . . ."

"Nope—not that. It's a pair of tickets to the Nuggets game Friday night. The owners want a big crowd to get the season started, so they're giving passes to everybody, from the city council to the Cub Scouts." A sardonic twist to her lips. "It's the council's duty to support our fair city's professional sports franchises."

"You mean like building the baseball stadium with public money only?"

That was still a sore point with Elizabeth. The publicized agreement between the club owners and the city said the stadium profits and costs would be shared between the private and public sectors. That was so the electorate would support the bond issue. The private agreement explained what was meant by "sharing": all stadium profits to the club, all stadium costs to the taxpayers. She'd fought against it, but it had been a battle she'd lost because too many people had been bought. "Our municipal government said they'd give anything to make Denver a major-league city."

"Yeah—and, boy, didn't they! Tell you the truth, I like Triple A better. Costs a hell of a lot less, the baseball's as good, and the players even talk to the fans."

"Unfortunately, the local boosters didn't think Denver should live or die by the Broncos alone." She smiled, "Come on—it should be a fun evening."

"The best I can do is try, Liz."

His tone cut through the relaxation she was feeling, and he was sorry to see that. "Is it that knifing?" she asked. "The one at the Blue Moon?"

He shook his head. "We got the perp on that one. This is an arson that's turning into a homicide with a lot of loose ends."

She held herself back from asking more questions about an open case. In the half-year they had been dating, she had learned that Wager didn't like to talk directly about cases that weren't closed. He might make oblique comments, statements that didn't seem to have any point, as he worked through knots in the skein of evidence, but he didn't like to present the details to her in a direct manner. It made it seem too much like a finished report, he said, and a finished report left no room for those faint nudges and suspicions that came when the details wouldn't quite fall into place by themselves. Those feelings were the difference between a half-assed job and one that got to the truth.

"There's also a case I'm helping Max with. And a problem with one of my snitches who's just out of the can. You name it, there's a lot of crap flying."

The waiter finally came with their entrées. Elizabeth finished her martini and cut into the side of fish hiding under a thin sauce. "Things get so hectic, don't they? Sometimes it seems as if the world's spinning faster and faster and no one's in control."

"Uh oh. You're in the pilot's seat, and you're wondering if things are under control?"

"I don't sit in that seat; I stand a long way behind it. But I suppose I'd feel better if I trusted the guy who's there. And if I wasn't trying to oversee so many other things to make sure they're being done right. That's one of the most frustrating things—I can no longer assume that people do in a capable manner what they're paid to do."

Wager could understand that. "Having trouble with the hospital budget?"

"Oh, Lord, yes!" She chewed and waved her fork for emphasis. "That's a big one—that really is one of the big ones! And if I could spend all my time working on it, I might get something done. But there are so many other demands, and they just seem to increase. . . . As Daddy used to say, I feel like a one-armed paperhanger with the hives. Sometimes I wonder if it's worth it."

He smiled at the woman across the small table. She seemed a point of intensity and life and ability in an empty waste of uncaring people. "But who could do better?"

She smiled back. "You sly bastard."

"We do what we can, don't we?" he asked.

She nodded. "And then some." She twirled her wineglass and watched a film of pale liquid spin up its side. "And thank God you understand, Gabe."

That was a reference to an ex-husband who had been jealous of Elizabeth's having any interests outside the home. "There's not much to understand. You're doing what you want to and doing what you're good at. I like to see able people doing good work."

"Surprising how few people think that applies to a woman. Still"—she sipped—"I wish these times together didn't seem so much like brief pauses between rounds." Followed by that wide, slightly crooked smile that heightened the life in her eyes. "Then again, maybe we should go a few rounds—just you and me."

Wager, too, grinned. "Two falls out of three."

• • • • • • •

It was midmorning when the replies from the West Coast finally began to come in. Wager was cruising District Four with Max, his eyes looking for Flaco Martínez but his mind on the Jane Doe, when the radio popped with his call number. The Crimes Against Persons clerk said one of the messages Wager was waiting for had arrived.

"Right. On my way."

Max pulled the unmarked car around in a U-turn and headed downtown. "This is on that arson-homicide?"

"Yeah. Telephone records. May or may not be something."

"Hope your luck's better than mine."

One of Max's snitches had said he'd heard Flaco was hanging out in southwest Denver along Federal Boulevard, so the morning had been spent driving from one likely spot to another to get a lead on the fugitive. No one admitted seeing the man recently, but there were whispers that he was in the area—someone told someone they heard from someone that someone had spotted him. That kind of thing.

"Albuquerque said they'll hold him if he shows up there." Max steered the car past the security gate and down into the dim levels of the Administration Building's parking garage.

"I think he's still in town."

"You mean because of this deal with the Tapatíos?"

Wager nodded. "If Flaco did kill Raimundo to show the Tapatíos what a stud he is, he'd lose it all by running away."

They were both silent in the elevator. What Wager said made sense to Max, and he was once more going over the list of Flaco's known associates in Denver, people who might risk hiding the man. Wager was mapping out steps on his own homicide case.

At his desk, he found two replies, one from Portland, the other from San Francisco. The San Francisco number had turned out to be a pay telephone at the airport; the Portland number was a Ramada Inn. But the detective in Oregon had gone out of his way to discover that on the night the call was made, the room was rented to a John Taylor, who gave his home address as 935 Jefferson Avenue, Richmond, Virginia. He'd paid cash for his room and listed his vehicle and license as a Ford Taurus, ZAC 338. "That's a rental plate, Detective Wager. The car agency had the same name and address on their contract. He paid cash there too."

"Thanks, Detective Yamamoto. If you ever need anything from Denver, give us a call and you've got it. Just ask for me."

"Will do, Detective Wager."

Yamamoto had done a good job, making more effort to check out Wager's request than a lot of cops would do. Strange that he often found it easier to work with officers on the other end of long-distance telephone lines than with many of the people at the other end of the room. Maybe it was because when most cops were on the phone, they tended to stick to business. No crap from Ross about union membership, no aroma therapy bullshit from Golding.

He dialed the Steamboat Springs sheriff's office to test his theory. A woman asked him to hold, and finally a man said hello. Wager told him what he wanted to know.

"Charles Pipkin? Hang on a minute." The voice came back.

"We don't have anything in our files on that name, Detective Wager. Could be a summer cabin."

"Can you get me an address?"

"You already got it—Rural Route 7. That's up toward Steamboat Lake, but exactly how far I couldn't tell you. Just a name on a mailbox—you'll have to ask the post office here. That's what we do when we're looking. Good luck."

"Thanks."

Maybe distance was a factor in his theory. He called San Diego and was finally put through to a detective who heard what Wager wanted and said "Hold on." Then another voice, more authoritative. It didn't bother to identify itself but asked for Wager's name, badge number, and office telephone number. "Someone'll get back to you in a little while, Detective."

So much for the distance factor contributing to harmony among the Blue Brotherhood. But at least the speaker had been businesslike.

Wager cleared his pigeonhole of the midmorning messages and found an additional report from Doc Hefley. The victim's bone structure and teeth indicated that she was in her mid-twenties. Her internal organs showed no presence of drugs or alcohol nor any indication of long-time abuse. She was a healthy female specimen, except for being dead. One of the other messages was a request from Lieutenant Watterson, the department's public information officer: Please call. Wager did.

"Anything we can tell the press about that arson and death over on Wyandot, Detective Wager?" Watterson took his meet-and-greet job seriously, and a good thing—it was about all the man, book smart and street dumb, was suited for.

"Who said it was arson?"

"The *Denver Post* this morning. The reporter talked to somebody in the fire department; now he wants to know what we have. What can you tell me, Detective?"

He didn't tell Watterson the first reply that came to mind. Maybe, for a change, a little publicity could work for the cops instead of against them. "Still no identification, Lieutenant. We're treating it as a possible homicide and arson. The victim's a female, probably in her twenties, and if anyone knows anything about it, we'd like to hear."

Watterson's voice got happy, "Ah! You saying we need the public's help on this one?" It was something he could use as a lead sentence for a press release. "Can we say, 'The Denver police are asking the public's assistance with . . .'?"

"Sounds fine."

"All right—thanks, Detective!"

Dialing Richmond, Virginia, Wager learned from the operator there that no John Taylor at 935 Jefferson Avenue listed a telephone. Nor was there an unlisted number for that name and address. Wager wasn't all that surprised, but it did give him something more to consider. A dope ring wasn't ruled out, but since the victim wasn't a user, it didn't seem as likely now. What did seem likely was some kind of organization that wanted to escape notice. The Posse Comitatus or some other right-wing antigovernment group? The nature poster and magazine hinted at a shared interest: radical environmentalists? But what reason would they have to hide? The missing renter wasn't Hispanic, so he wouldn't be a member of one of the more militant La Raza offshoots. Mormon polygamists? Wager had run across those before, but so far nothing fit that life-style—no children, no "sisters" sharing the same roof. Still, there was evidence of a group of people from out of state who visited the address for a few days, kept a low profile, and tended to escape notice. It was possible that, for some reason, they valued their secrecy enough to kill for it.

When his telephone finally rang, Wager expected the authoritative San Diego voice, but it was another man, who said, "This is Special Agent Bunting of the Denver office of the Federal Bureau of Investigation. I understand you called San Diego to speak with William Johnson."

"Who?"

The line hummed a moment. "Are you the officer who called the San Diego police for some help with a telephone number?"

"Yes. But they haven't gotten back with a name yet."

"I see. Care to tell me what your investigation's about, Detective Wager?"

"Homicide. I'm trying to identify the victim. What's the FBI's interest in this?"

Another pause. "A homicide victim?"

"Happened late on the twentieth or early on the twenty-first. A female, but she's burned too badly to get any identification. Now, what's this have to do with the feds?"

"I'll get back to you."

Wager was left holding an empty line and the easily stirred resentment of any cop who gave information to the FBI and was offered nothing in return.

Bulldog Doyle held an unlit cigar just off his lips. "The FBI? How the hell do they come into it?"

Wager told him about tracing the San Diego number.

Doyle pushed one of the intercom buttons. "Michelle, get Dr. Hefley for me."

The woman's voice came back. "Yes, sir."

He turned to Wager. "Bring me up to date."

That didn't take long, and Doyle reached the same conclusion Wager had. "This Marshall was in hiding before the victim was killed."

"Unless he planned the murder this way."

"You believe that?"

Wager didn't, but he knew better than to rule out anything until the evidence said otherwise. "It's one possibility."

"Um." Doyle finally lit the thick cigar with a long wooden match. A cloud of gray smoke swirled in front of his face. "What about WIPP?"

The federal Witness Protection Program. Wager had considered that too. "Another possibility. But I don't like it. Marshall had too much contact with people who aren't local: visitors to his house with out-of-state plates, long-distance calls."

"Yeah. Those visitors. People who stayed only a short time and didn't mingle with the neighbors." Another large puff. "Did Douglas run any tests for dope traces in the house?"

Wager nodded. "He didn't find a thing. But the fire makes it tough to be sure." He added, "No traces in the victim's organs, either."

"Um." Slowly, Doyle shook out the wooden fireplace match he ritually used to light his cigars. His desk held other instruments for the ritual too—an engraved cigar cutter, a large wooden box with a nameplate on the lid and a doodad inside to hold moisture. It was a Christmas present he'd once shown off to Wager. "And now the FBI. This whole thing is starting to stink."

Maybe it was a case for Golding. The intercom buzzed, and Wager watched Doyle press the Communicate switch.

"Dr. Hefley on line one, sir."

"Thanks . . . Doctor! How are you this morning?"

Doyle always had to use preliminary bullshit before he got to the point. Wager figured it was part of the department's new Intensive Public Relations Enhancement Program, whose memos came through headed I-PREP.

"Has anybody from the FBI contacted you yet?" Doyle paused for the answer. "Good. But they probably will. If they do, don't release anything—it's an ongoing case; it's our jurisdiction. Refer all requests and inquiries to me, understood?" Another pause. "Good. . . . Right. You too. And don't forget that Boulder River trip." He hung up and smiled at Wager. "Fishing trip. Up in Montana. Get in before the snow flies."

Wager didn't give a damn about vacations, Doyle's or anybody else's. "That's fine."

Doyle's smile went away. "Right. Well, the same goes for you, Wager: I don't want any information released to the FBI without my approval. Clear all requests with me, and pass that word to Douglas as well."

"What about our I-PREP campaign? Does that include the media?"

The Bulldog chewed on his cigar as he stared at him. "That program comes straight from Chief Sullivan. You having trouble with it, Wager?"

"I'm only asking, Chief."

Another chew. "Refer all press inquiries to Watterson. I'll brief him."

Wager nodded and stood.

As usual, Doyle wasn't through. "You need any help?"

"Not yet. Maybe after I know a little more about what we have."

The chief studied Wager. "It's your case, of course. But you keep me informed."

Relations between the Denver PD and the FBI ranged from touchy to terrible. A lot depended on which agents were involved and what the case was. But like many large police departments, Denver's was leery of getting in bed with the feds. FBI, NSA, DEA, ATF, you name it—whatever alphabet group it was, they tended to come into a local jurisdiction and stomp around until they closed out the part of the case they were interested in. Then they grabbed as many headlines as they could and ran off, leaving the locals with a pile of crap that was too compromised to bring into court. The Secret Service was that way too, even if they didn't go by their initials.

When Special Agent Bunting called back, to get more information on the homicide, Wager asked again what the FBI's interest was.

"I'm not at liberty to discuss that with you, Detective Wager."

"Bu you're at liberty to ask about one of our ongoing homicide investigations, Special Agent Bunting."

The man understood. "If it was my case, Detective, I'd be glad to give you all I have. But it's out of the San Diego office, and in addition to not knowing a damn thing about it, I can't speak for them."

"Then, Special Agent, San Diego better send somebody who can. Have a nice day."

Eighteen minutes later, Chief Doyle rang.

"Chief Sullivan called down—somebody in the San Diego office of the FBI squawked about our lack of cooperation. Sullivan wants to see us right now."

"I'm on my way."

Doyle and Wager rode up to the top floor. The office of the chief of police was a pair of large and quiet rooms whose windows looked toward the shiny gold dome of the state capitol and the hot glitter of traffic that circled it like hungry flies. The good-looking Chicana receptionist smiled hello and murmured something into her intercom, then she nodded at them. "Please go in, Chief Doyle."

Wager went too.

"Doyle, Wager. Sit down, gentlemen, and tell me what the hell's going on."

The chief preferred civilian clothes, but he nonetheless wore them like a uniform. A set of dress blues, freshly pressed and glittering with brass, hung in a plastic bag on a coatrack behind the door. On each side of the large, neatly organized desk, standards held the flags of nation and state, city and police. Wager sat in a black leatherette chair that caressed his back with the embossed seal of the City and County of Denver. He kept his mouth shut while Doyle did the talking.

Sullivan listened and rubbed a forefinger at the baggy flesh under one gray eye. He turned to Wager. "The Denver office called you? Not San Diego?"

"An Agent Bunting. I don't know him."

"I do—he's not so bad. At least it wasn't Wilmore."

Doyle snorted. "He should have retired years ago."

"He did," said Sullivan. "He just hasn't turned in his badge. How important is this William Johnson, Wager?"

"I don't know anything about him. Bunting let the name slip when he called me."

"Nothing on him in our files?"

"I counted about forty William, Willy, Will, or Bill Johnsons. Fifteen or twenty have convictions or old addresses in southern California. None of them were linked to Marshall or to that address."

"Yeah. I suppose that was too much to hope for." Sullivan made a decision. "OK, I'm going to call San Diego. I'm going to tell them we'll be happy to"—he stressed the next word—"exchange information with them. I'll tell them to work through you, Wager—you're the officer of record on this homicide. Use your own judgment about how much to let them have. But make damned sure we get something for what we give."

In the elevator on the way back down, Doyle reminded Wager, "Sullivan wants to be a nice guy. But if you need additional horsepower, I'm on call. Just don't forget it's our jurisdiction. And by God a homicide."

Homicide, even for the feds, was the ranking offense, which the next caller apparently knew. He was a Special Agent Mallory of the San Diego office, and he spoke softly as he apologized for the mixup—"Unfortunately, that can happen when a request goes through too many hands"—and explained that Bureau policy required field offices to work through each other when a case crossed territorial lines. "It's our policy here in San Diego to work closely with local law enforcement agencies, Detective Wager, and we'll be happy to work with you."

It all sounded very nice and cozy, but so far Agent Mallory hadn't told Wager a damn thing. "Who is William Johnson?"

Only a slight hesitation. "He's a person who serves as a liaison for us. I can't tell you more than that over the telephone. I understand you have a homicide there involving a young woman?"

Wager had told Bunting only that the victim was a female, nothing about her age. "You know who it might be?"

"Nothing definite. We have an informant who's missed her contact. But she's done it before."

"Want to describe her?"

"Twenty-three years old, blond and blue, five eight, one twenty-five. A small rose tattoo on the back of her left shoulder, no other identifying marks or scars."

"Name?"

". . . Pauline Tillotson. Does this description fit your victim?"

"It fits a young woman who was seen at the house before the fire. She may or may not be the victim. The pathologist says she's in her twenties, all right, but the only means of identification we have are the teeth."

"Do you have a forensic dentist? I can send you Tillotson's dental records."

"I'd appreciate that. The house was owned by a John Marshall—possibly an alias. Have anything on him?"

Mallory was silent a moment. "No, I can't place that name. Is he a suspect in this?"

"The fire was an arson, but the woman was dead before it started. Marshall may have been the last one to see her alive."

"I see. . . ."

That was more than Wager did. "What's going on, Agent Mallory? What was Tillotson tied up in?"

"I'd feel a lot more comfortable telling you if I knew for certain who the victim is."

"I don't expect a positive ID for another six or eight weeks. And then there might not be one."

"Six or eight weeks?"

"We sent the hands and dental X-rays to the FBI lab. It takes your people a long time."

"Jesus, they can do better than that! Let me call them. I'll get back to you."

Wager had gambled by telling Mallory about sending the X-rays and hands to the FBI lab. But the payoff could be an early positive identification. That would open the victim's world of relatives, acquaintances, credit and bank accounts—the things that would fill out her life and possibly lead to her killer. The danger was that those things could also lead to motive, and motive could involve whatever it was the FBI was interested in. Mallory might get his positive ID and then go about his business, leaving Wager to wait the six weeks or more for the routine identification while the FBI worked its own side of the case.

That worry nagged at the back of Wager's mind as he labored through the early afternoon, and it wasn't relieved by a phone call from Stovepipe, who was upset when he learned what the bank officer had said.

"My father's signature! That bastard skipped when I was ten years old, Gabe!"

"Or certification of his death."

"But I don't know if he's dead or alive—I don't even know where he is!"

"Look, Stovepipe, if you put anything up for collateral—

house, car, dog, anything—it has to be yours. If it's not, the people who do own it have to agree to it."

"Aw, man, this is so much shit. My old man never made a payment on that place after he split. My mother paid it off—almost twenty goddamn years, she paid it off, one month at a fucking time. It's hers!"

"That's not what the papers say."

A long silence, followed by a deep sigh. "All right. What the hell do I do now?"

"Maybe she can have him declared dead. Maybe she can claim desertion and get the property title cleared that way. It's something a lawyer will have to tell you."

"Lawyer—I went to the pen because of a fucking lawyer!"

There were also the aggravating circumstances of breaking and entering and a record of unauthorized withdrawals from banking institutions. But Wager let it pass. "I don't know what else to tell you, Stovepipe."

"Goddamn, Gabe, it was a hell of a lot easier to get my money the old way."

"Maybe it won't be so bad. Talk to a lawyer and see."

"Lawyer," he said, before he hung up. "Crap. Put them bastards in and let the inmates out, and the goddamn crime rate'd go down fifty percent."

Max stopped at Wager's desk to ask if he'd ever heard of Inez Suazo. "She's supposed to be Flaco's local squeeze. I'm on my way to see her—like to go along?"

It beat shuffling papers and counting the minutes between phone calls. Besides, it was obvious Max wanted him to. "How'd you find out about her?"

"I went back and leaned on Urbano—the owner of that bar where Flaco hangs out. He said Inez came in with him a few times. She's a local girl; he knows her. Said she and Flaco looked like they were getting it on."

Max drove. Suazo lived across the city-county line, in the

small municipality of Mountain View. A few streets away, the spidery arches of the Lakeside Amusement Park's roller coaster lifted above the trees hanging over blocks of tired-looking cottages. Suazo's was a flat-roofed duplex behind a sagging picket fence that had once been white and once had a gate. The duplex had once been white too, but the paint had flaked away to leave crumbly red brick showing through in ragged patches like mange. A boy of about ten answered Max's knock. He stayed behind the rusty screen door that opened directly to the sidewalk.

"Is Inez Suazo in, please?"

Over the boy's shoulder, from a dim living room that looked too small for its sagging furniture, came the chatter of a televised cartoon adventure. "No, sir. She's not home from work yet."

"Can you tell me where she works?"

The boy hesitated, dark eyes wide with a confusion of surprise, worry, and hopeful trust.

Wager showed his badge, and the boy's eyes got wider as he stared at it. "We're police officers, son. We'd like to talk to her about some people she might know."

The eyes blinked. "She works at her office. She's a secretary."

"Can you tell me where the office is?"

"Over on Federal. It's an insurance office. I think it's called the Colorado Agency or maybe the Columbine Agency."

"What time does she usually get home?"

"Five-thirty. Sometimes six."

Max glanced at his watch. It was a little after four. "Are you a relative of hers?"

"She's my mom."

"Did she leave you a phone number to call her?"

"Yes, sir. But she don't like me to call her at work unless it's real important."

"Can you give us the number? We'll call—it's important."

"I guess so. Just a minute, please."

He came back and read it from a square of paper with a thumbtack hole in the edge. Wager copied it down. On their way back into Denver, Max said, "Nice kid."

"Yeah." Wager thought about latchkey children and working parents and single moms who tried to make a home for their kids and also have a social life of their own. He was glad he and Lorraine had not had any children. For one thing, it made the divorce easier and cleaner. More important, his would not be the lonely kid who had the television blaring to drive away the emptiness of the house.

They stopped at a pay phone, where Max called in for an address on the telephone number. Back in the car, he said, "It's the Columbus Agency. Nine hundred block of Federal. Kid doesn't even know the name of the place his mother works."

It was a wooden cottage that had been moved to a commercial lot and converted into an insurance office. The steeply pitched roof and scalloped shingles that decorated the pinched second story reminded Wager of his old barrio, now disappeared into urban renewal. A brightly painted sign at the top of the porch said COLUMBUS INSURANCE—AN INDEPENDENT AGENCY. A slender Hispanic woman looked up as they entered; in her mid-twenties, she smiled without showing her teeth, which made her seem prim, but she had an attractive and friendly face.

"Are you Inez Suazo?" Max showed her his badge.

She stared at the badge. Then her face went white, and her mouth gaped open to spoil her looks. But it wasn't her appearance she worried about. "Ramón! My son—something's happened to him!"

"No, no—he's all right, ma'am," said Max. "We just stopped by your house and talked to him. He told us where you work."

She gasped with relief, and her metal-and-leatherette chair creaked as she sagged back against it, eyes closed. *"Dios!"*

The other rooms in the cramped building seemed empty. Inez used what had been the living room, and her desk, computer station, and filing cabinets took up most of it. A doorway led to another room, converted into an inner office. It, too, had a desk and computer station, as well as a pair of comfortable chairs. Wager couldn't see beyond that, but guessed a kitchen and bath made up the rest of the space. There would be one, maybe two rooms upstairs, jammed under the steep roof, with windows in the gable ends. It was possible that the house had been trucked from his old barrio to serve as the agency office.

"Didn't mean to frighten you, ma'am." Max smiled. "Is your boss here?"

Her color had come back. "No—he's gone for the day. Is there something you need?"

Wager turned back from inspecting the offices. "I understand you and Flaco Martínez see a lot of each other."

"Flaco?" Her fear had gone, but now caution replaced it. "I know him. Why?"

"We're just looking for him, ma'am," said Max. "We'd like to ask him a few questions."

She weighed several things in her mind. "I don't know where he is. I'm sorry."

It was Wager's turn. "We want to talk to him about killing Ray Moralez. Do you know anything about that?"

". . . No. I really haven't seen him for a while. We sort of stopped seeing each other a while back."

Max asked, "Do you have any idea where he might be, Ms. Suazo?"

She shook her head, eyes on the papers stacked by her computer keyboard.

"You ever heard of section 40-8-105 of the Colorado Criminal Code?" Wager waited until she looked up, puzzled. "It tells what accessory to a crime means: 'Any person is an accessory to a crime if with intent to hinder, delay, or prevent the discovery, detection, apprehension, prosecution, conviction, or punishment of another for the commission of a crime, he'—or she, Ms. Suazo—'renders assistance to such person.' It's a class four felony. That means one to ten years, plus a fine of up to thirty thousand dollars. In your case, it could also mean turning Ramón over to his grandparents or to the state. Or to his father." Wager leaned close so he could study the woman's dark eyes. "Is your boyfriend worth that?"

"He's not my boyfriend! I told you!" She glared at Wager, then added in a weaker voice, "He never was, really."

"Ms. Suazo, Detective Wager's only trying to explain just how serious it is to protect a suspect. Especially in a murder case. If you know anything that might help us—anything at all—it's to your advantage to tell us."

She wasn't as pale as when she thought her son was hurt, but her color was sallow. "Flaco can be mean. He scared me. That's why I stopped dating him."

"Flaco won't know we talked to you if you don't tell him." Max smiled again. "That's a promise, ma'am."

Suazo chewed at the dry flesh of her lower lip. The grimace showed badly crooked teeth, poor people's teeth, and Wager understood why she liked to smile with her mouth closed. "He knows where I live. He knows about Ramón."

"But he doesn't know we've talked with you. And we'll keep it that way."

Wager added, "You want him hanging around you and Ramón for the rest of your life? Or do you want us to get rid of him for you?"

"Did he tell you anything about Ray Moralez, Ms. Suazo?"

The woman hesitated and then sighed. "No—not exactly. But one night he came by the house all wound up. Excited and jumpy, you know? He drank a lot—beer, water, anything— like he was real thirsty." She shrugged. "He just acted kind of funny. It was kind of scary."

"When was this?"

She shrugged again. "A week ago, I suppose."

"What time?"

"Pretty late. One in the morning, maybe. He woke me up, knocking on the window."

Moralez had last been seen alive around eight-thirty at night. The body temperature, lividity, and autopsy showed he was killed before midnight. "What'd he say?" Wager asked.

"Just that he'd done the big one. I asked, 'Big what?' and he didn't say. He just smiled and asked if I had something to drink—he was really thirsty, he said."

"He didn't mention Moralez by name?"

"He didn't mention anybody by name. He was . . . funny—different. Like I say, excited. That's when he started to get rough."

"What do you mean?"

Her voice lost some of its inflection, as if she were reporting something unpleasant that happened to someone else. "Sex. He drank a lot of beer and was getting drunk real fast. He started acting rough, and I wanted him to leave. He was getting noisy, you know? I didn't want him to wake up Ramón. I wanted him to leave, so I told him it was my period. He started getting nasty—wanted me to give him head or do it up the *culo*. I got mad and told him to get out or I'd call the cops. Then he just laughed and called me a dumb bitch and walked out. That was the last time I saw him."

It sounded to Wager as if she was telling the truth. If they had to build a circumstantial case against Flaco, the woman's testimony might sound truthful to a jury too. But she didn't have to know about that possibility yet—no sense losing her if she decided to run rather than show up in court. "How'd you meet Flaco?"

"In that bar. The Chihuahua. I go there sometimes—the bartender, George, we went to North High together." She shrugged. "Flaco bought me a drink; one thing led to another."

"Flaco and George pretty tight?"

"No, I don't think so. George's been there a long time; I think Flaco just started coming in."

"He ever talk to you about his business?"

"Flaco? No. I asked him what he did. He said he worked around here and there. But he always had money."

Max asked her about any friends Flaco might have introduced her to, and she mentioned Sol Atilano and Dave—she couldn't remember his last name—and she didn't know where either one lived. Wager asked if she'd ever seen Flaco with any members of the Gallos gang.

"I guess so, sometimes. Roy Quintana—Flaco told me Roy was a Gallos, but I never saw him wear colors. I don't know much about the gangs—I don't like them. George doesn't let gang colors in his bar."

She didn't know where Roy Quintana lived, either, but Wager guessed Fullerton would have the name in his files. He asked the woman if she had any idea where Flaco might be hiding.

"We went to his place once. It's over on Thirty-eighth." She didn't know the number but said she drove by it sometimes on the way to work. She told them where it was and what it looked like. Wager remembered the building from his years of patrolling the neighborhood, a brick row of sagging one-bedroom apartments whose doorways opened onto small pads of concrete one step up from the sidewalk.

"That's the only place you know where he might be?"

She nodded. "Mostly we'd meet at the bar when I got off work." She added, "Sometimes he'd come over to my place later—after Ramon was asleep."

"What kind of car's he drive?"

"A hot one—a white Z car. Calls it his baby."

Driving up Federal Boulevard, Max asked, "You want to call for backup?"

Wager shook his head. "Waste of manpower. He's probably long gone."

They turned onto busy Thirty-eighth Avenue, and Wager told Max to stay in the left lane. In a couple of blocks they saw the row of single-story apartments, and Max waited for a break in the steady flow of cars. "Looks like a long dog kennel."

The series of eight or ten doors with their flanking pairs of grimy windows made a crooked line a pace or two back from the sidewalk. Half the doors sagged open for air, but all they caught was traffic noise and fumes. A knot of kids hung like flies around one doorway, peering in, their voices shrill against the rush of cars. They didn't notice Wager and Max park.

"She said the third door from the west end."

It was closed, the two windows dark behind their rust-colored screens.

"I'll go around back," said Wager. "Give me a couple minutes, then knock."

He tried to listen for Max's large knuckles rapping on the warped door, but the steady noise of tires and car engines on the avenue filled the afternoon. Wager stood in the trash-littered alley that ran behind the row and watched the back door of the third unit. Patches of dirt provided back lawns for each apartment, and a lot of them had kiddie toys scattered here and there. Most of the back doors were open, and from this side the inhabitants enjoyed the sour smell of Dumpsters and scummy water caught in the alley's potholes. A woman leaned out and stared at Wager for a long moment, then she said something to someone inside and her door closed gently. Beyond the unpainted board fence behind him, Wager could hear the monotonous pat-pat-pat of a basketball on somebody's driveway. Max showed at the building's corner and shook his head.

"No answer," he said. "I called in for a warrant. You want to take the left-hand neighbors?"

The residents probably spoke English, but they were more comfortable with Spanish and got talkative when Wager used it. No, they didn't know anything about the *hombre* next door; he wasn't real friendly and was gone a lot. He moved in maybe a month or two ago—people are always moving in and out of these places. No, no visitors—he stayed to himself and a lot of times came in real late. They could hear his car—he liked to pull it up into the backyard under his window in case somebody tried to steal it. It was real fancy—one of those Z cars—and made this deep rumble when the motor ran. They hadn't seen the car or him for a few days now.

Max had pretty much the same results. "The warrant's been signed. Try the door?"

Wager did. It was unlocked. Front room, kitchen, bedroom, and shower—the whole place might have fit into a single medium-size living room. The drawers hung open, scraped clean, and the stained mattress on its rusty springs and plywood support had been stripped. The bathroom cabinet was empty of everything except a little trash and grime. The refrigerator held some milk and bread and a couple of eggs, and in the sink a frying pan caught a drip from the faucet. A crust of gray grease had gathered where the pooled water met the iron sides of the pan. No telephone, no television.

"The people next door recognized his picture," said Max. "I told them to call if they saw him."

"He won't come back here. No reason to."

Max agreed. "You know anything about Roy Quintana?"

"Never heard of him." Wager smiled. "But I bet Fullerton has."

"Right. Thanks."

They reached the Admin Building around seven-thirty. Max didn't bother to take the elevator up to the office; Francine had wanted him home early and was probably royally pissed by now. Wager checked him out on the location board before looking in his own box for any messages. A brief one had been phoned in from San Diego: "Agent Mallory, FBI San Diego, CA, arr. Stapleton tonight, United 358, ETA 2314. Positive ID victim."

Wager dropped Elizabeth off at her home after dinner and prom-ised to call in the morning. He'd stay at his own place tonight; there was no telling how late he'd be with the FBI man, and no sense disturbing her when the meeting was finally over. He arrived early at Stapleton airport, and so did the flight. He didn't know what Mallory looked like, but he had seen plenty of FBI agents, so he stood by the exit and watched the passengers trail off. A lot were families with hyper kids who tugged on stretched arms or others who hung asleep over weary shoulders. College-age people carried backpacks and wore T-shirts advertising various products and messages. Elderly men and women trailed out anxiously looking for relatives and friends. A few businessmen carried attaché cases and dangled jackets over one shoulder. One tall, dark-skinned man with a conservative suit, gray hair whose tight curls were clipped close, and almost black eyes seemed to be looking for Wager.

"Mallory?" Wager showed his ID.

"Yes." A brief and proper smile. "Wager—good of you to meet me."

"Any luggage?"

The man hefted his clothes bag. "Just what I'm carrying."

They began walking rapidly past the clumps of passengers in the long concourse. "The victim has been positively identified?" Wager asked.

"Pauline Tillotson: dental charts and two surviving fingers on the left hand." He explained, "It was clenched tightly enough to protect the flesh. The lab managed to get prints from the inner skin."

Wager didn't say anything until they reached his car in the no parking zone just outside the luggage carousels. "Where to?"

"The Marriott City Center—it's near the Federal Building." They were halfway down Martin Luther King Boulevard before Mallory asked, "Any leads on the man you're looking for?"

"Just that it's someone who knows how to hide his identity."

That was no surprise to the agent. "If it's who I think it is, he's had a lot of practice."

They were silent for the rest of the ride. Mallory checked into the hotel and sent his bag up to the room; then he and Wager went into the bar. This late on a weeknight, it was quiet and the large piano stood silent. They sat away from the escalator that formed one wall behind the serving counter, and took a table half-sheltered by a plant with large, shiny leaves, whose name Wager didn't know. He thought the place was more like a patio café than a real bar: open to strollers in the lobby and filled with light from the large chandelier. Maybe all the plants were supposed to make people think they were outside, but it only made Wager think about bird crap. He had a beer, Mallory a martini—"dry, up, with a twist." After the waitress brought the drinks, the FBI agent took a long sip and sighed comfortably.

"All right, Detective Wager, I suppose your patience has been tested enough." Another perfunctory stretch at the corners of a thin-lipped mouth. Wager drank at the foam in his tapered glass and watched a couple ride up the escalator to the second floor. Mallory wouldn't have come this far if it weren't important and, Wager suspected, if he didn't need something from DPD.

"Pauline Tillotson was working for us as an informant." Mallory leaned forward slightly, his voice barely carrying across the table with its glasses, cocktail napkins, bowl of salted munchies. "She volunteered. She came to us—to our San Diego office—when the activist group she was affiliated with split off from Earth First!"

"Earth First!? The kiss-a-tree people?"

Blinking, Mallory smiled briefly. "I suppose that's one way of describing them. Ecology, utopianism, Greenpeace, socialism, the Green Party—it's a mixed bag of isms; but yes, that's where these people originated. If the splinter group has a single leader, it's William Libeus King—he prefers his middle name. He's been implicated in the bombing of a high-power transmission line near the atomic warhead plant in Amarillo."

Wager tried to dredge up what he'd read in the newspapers about power line bombings. "Somebody tried something like that out at Rocky Flats a few years ago. Was he in on it?"

"We don't think so—we attribute that job to Dave Foreman, who founded Earth First!" Mallory's thin lips twisted in an ironic smile. "Now Foreman's one of the people King thinks isn't radical enough."

"The Amarillo plant's a federal installation, right?"

Mallory nodded. "Right. That's when we got interested in Libeus King."

"I thought that was Department of Defense or Department of Energy territory."

Filling his hand from the snack bowl, the FBI agent finished chewing before he answered. "By charter, DOE is supposed to provide security for the installations, that's true. And they do a fine job! They do indeed. But domestic espionage and sabotage are clearly the Bureau's responsibility. There's an overlap of authority there, but we work quite closely and harmoniously with DOE security forces, of course."

Wager nodded as if he believed the man.

And Mallory, as if he didn't believe Wager's nod, emphasized, "After all, we all want the same thing—the safeguarding of federal installations." He rinsed his mouth with icy gin. "Anyway, Tillotson came to us after King's group split off from the main movement. She didn't like their increasing emphasis on violence, and she was worried because King started focusing on what he called the 'pollutions of the military-industrial complex.' In fact, the incident that brought her to us was an attempt to set fire to a nuclear submarine at the pen in San Diego harbor."

"I didn't read anything about that."

"That's because the attempt failed. And we kept it out of the papers. All we need is a series of copycat arsonists going after nuclear subs! Anyway, Tillotson had been part of it, without—she says—fully realizing what she was participating in. It scared her enough so that she came to us to cover her tail."

And that gave the FBI leverage over the woman—the usual immunity from prosecution in exchange for cooperation. "So you had a snitch."

"We had a snitch."

And Wager had a good motive for the homicide. He took the police sketch from his breast pocket. "This is the man who rented the house. Is he familiar?"

Tilting the paper to the bar's dim light, Mallory studied it carefully. "It certainly could be Libeus King. Do you have a physical description?"

Wager told him what little he knew about Marshall. "Can you get me a copy of his jacket?"

"Sure. No problem. I'll have his file faxed in the morning." The tall man amended, "It'll have to be sanitized, of course, but it'll still give you plenty to go on."

"What about known associates?"

"Do you have additional suspects?"

Wager told him about the other people seen at the house, and the agent sipped again. "So he's had his brigade meetings."

"He what?" asked Wager.

Mallory explained, "They think of themselves as 'Eco-warriors.' Libeus King calls his group the Edward Abbey Brigade of the Green Army." He saw Wager's look. "Hey, they're not the only militant ones; a number of small groups think of themselves as ecological guerrillas. The Sea Shepherds out of Redondo Beach even run advertisements soliciting money and volunteers for guerrilla actions. They claim to have sunk seven illegal whaling ships." Mallory smiled, "It's unclear who defines the ships' legality, and so far, they say, it's without loss of life. But it's only a matter of time. Fortunately, they do their work outside our jurisdiction."

"King is part of a whole army?"

"It sounds a lot bigger than it is, which is what they want. But it's big enough to cause trouble. We estimate at most a couple hundred members and associates of the 'army' nationwide; they're loosely affiliated, but they share the same feeling that they can use any means necessary to save Mother Earth." Mallory's hand emphasized what he said. "King's is one of the best-organized brigades—and potentially one of the most violent. He may have as many as thirty people spread across the western states. Despite the man's pretensions, we don't take his group lightly. They're dedicated, they're imaginative, and they've made some serious threats and attempts." He added, "And Tillotson's latest reports indicated that King's attitude is increasingly hostile. He apparently feels the federal government is actively working against all that he's trying to defend."

"Is it?"

The agent's dark eyes rested on Wager's face to see if he was joking. "He accuses the government of being unresponsive to the need to save the earth. Of sacrificing the citizenry to the interests of industry and the military. He thinks people should strike back before it's too late."

"Strike back how? And too late for what?"

"Too late to save the earth, for humanity to survive, for democracy to triumph—I'm not exactly certain what demons he's fighting, except they seem to be embodied in the federal government. Tillotson said that the submarine attempt showed King's increasing desperation. He felt he had to strike back in some major way. He wanted to make a public statement that people couldn't ignore."

"Is that why all those people were meeting here?"

The quick lift and fall at the corners of Mallory's mouth. "That's what we wanted to talk with Tillotson about. Her last information was that King had called a war council with his brigade lieutenants, and in the past a war council has meant some kind of action."

Wager thought about that. "How many lieutenants?"

"Anywhere from four to eight." The man hesitated and then shrugged—Wager might as well know it all. "They're people King's known for a long time, people he goes camping and river rafting with, people he's learned to trust. They think like he does and do what he says. Each lieutenant has his own 'company,' recruited in his own area. Who they are, and how many, only that lieutenant knows. But they're supposed to be experienced outdoor people and long-term acquaintances before they're invited to join. The lieutenant is the only liaison with the brigade, and they never meet as a group; the lieutenants come to see King one or two at a time, so it's possible even they don't know who all of them are. Or how many."

Wager took a long swallow of his beer. "Organization that tight, you were lucky to get a snitch."

"Very lucky," Mallory agreed. "Even Tillotson didn't have full knowledge of the brigade's membership or of King's plans."

"Most of Marshall's visitors came in the last couple weeks, the neighbors said."

"Individuals and small groups? One after the other?"

"That's what it sounded like. Apparently they drove there

—some of the residents complained about losing parking places on the street. But they were quiet. Nobody remembered any loud parties."

Mallory raised his glass to the waitress for another round. "It fits." He waited until the waitress had come and gone again before telling Wager the rest. "Tillotson told us they were talking about a major strike in the Denver area. A real headline grabber, she called it."

"Where?"

The agent shook his head. "If she did find out, she didn't get a chance to tell us."

Denver had a long list of military-industrial targets where sabotage would make headlines. The Rocky Flats plant was already in the news—that's where they made the plutonium triggers that were shipped to Amarillo for assembly with the warheads. The Rocky Mountain Arsenal, with its nerve gas stores, was on the north edge of the city. There were half a dozen military reserve centers. The space and rocket industry was served by a lot of big companies all along the Front Range—Martin Marietta, Ball Brothers, computer companies. A bit farther south, Fort Carson and its stockpiles were just outside Colorado Springs, and the Pueblo Depot held military supplies. There was even the Space Defense Command and NORAD headquarters inside Cheyenne Mountain, though Wager didn't think they'd have to worry about that one. It could withstand a direct hit by an ICBM and had elaborate defenses against both conventional and biochemical assault. There were lesser targets, too, around Denver, which would generate both chaos and headlines: the air force personnel and finance computer center, the Denver Mint, NASA's western facilities, with their new supercomputer, the St. Vrain atomic power plant, even some special-weapons development units at the Federal Center on Denver's western edge. Wager didn't know much about that very secret activity, but there were always rumors about the latest toys some of the feds out there had come up with. Mallory probably knew of even more targets, ones that Wager had no knowledge of. "There're a lot of possibilities around here."

The agent pushed his empty martini glass in a small circle. "So many it's scary." Glancing up, Mallory warned Wager, "This information is highly confidential, of course. I'm giving it to you because I want you to know what the stakes are."

Wager understood the man. He understood, too, the large quantity of information Mallory had given him. "I'm interested in the homicide only. If this guy Marshall, or King, is cleared, he's all yours. If I learn anything that might help you people, you've got it."

That didn't cover everything Mallory wanted. "If you charge him, we'd like access to him."

"I have no trouble with that." Depending on what Mallory meant by "access"; that could be worked out when and if the time came. It was Wager's turn to warn the agent. "But my chief has to know what the stakes are too. I'll tell him it's confidential and that I've promised you it would stay that way. But he should know."

"I understand."

They talked a little about the next day—Mallory promised again to have a copy of King's FBI sheet faxed to Wager and then drop by the homicide office later in the morning to brief Chief Doyle. Wager would use his new knowledge to go over everything he had on Marshall and the victim to see if anything new turned up. He and Mallory would then meet at eleven to compare notes.

On his way to the car, Wager asked another question that had been at the back of his mind, "Does King have any lieutenants in this area?"

Mallory nodded. "A Richard, or Dick, Simon. We don't know much about him except that he lives up near Boulder in a mountain cabin. Tillotson said Simon has the Front Range region from Cheyenne, Wyoming, to Pueblo, Colorado."

"Where near Boulder? Do you have an address?"

The FBI agent looked embarrassed. "Yes—it's on Magnolia Road. But neither King nor Simon are there. I—ah—that is, when you called this morning, I asked one of our agents from the Denver office to check out the cabin. I got his report just before I boarded my flight. The cabin is vacated."

Simon had slipped through their fingers, and that explained a lot of Mallory's cooperative spirit. Wager asked the man for Simon's address anyway—otherwise, it would be one of those tiny blank spots that irritated. As he jotted down the cabin's route and fire-fighting numbers, he heard the jangle of distant sirens a few blocks to the north. A large fire, maybe, or a major accident—something that stirred up the rescue and emergency vehicles and echoed their mechanical wails from a dozen directions through the cold concrete walls of the streets. The noise's piercing discord, its driving pulse, made a fit background for Wager's feelings about Tillotson's death. Every homicide had its urgency, but this one had gained an additional impetus as well as a dimension Wager wasn't familiar with. If Mallory was right, then perhaps what Tillotson learned was vital enough—dangerous enough—for Marshall/King to risk a murder conviction. Maybe he planned a terrorist act that would make the death of only one person seem unimportant. Even if that aspect of the case was the FBI's responsibility, the man planning that act, as a homicide suspect, was Wager's responsibility. And despite what Mallory promised, if one of the agent's bosses felt the FBI would gain from it—and if they got to Marshall first—they could offer him immunity from the homicide charge in return for information about his and other guerrilla groups. Marshall would not be the first murderer to disappear into the federal Witness Protection Program. At least Mallory had said nothing yet about expanding the case by bringing in the Denver FBI office. And Wager hadn't asked him.

• • • • • • • • • •

But as he came in the next morning, his first call was from Special Agent Bunting. "Did the San Diego office make contact with you, Detective Wager?"

"Yes. I think we've worked things out."

"That's fine . . . fine. You—ah—discussed the case with a Special Agent Mallory, I believe?"

"Mallory. Right."

"I understand he's in town now."

"Came in last night."

"I see." Wager was beginning to see too. Bunting asked, "Did he give you information that our office—ah—should be apprised of, Detective?"

"Nothing you don't already know, I guess." Wager smiled at the telephone. "Were you the agent that checked out the Simon cabin on Magnolia Road near Boulder?"

"No. . . . That was another agent. I of course didn't see his report. But I'm sure Agent Mallory will share it with you on a need-to-know basis."

"Right. And you people always work together on these cases, right?"

"Yes! Of course."

"Fine. Then I'll tell Mallory you called."

He hung up and stared a long moment at the collection of Wanted posters, cartoons, notices, and messages tacked to the bulletin board. Wager had heard about the rivalries between FBI regional offices and how jealous each office was of its cases. Publicity was important to every law enforcement agency, including DPD. But it was really important back in Washington and therefore to the regional FBI offices. In fact, it was rumored that the agent in charge of the Denver office had a secretary whose primary job was to clip every press notice about local FBI activity and fax it back to Bureau headquarters. There was also a standing joke that the FBI didn't mind who did the work as long as it got the credit.

There was another wrinkle: Mallory was an Afro-American, one of a group that was not as rare in the FBI as it used to be. But Mallory still had to put up with a lot of things that Anglos didn't, and he would be eager to prove that he could handle the case as well as if not better than any other agent. Wager could understand that feeling. So far, Mallory seemed to have played fair, and Wager would too. And as for helping the Denver FBI office take away the San Diego agent's case, Wager didn't owe Bunting and his people one damn thing.

The papers Mallory had promised came through from San Diego a little after eight. It was obvious that the information was incomplete, and even what Wager was given had heavily inked gaps in the narrative of criminal activity. But the vitals were there: photographs and fingerprints, physical descriptions, brief biographies, lists of known associates and customary behavior patterns, threat assessments. Wager compared King's photograph with the sketch of Marshall, and as Mallory said, they could be the same man. If Archy could find a fingerprint in the house that matched any of these, it would be definite. Even if it wasn't, the physical likeness made King a strong lead.

Tillotson's front and side photographs showed a young woman with large, frightened-looking eyes caught as they gazed slightly away from the camera. She had high cheekbones, accentuated in the photograph by shadowy, hollow cheeks; lips whose possible fullness was pinched with tension; and a long, rounded jaw. Accompanying Tillotson's dossier was an abstract from the FBI lab's report identifying the dental X-rays and hands of the victim as those of Pauline Elizabeth Tillotson, WF, DOB 7 August 1969. It also provided her Social Security number, gave her last known address as 3144 Country Day Road, Poway, California, and named her nearest relatives. Phyllis and Gordon Tillotson, mother and father. They lived at the same address. Wager jotted down the telephone number; as case officer, he was responsible for having the next of kin notified.

He telephoned the morgue and left a message for Doc Hefley, saying that the Jane Doe had been identified, then he called Archy Douglas. "The FBI lab came back with a positive on that arson-homicide victim."

"Already? Jesus Christ, that's a miracle! How the hell did that happen?"

"Hey, I didn't ask questions; I just said thanks." He told the forensics detective Tillotson's name and vitals and promised Archy a copy of the FBI report. "How're you doing on the fingerprints?"

"I finally got all the elimination prints. I haven't had a chance to start comparing yet."

"We have a possible suspect—and a complete set of prints. If I bring it over, how soon can you get a match?"

"How soon? Jesus, Wager, I'm still on duty from yesterday —I spent the whole goddamn night at the Blue Moon."

"What happened?"

"You haven't heard yet?" The outraged voice didn't wait for Wager to say no. "Two people from patrol: Rosener and Markowsky. Both shot. Rosener's in the ICU, Markowsky's still under the knife—they're asking for type AB blood, if that's you. Sniper. Some son of a bitch phoned in a fight in the alley behind the Blue Moon. Said a man had been cut. A fucking setup."

"Who's on it?"

The rage ebbed from Archy's voice, to leave him sounding very tired. "Assault. And Ross from Homicide—he's part of the shooting team. Between you and me, Wager, I wish it was you."

That explained those sirens last night and the silent emptiness of the homicide offices this morning; detectives who could give blood were lined up over at Denver General with the officers of the patrol division. Those who could drop current cases were out on the streets, looking for the sniper.

"Did you know either of them, Gabe?"

"I've seen Rosener around. I don't know Markowsky."

"Yeah—he's just out of the academy. Rosener was his field training officer." Archy added, "From what I put together so far, Markowsky was hit first, and Rosener returned fire. Then he tried to pull Markowsky to safety. That's when the bastard got him."

"Suspect?"

"Nothing yet. And those sons of bitches in the Blue Moon won't say a thing. Check with Ross when you see him. Ask him to let me know what he's got, OK?"

Wager said he would, but he had to add, "I know first things first, Archy. But this ID I'm asking you for is important too— I need it."

A pause. "Jesus, Wager. I'm talking a cop-shooter here."

And Wager was talking a possible terrorist, but he couldn't tell Douglas about it. "I'm just telling you it's important, that's all."

"Yeah. Your cases are always important, aren't they?" The line clicked.

Like everyone else, Chief Doyle was out of his office; Wager had the dispatcher call him at Denver General, where the man was in line to give blood. A few minutes later, Wager's phone rang, and Doyle, his voice revealing the tense anger that had spread like a virus through the whole department, asked Wager what he wanted. He told the chief about Agent Mallory and added that it involved classified information. "Mallory told me about it last night, and I don't want to talk about it over the phone. He wants to meet with you this morning and fill you in."

"Christ!" An angry silence. "All right; what time?"

"He said he'd call your office first. Your secretary's probably talked to him by now."

"All right. Tell Michelle I'm on my way in and that I'll see Mallory whenever he's available."

Wager said he would. "How're Markowsky and Rosener?"

"Markowsky's out of surgery. They're both still alive. That's about it."

Gradually, the routine demands of Crimes Against Persons drew the detectives back to the office and the ringing telephones on their desks. But anger hung like a bad smell in the air, and whenever someone asked a new arrival if anything had turned up, everyone knew what was meant, and everyone listened to the reply.

Elizabeth, her voice tense, had called to be sure Wager hadn't been involved in the shooting and that he was all right. It felt kind of odd to learn that someone had been thinking about his safety, and after he hung up, Wager worried that he might have been too casual in shrugging off Elizabeth's concern. It wasn't that he didn't appreciate it; he was just unused to it. He tried to call back and tell her that, but her line was already busy, and he had chores to do as well.

One was to talk to the victim's parents. Wager telephoned the police department in Poway, California, and asked them to send a courtesy officer to notify the Tillotsons about the death of their daughter. He'd left his name and number for further information, and a little after nine the call came from Mr. Tillotson.

"Is this the officer who called about Pauline—about my daughter?"

"Yes, sir. I'm sorry it happened."

"What . . . Can you tell me what did happen, Officer? The police told us only that she's dead. They said you'd have to explain . . ."

He tried not to sound officious. "It happened on the twenty-first, sir. She was a homicide victim."

"Homicide? My God . . ." Wager could hear words muffled through a hand over the mouthpiece. "The twenty-first? That was three days ago!"

"Yes, sir. We couldn't get a positive identification until late last night."

"Positive? You mean you're not sure it's Pauline?"

"Well, we are now, sir. There was a fire, and—ah—her body was badly burned. Identification had to be made from dental records and fingerprints." He finished with lame consolation. "She was dead before the fire, sir."

"Oh, God—oh, my God."

He waited, but the line was silent. Finally, he asked, "Mr. Tillotson, we need some help to find your daughter's killer. Can I ask you a few questions?"

"Yes . . . I suppose so."

"Did your daughter say anything to you about why she was in Denver or who she was staying with?"

"No. We didn't even know she was there. She was in Arizona—she was with—" The voice stopped. "Her boyfriend, Libby, what happened to him? Where is he?"

"Would that be Libeus King?"

"Yes. Isn't he there? Why didn't he call?"

"He seems to have disappeared, sir. Do you have any idea where he might be?"

"Is he the one . . . ? Do you think he did it?"

"Did he ever threaten your daughter, sir?"

"No—not that I know of. But the way you said it . . . You make him sound like a suspect."

"We don't have any suspects yet, sir. She was staying at a house rented by a John Marshall. Did she ever mention that name?"

"Not to me." The hand over the mouthpiece made another interruption. "Her mother doesn't remember it, either."

"Can you give me the names of any of her friends who might know why she came to Denver?"

"I don't know. I really don't. She hasn't lived at home for several years. Not since she went to college. I . . . I guess I don't know who her friends are anymore."

"Would you mind asking your wife, sir? Anything might help us."

He did, but the answer was the same, and Wager guessed that the girl, conscious of security, had said little to anyone about the new friends and acquaintances she met while going with King.

"Is there anyone she might have written to? High school buddies, hometown friends—anyone at all I can talk to just in case she told them anything?"

"Just a minute." The voice came back. "You might try Sheila Riggs. She used to be Pauline's best friend—they went to high school and college together." He gave Wager the number after his wife looked it up. Then he asked, "Mr. Wager, was Pauline . . . Was it . . . sexual? Was she hurt before . . . ?"

"We don't have any evidence of sexual assault, Mr. Tillotson. It looks like death was caused by a blow to the head."

"Why?"

"I don't know, not yet." He told the man what Colorado number the California mortician should call for his daughter's body. "He'll make all the arrangements, Mr. Tillotson." He again said he was sorry about the man's daughter, thanked him for the information, and left his name and number if the Tillotsons remembered anything else, no matter how trivial.

Hanging up, he dug his fingers into the tense muscles at the back of his neck. It didn't bother some of the detectives to give relatives the gory details of their loved ones' death; it did bother Wager. He kicked away from his desk and poured himself another cup of the sour coffee that steamed gently on the hot plate in the small utility room. Ross, baggy-eyed, his mouth tight at the corners, strode down the hallway. Wager caught his eye.

"Archy Douglas wants an update as soon as you have something."

"No shit, Wager. So does everybody else."

"He asked me to tell you, Ross. That's all."

"Fine. You told me."

The dark-haired detective turned his back on Wager to grab the handful of messages from his pigeonhole. Going to his desk, he ignored the glances of the other detectives and began making telephone calls. Devereaux, Ross's partner, stopped by the utility room to rinse out his coffee cup for a refill. "Ross is pretty wound up over this, Gabe. He worked the same district as Rosener."

"Any names yet?"

Devereaux shook his head. "Some of those people at the Blue Moon know something. But nobody's talking. Not yet anyway."

"If you're getting up a reward, count me in for a hundred."

"Thanks, Gabe."

At his desk again, Wager called the dispatcher for another statewide BOLO on King's car and plate. No one had yet reported seeing it, which could mean that it was out of state or parked somewhere off the streets. Or—most likely—the patrol officers were paying less attention to wanted plates than to many other things, such as a fugitive cop-shooter. Sliding his name across the locator board, Wager headed back to the west side with the photographs of Libeus King.

Angela Cruz was at her cash register in Payless Drug. Under the cold light of the fluorescent ceiling, she looked at the collection of photographs. Wager had put them into a large manila folder that had rows of little cut-out windows. Most of the faces were roughly similar to King's; a couple were radically different. Arranging the display was an art form, and Wager had been careful to choose faces that were close but still different enough not to cause confusion for a witness. The manila windows showed pairs of photographs, one full face, one profile with the hair pulled back to show the ear. The frames of the windows were supposed to hide the fact that the photographs had DPD identification numbers below them. That way, the court said, the suspect's rights wouldn't be violated by prejudicing a witness against someone who had an arrest record. Wager figured the court thought all civilians ran around getting mug shots.

The girl's finger ran halfway across the second row and stopped. "That's the one—that's him."

"You don't want to look at the rest?"

"No. That's him."

It was King's FBI photograph.

The answer was the same at the liquor store, and just as

positive. But the newsstand manager frowned. "It could be this guy, or him, or this one down here. I really can't say—I see so many people every day, they all sort of fall into categories, you know?" He handed the folder back. "These three are all from the same category, see? Dark hair, kind of bushy; eyes kind of like triangles and going down at the corners. Kind of an oblong face. But whether it's the same individual, I really can't say."

Wager thanked the man and crossed him off the potential-witness list. King's photograph was among the three he'd pointed to, but if a case went to court, Wager would want an ID stronger than "maybe." After all, Kolagny might be the prosecutor.

The last stop was the used car salesman out in Aurora. He, too, indicated King's picture and said that was definitely the man who bought the Toyota. Then he added something. "I remembered after you left. He asked if the car was adjusted for high altitude. He said he wanted to take it up into the mountains."

"Did he say where?"

"No. Just that he wanted to make sure it would run OK at altitude."

Back at his desk, Wager pasted a new name tag over the lip of the Marshall folder and inked in "KING, William Libeus, aka John Marshall." Then, checking the wall clock, he called the Bulldog's office to find out if Special Agent Mallory had arrived yet. The secretary said the agent was in with the chief now; did Wager have an urgent message for them? He didn't.

Mallory would get down to the homicide office when he could; Wager began catching up on the routine paperwork that never stopped. He was in the middle of a survey of overtime hours when the telephone rang and a familiar voice brightened his day. "Wager—I understand you're sitting on a story that you don't want the press to learn about."

"Good morning to you too, Gargan. If there's something I don't want the press to know about, I'm sure as hell not going to tell it to you."

"You know that doesn't at all surprise me? But I'll tell you what does surprise me: blatant disregard of the police department's Public Relations Enhancement Program by one of its own detectives. Or are you the only cop in DPD who hasn't heard of I-PREP?"

"I'm a cop who doesn't discuss open cases."

"You haven't even asked me what case I'm interested in! If I had to tell Chief Sullivan, I'd have to say you don't care what case I'm interested in—you just want to be uncooperative with the press."

The reporter was right on both counts: Wager didn't care and he was uncooperative. But in support of the Public Relations Enhancement Program, he asked, "All right, Gargan, what case are you interested in that I can't talk to you about?"

"That arson and possible homicide over on Wyandot Street. Female victim in her twenties. Lieutenant Watterson gave us a press release yesterday and asked for any witnesses to come forward. Guess who he wanted them to call, Wager?"

"You a witness?"

"Har-de-har. Was it a homicide or not?"

"Why aren't you on the Blue Moon cop shooting, Gargan? A sniper attack on a cop's a hell of a lot more exciting than an unidentified corpse. And maybe you could even do some good for a change—talk one of those barflies into identifying that goddamn sniper."

"The editor put a team on that one. Now, was it a homicide or not?"

"Yes."

Gargan waited. "That's it? You're giving me a one-word story?"

Wager could think of two or three more words to give Gargan, but they would violate the good-relations policy. "It's an ongoing case, Gargan."

"Right. So I suppose you don't want to tell me why the San Diego FBI office sent a man to investigate it."

Wager hadn't told Watterson about that. "If you know so goddamn much about it, you don't need to talk to me."

"I know you're the officer of record, Wager. Now, do you tell me about it, or do I file a complaint with Chief Sullivan?"

"What you do, Gargan, is talk to the public information officer. Either that or go to hell." He hung up on an indignant squawk and stared at the wall as if it could tell him where the reporter got his information. They had their sources—their juice—all over the department. For the price of a dinner or a few beers or a flattering mention in the news, cops and support staff would tip reporters to the confidential details of cases. Every cop wanted his payoff case, the case that would get national headlines and make his name famous. Promotion, better job offers, book and movie money—Wager had heard the squad room talk about how this detective or that one had milked a case for its payoff: "Like that French Connection cop—man, didn't he hit a big one! And thing is, guy like that's not a damn bit better than you or me or any other cop. Lucky, that's all—lucky to be in on a big case and lucky to have the right connections with the press, man."

He had heard the talk, but just who Gargan could flatter to get information about the FBI, Wager didn't know. Nevertheless, he had a suspicion that it wasn't any of the very few people in the department who knew about the case. And when Mallory finally showed up, Wager asked him.

"How much have I told the Denver office? Why?"

"I had a call from a reporter a little while ago. He wanted to know if you were here because of the Tillotson homicide."

Mallory's dark eyes studied Wager's. "A local reporter?"

Wager nodded.

The FBI agent came to the same conclusion, and a flash of anger tightened his lips. "Bunting knows I'm here. We're required to check in with the regional office, under normal circumstances. I have no doubt he has his contacts in the San Diego office who could tell him what brought me here."

"Bunting called first thing this morning. Asked me what was going on."

"What'd you tell him?"

"Talk to you."

Mallory nodded. "You don't think the leak came from this department?"

"It wasn't me. The only other one who knows anything is Chief Doyle. And you were still briefing him when the reporter called. Who else is left?"

"Goddamn it—Bunting would do it: use publicity as leverage to get the case away from our office."

That wasn't what worried Wager. "Would a story scare King off?"

"It certainly could. Worse, if he is planning a strike, it could push up his timetable." The agent ran a hand through his short gray hair. "I explained that to Chief Doyle—he said he'd go along with a news blackout on the story for now."

"That's fine. But maybe you better explain it to the reporter too."

Mallory reached for the telephone. "What's his name?"

It took three or four calls. The first was to Mallory's home office. It was hot and terse, and the name Bunting came up several times. The other calls were to the *Denver Post,* where finally an editor in chief agreed to hold the story. But he demanded an exclusive interview with Mallory when it was over. The agent said that since the newspaper had him over a barrel, he would agree, though reluctantly, to that stipulation. Then he smiled as he hung up. "I'll of course give due credit to you and the Denver Police Department, Wager."

Wager grunted. "Provided things work out."

"Well, yes, always that proviso." Which he dismissed with a wave of his hand. "Let's go get some lunch. We can tell each other where we're at."

———

Mallory knew a little about Denver—"I've spent some time here on cases"—and had his favorite restaurants—"I'm on per diem this trip; I can afford it." The one they went to wasn't one Wager would have chosen. For one thing, it was in the heart of tourist country, Larimer Square, and for another, you had to wait in line for a table, then wait at the table for the menu, then wait after the menu for the food. The only thing quick was the check. At least there weren't any trees growing over their table.

Wager told Mallory that he had positive identification from three witnesses that Marshall and King were the same man. "I also have a description of his car and his license number, but nothing's turned up on that yet. I talked to Tillotson's parents. They didn't even know she was in Denver. They gave me the name of one of her friends, but I haven't reached her yet."

Mallory pulled a slip of paper from his vest pocket. "Here's a roster of her known associates. It's up-to-date, but as far as I know, none of them are in the Denver area."

Wager glanced down the list. He recognized a couple of the names. "Any word on this Simon guy? The one up in Boulder?"

"Nothing new."

"What can you tell me about Charles Pipkin?"

"Oh? You've run across him?"

He told Mallory about the telephone calls listed to the Wyandot number. "One of them was to Pipkin. It's a rural route address outside Steamboat Springs."

The agent cut into the chicken swimming in its special house sauce and chewed for a moment. "Pipkin. I didn't know he'd left the San Diego area. No arrest record, graduated San Diego State University about six years ago, now a science teacher in a junior high school. Active in Greenpeace and a couple other conservationist political movements; became associated with King's group two years ago, and that's when Tillotson met him."

"What would he be doing in Steamboat Springs?"

The man shook his head. "Last I heard, he was still in En-cinitas. Tillotson didn't tell me anything different in her last report." He added, "She did say that King once called Pipkin their special-weapons expert. He knows a lot of chemistry and physics, she said."

Chemistry and physics. Wager recalled a little something that made his expensive fish suddenly taste like mud. "One of the people who recognized King—a news vendor—said one of King's visitors made a joke about the Rocky Mountain Arsenal."

Mallory, too, stopped chewing. "What kind of joke?"

Wager told him.

"They've moved most of that stuff to Utah. But not all." He stared into space for a moment, then his eyes returned to Wager, worried. "My God—something at the arsenal would be a 'real headline grabber.' All over the world."

"Another witness said King was worried about his car and high altitude." Wager told Mallory what the used car salesman remembered.

"King said that? High altitude?"

"That could be almost anywhere in the state."

"But he'd have to drive over a high pass to get to Steamboat, right?"

"A couple. Ten, eleven thousand feet."

Wiping his mouth, the agent signaled for the check. "You have jurisdiction in Steamboat?"

"I can get it. It'll take some time, but Routt County's been pretty easy to work with." Unlike one of the other mountain counties, where rumor had it the sheriff owed the local dope dealers more than he owed the law.

"We'd better get up there."

"It's a good four-hour drive. One way."

"Maybe Bunting can get us a plane. Son of a bitch owes me something after what he pulled."

They split the check—Mallory's per diem went only so far—
and the FBI man said he would call as soon as he'd arranged
for an airplane. Wager went back to his desk and his telephone.
Max came in as Wager was giving Sheila Riggs's number another try.

"Fullerton's got a lead on Roy Quintana, Gabe."

He hung up on the still-unanswered ringing. "Where is he?"

"Not him. A cousin he hangs around with—Eddie Barela."
He showed Wager a thin police folder. "Did some time in Buena
Vista for car theft. Works at a rendering plant out in Commerce
City. Want to come along?"

Max wanted him to, and he wasn't doing a damn bit of good
sitting and waiting restlessly for Mallory. "Why not?"

The plant was a collection of Butler buildings, whose tin roofs
shimmered in the hot afternoon sun. Cars were already starting
to leave the employee parking lot as the shift foreman led Max
and Wager down the shaded side of one of the buildings toward
the changing room.

· "Barela in trouble?" The stocky man squared a dirty gimme
cap on his head. Its logo read MoPar.

"No," said Max. "We just want to ask him about somebody he knows."

The foreman nodded. From under the cap a sweaty tangle of long graying hair lifted, then fell on his tanned and seamed neck. The lines on his face were engraved too, as if his eyes and nose were permanently pinched against the thick, rank smell of bloody hides and boiling flesh. "He's a good worker. Hate to see him go."

"We're not taking him anywhere," said Max.

"You hire a lot of ex-cons?" Wager asked.

"Goddamn right. And a lot work out too. A few don't." He glanced at Wager and then, narrow eyes flat, away again. "I'm one."

"I guess you worked out."

"I guess I did." He opened a door bearing the sign EMPLOYEES ONLY and leaned in. "Barela? Barela here?"

The foreman had told them that work started early at the plant, and the shift ended at three. Through the half-open door, Wager could see a dozen men, Hispanic, Black, Anglo, changing in front of lockers that held their street clothes and hard hats. The murmur of tired voices in Spanish and English was punctuated by occasional laughter. Splattered, crusty overalls intensified the odor, and a liquid film made the concrete floor sticky.

"Anybody seen Barela?"

"He punched out, Otis. Got a league game starts four o'clock."

The foreman shrugged. "I guess I can't help you, gents."

Wager stepped past the foreman so he could see the man who had replied. "Where's it at?"

The answer was sudden silence and a lot of expressionless stares from people of all colors who didn't like cops. The one who had spoken, a young Hispanic, looked uncomfortable.

The smile on Wager's lips didn't make it to his voice. "What kind of league and where is it?"

The young man looked around; no one looked back. Finally, he muttered, "Metro Mexican League—they play at Montbello High School."

"Thanks. Have a good day."

Back in the car and heading east on I-70, Max asked, "What the hell's the Metro Mexican League?"

Wager didn't know too much about it. "Local amateur ball teams. It's been around awhile—mostly players from Mexico."

"Softball?"

Wager shook his head. "Hardball."

The baseball diamond was set off from the rest of the high school's playing fields by a tall mesh fence. Max and Wager walked across the lawn that surrounded the parking lot. The brick school's long windowless wall looked like a high-tech factory and already had an empty, after-hours feel about it. On the running track, a cluster of athletes stretched and sprinted; the sound of a football coach's angry voice carried from beyond a blocking sled in the middle of an open field. At the baseball diamond, the freshly dragged dirt of the infield held a noisy team in green and yellow; a team in white with blue pinstripes was at bat. A small crowd was scattered over the open bleachers behind the backstop. It seemed to be made up of friends and family who knew the players by first names. Shouts, hoots, and cheers marked a hard swing.

"That's a pretty good pitcher," said Max.

Across the flat green of the fenceless outfield and the park space beyond, a line of distant roofs and trees marked a residential avenue. Max and Wager watched another fastball pop dust from the catcher's mitt; the umpire straightened and glanced at his counter before calling, "Two and two."

A chorus of hoots and whistles followed the call, and a woman's voice from the far bleachers jabbed through the noise. "*Era un* strike, man! You *no tiene* eyes!"

"What team's Barela on?"

Wager should have asked the kid at the rendering plant, and

he was irritated at himself that he didn't. "I'll take the green. You take the white."

A stocky, uniformed man stood at the entrance to the fenced dugout and studied his clipboard. Across the yellow shirt, green script spelled LOS AMIGOS. The weight of his stomach rolled down the elastic band at the top of the green baseball pants.

"Sus jugadores son de México?"

The dark face looked up, surprised. *"Sí, la mayoría. De Jalisco. Algunos, no."* The stocky man bobbed his chin at a black kid and an Anglo sitting on the bench. The pitcher, too, was an Anglo. *"Quiere jugar?"* The brown eyes measured Wager's shoulders.

"No. Busco a Eddie Barela. 'Stá 'quí?"

"Sí—es lef' fiel'."

The batter swung again, wood cracking hard. The ball was a blur along the third base line. The infielder dove, stretched flat, to spear the ball with his glove and smack hard in the dirt. He rolled once and rose in triumph, the ball pinched in the tip of his glove.

"Ah—magnífico! Buenobueno! OK Pitano!" The manager grinned widely at Wager. *"Como un profesional, no?"*

"Por supuesto." It was a good play, as good as any Wager had seen on television. Whether the third baseman could do it every time, like the pros were paid to do, was another thing; but it was a good play. The uniforms jogged in through the applause and shouts of the stands. Wager caught Max's eye and gestured; the large man squeezed past the corner of a tamale vendor, whose pickup truck with its aluminum camper had been pulled close behind the stands and who turned from watching the last play to chatter excitedly at his cluster of waiting customers.

"He's coming in from left field."

"That's a hot third baseman! How many teams in this league?"

Wager shrugged. "I'm not sure—it doesn't get much news. Most on this team are from Jalisco."

Max looked at the green uniforms. "That's where the Tapatío gang's from, right?"

"So they claim. Their fathers or grandfathers anyway."

"*Queremos* runs, man! Get a hit, man!"

The players filed into the dugout, drinking thirstily from squeeze bottles, and settled on the bench. Wager moved down the fence in back of the dugout until he stood behind Eddie Barela.

The man, in his early twenties, glanced over his shoulder without recognition, then back at the game, where an Amigos batter dug a cleated shoe into the clay at the plate. "*Debe un hit, Jaime!*"

The same woman's harsh voice carried across the field: "*Si no eres un hombre, venga al rancho y te hacemos un hombre!*"

Laughter answered from both bleachers.

"What's that about?" Wager asked Barela.

The grinning man half-turned to answer. "That's *una ranchera*. You know the El Rancho Bar? They sponsor that club." He wiggled his little finger. "She works at the club, you know?"

"*Una fichera?*"

Barela shrugged a careless affirmative. "They come out to the games, get pretty raunchy sometimes. Raunchy Rancheras, we call them."

The first pitch was a sharp curve that broke wide. Cheers from the Amigos, whistles and catcalls from the other side.

"Got a couple minutes, Eddie?" Wager cupped his shield in his hand so only the young man could see it. "Denver police."

His brown eyes tightened, and the grin went away. "What for?"

"To talk about your cousin Roy. Talk about Ray Moralez, who got shot. About Flaco Martínez, who did it."

"Aw, man! I don't know nothing about that shit."

The batter popped a high, arcing ball down the first base line. They both watched the outfielder race for it. He stretched and missed, the dropped ball bouncing past him. The batter turned at first and paused, as Barela joined the cheering, "*Andale, Jaime*—all right!"

"Fielder should've had that," said Wager.

Barela's head wagged, "Yeah, but we'll take anything they give us!" Then he remembered Wager was a cop. "Look, I don't know nothing about Ray Moralez or Flaco whoever. That's gang shit, man. I'm not part of that."

Max leaned against the fence, his bulk making it creak. "How many teams in this league?"

"Seventeen." He looked up at the large man. "You play?"

"Used to—high school." Max watched the pitcher try a pick-off at first. "You've got some good players here."

"Yeah. It's a tough league—you play with these people, you got to like the game, man. You a cop too, right?"

Max nodded and introduced himself. "Are most of your league players Mexican?"

"Yeah. A lot from Chihuahua, Zacatecas, Aguascalientes. But we got a lot of Chicanos too. Like me—real Yanquis, you know?"

Wager asked, "Your cousin Roy play too?"

Barela shook his head. "He should. He's got a pretty good arm."

"When'd you see him last?"

A deep sigh. "You people just don't quit, do you?"

Wager smiled. "Don't win any games by giving up."

The young man looked at Wager as if he'd never thought of it that way. Then he sidled through the narrow dugout gate, and the three men walked to the vacant end of the noisy bleachers. "Roy didn't have nothing to do with it. That's what he told me, and I believe him." Neither Wager nor Max contradicted him, so he went on. "Fights, macho stuff, OK. I mean, he lives in the barrio, you know? You live there, you got to prove yourself. But he's no *calavera*—none of this *homicidio* crap."

"Flaco's not from the barrio," said Max. "It'll be a cleaner place for everybody when we get him off the street."

Wager nodded at Barela's teammates, who were shouting loudly as another batter stung a single past the pitcher and over second base. "A lot of these people are from Jalisco. Your cousin's a Gallo. Maybe your teammates have cousins in the Tapatíos. The Gallos and the Tapatíos start killing each other because of this Flaco guy, how you going to feel?"

Max added, "All we want to do is talk to Roy. And all we want to talk about is Flaco. If he doesn't want to tell us anything, that's up to him. But we won't know unless we find him."

The young man stared at the worn grass. A clutch of children in shorts and tennis shoes ran shouting to swirl around them for a moment and then clatter up the bleacher seats. "OK. Just don't tell him where you found out, OK?" He waited until both Wager and Max nodded. "He's got a place over on Caithness. I don't know the number—second block. Brown brick apartment house—top floor, number eight." He added, "He's usually there nights—late, you know."

Max nodded thanks. "Who's winning?"

"We got the tying run on second."

"Buena suerte."

Wager's radio called his number as they pulled onto Interstate 70. It was the message he'd told the division receptionist to forward immediately: "Broomfield airport, five-thirty P.M. Mallory."

"Thanks."

Max looked at his watch. "It's almost five now. Want me to run you out to Broomfield?"

"Yeah." Rush hour traffic would make the trip from downtown to the outlying airfield slow. Max swung onto I-270 and headed north in the heavy traffic that looped around the city. "You want me with you when you talk to Roy tonight?"

"I can handle it, Gabe."

"Didn't say you couldn't. But I shouldn't be too late. I'll give you a call when I get back."

XV

9/24

1745

•   •   •   •   •   •   •   •   •

The small, two-engine plane spiraled upward to gain altitude
before crossing the mountains. Mallory sat up front in the co-
pilot's seat; Wager had strapped himself into one of the four
seats in the cramped cabin. Beneath the wing, the ripple of flat,
brown prairie dropped away, mottled by the shadows of puffy
clouds, which always built up in late-September afternoons.
Almost directly beneath the plane Wager could see the Rocky
Flats weapons plant, a heavily fenced rectangle of square buildings and paved streets and vehicle parks. Around it was a wide
band of vacant land marked here and there by gullies, an occasional stunted tree, and the twin dirt tracks of vehicle patrol
routes. A busy two-lane highway led north to Boulder, where
a sprawl of red-tiled roofs surrounded by trees and homes
marked the university. Then the plane was over the abrupt
foothills and straining hard to gain altitude to cross the Continental Divide.

Wager figured that by the time Mallory had arranged for a
plane, pilot, and ground transportation at both ends, they could
have made the drive to Steamboat Springs. But then they'd face
the long drive back; and besides, Wager suspected that saving
time wasn't the real reason for the flight. The real reason was

that Mallory wanted to make the Denver office kiss his butt with a little personal service by way of apology for that news leak. So they made use of the plane and pilot that the local office leased for short trips in the region. It was what he'd told Elizabeth when he called to say that tonight was going to be another long one.

"Steamboat? Why in the world are you flying out there?"

"I'll tell you when I get back." Some of it anyway—as much as he could.

"Any idea what time?"

He told her no and added that he and Max had a job to do later in the evening.

Her soft laugh mixed exasperation and wonder. "Your day sounds worse than mine! Doesn't it seem as if life's going faster and faster in more and more directions?"

"I haven't had time to think about it."

Another laugh. "I suppose that's the best way to handle it. I'll leave the light on."

That would be the small lamp by the sofa in the living room. Wager could see it in his mind's eye and, sinking into the isolation caused by the roar of the straining engines, savored the warmth in the thought that Elizabeth was willing to waste electricity on him, and—more important—that she would be waiting.

He gaped to relieve the pressure on his ears and watched jagged spires of shattered, naked rock pass very, very close beneath the wing. In fact, a couple of the ice-crusted peaks seemed to rise higher than the plane, and Wager figured the pilot was crossing one of the passes between mountains. Pawnee, maybe, or Arapaho. It was hard to tell, looking down on them from this angle. The rocky cliffs writhed and dropped away, marked here and there by ledges of green tundra and small turquoise lakes tailing out from cirques and snowfields. Then the close, shattered ridges were gone, and the engines stopped straining as the plane tilted into a long, shallow glide.

Below, gorges widened into canyons and then broader valleys that were scored by the straight lines of section roads marking ranches and farms.

"You have anything yet on King's automobile?" Mallory raised his voice over the buzzing drone of the engines.

Wager shook his head. Something might have come in this afternoon, but he wouldn't know until he got back to the office.

Mallory turned back to the windshield. The pilot said something to a hand-held microphone, and the plane banked slightly. The level green of Middle Park started rising again into the wooded peaks of the Gore Range, and the small plane bounced in its updrafts as they passed over dark pines and golden swaths of changing aspen. Then the pilot banked more sharply and began a steeper glide. On the flanks of one mountain, the trees had been shaved away in long streaks for now-grassy ski runs. A network of roads, paved and unpaved, began to converge on a spread of ranches, mountain homes, condominiums, and finally the cluster of brick buildings that was Steamboat Springs. The pilot said something else and banked again, and a few minutes later, Wager felt the wheels jolt softly against the runway.

A tanned and smiling blond woman handed Mallory the keys to a rental car, and they headed north on a narrow two-lane road that cut across an empty expanse dotted with sagebrush and wire fences.

Neither man said much; they concentrated on reading the names and numbers on the mailbox posts as the road crested a long ridge and dipped gently into another broad valley. Ahead of them, the horizon was a line of mountains mottled with green and yellow and orange.

"Getting close," Mallory said once. "It should be one of these up ahead."

It was, a mailbox whose post was anchored in a plastic bucket filled with concrete. No name, just the route number and two dusty ruts across a cattle guard and winding over a ridge of blue-green sagebrush. Mallory nosed the softly sprung car carefully down the rough path.

The cabin was a good half mile in, an A-frame set at the edge of the woods whose shimmering yellow was touched here and there by the pale green of late-turning leaves. A sun-glittered car was parked in a turnaround at the cabin's front. Mallory stopped to study it through a pair of small binoculars. He had his look and then handed the glasses to Wager. "It's not the Toyota."

Wager looked. It was a light car, not a dark-blue one, and it didn't have Denver plates, either. The license plate was the cheery blue-on-white of California's latest style.

They coasted to a halt at the edge of the turnaround and got out, both men closing the car's doors softly. Mallory checked the cylinder of his two-inch Police Special and replaced it loosely in his shoulder holster. Wager chambered a round to load his Star PD. Before walking nearer, they looked the cabin over. Two-story, it had a small balcony tucked under the roof's peak, probably off the main bedroom. An LP gas cylinder glinted in an open area a hundred yards from the house. An electric wire ran into the trees behind, probably to a well pump. Higher up the hill, in a clearing, a television dish pointed skyward. The only sound was the tiny whisper of aspen leaves that quivered and shook in the cool breeze.

Standing to one side of the doorframe, Mallory knocked loudly. Wager remained at a corner of the building, where he could watch the back.

Mallory knocked again and called through the open door. "Mr. Pipkin?"

A startled answer. "Yeah—just a minute!"

The sound of bare heels on the plank floor, and a man stood buttoning his flannel shirt and stuffing its tail into his jeans. "Caught me sleeping." His dark hair was tousled, and a stubble of whiskers made shadows on his lean cheeks. He glanced at Wager, then back at Mallory, caution coming into his eyes.

Mallory showed his card and identified himself. "This is Detective Wager, Denver police."

Pipkin didn't offer to shake hands or open the screen door. He was around six feet, slender build, and the caution deepened into suspicion. "What's the problem?"

"We're looking for Libeus King. We thought you might know where he is."

Pipkin scratched at his jaw. "You mean you thought he might be here."

"That too, Mr. Pipkin. Mind if we come in?"

He pushed open the door and held it for Mallory and Wager. "Well, he's not. You can look around if you like."

Wager would like, and Pipkin's invitation took care of any need for a warrant. He walked through the open room as he listened to their conversation.

"When did you last see King, Mr. Pipkin?"

"Not for a long time."

"Do you have any idea where he might be?"

"No."

"Has he contacted you in any way?"

Wager went up the spiral iron staircase to the second floor. Here, the angled walls pinched together at an overhead rafter, but plenty of light came through the glass triangles at each end of the building. A bathroom, one bedroom, with an open doorway, a sleeping loft that also served as a television room. The downstairs was a large open area marked off by furniture groupings rather than walls: kitchen and dining, living and lounging, with a stacked cabinet of stereo components, a worktable, and a bulletin board with a series of schematics tacked to it. They looked like engineering projects of some kind. A large bookshelf held loose-leaf notebooks, spiral-bound texts, and a few volumes with titles like *Stress Factors in Concrete Structures*.

"He sent me a postcard from Arizona a few weeks ago. Just to say hello."

"He didn't telephone you from Denver?"

Pipkin shook his head.

"Strange. Detective Wager has a record of a call to this number from King's Denver residence."

"You asked if Libby called me. He didn't."

"Who was it?"

"Why all these questions, Mr. Mallory? Libby's not here, and you have no reason at all to harass me. I don't know where he is. That's it."

Wager turned from studying the quiet, golden view out the back of the A-frame. The shimmer of leaves, the pale tree trunks, the calm blue of clear sky, all underlined the distance from the frenetic pace of Denver. But even here was no refuge. "King's a murder suspect."

"A what?"

"We think he killed Pauline Tillotson."

"Pauline? Pauline's dead?"

"Killed and her body burned in an arson."

Pipkin groped to pull a stool from under the breakfast shelf and sit on it. "My God. Pauline."

"Who called you from Denver?"

The man looked up at Wager, the question finally registering. "She did. Pauline."

"What about?"

He shook his head. "Just . . ." His fingers scratched at his neck, rasping in the whiskers. "We just talked."

"Were you good friends?"

"Yes. I liked her—she . . . she was sincere. She really wanted to make the world a better place."

"She was good-looking too."

Pipkin's eyes focused on Wager. "I said I liked her. I wasn't in love with her. We were friends. She and Libby were together anyway."

"Did they fight a lot?"

"No." He stared at something only he could see. "You don't

fight with Libby. You either agree with him or . . . or leave."
Wager thought that was bullshit; everybody fought at one
time or another. "What do you mean, 'leave'?"
"Walk away. Leave. He's that way: either you go along or
you don't. No argument, no questions, just yes or no."
"What happens if you say no?"
"No hard feelings—it's your privilege." Pipkin tried to explain. "Libby believes everyone should act from the heart. Do
what you really believe in. If someone comes up with a"—he
glanced at Mallory—"proposal for a project, say, then they talk
it over and think about it. Anybody who wants to join says
yes. If Libby says no and somebody else wants to go ahead,
they can."
Mallory asked, "What about fundamental differences of opin-
ion? Philosophical differences?"
The man shook his head. "No problem there—we all want
the same thing: an end to environmental destruction. Any"—
he shrugged—"debate—I couldn't call it argument—would be
over specific tactics."
"That's what you mean by a 'project'?" asked Wager.
"Yes."
"Suppose somebody wanted out of a project?"
He tried again to explain. "Look, somebody comes up with
a project, it's discussed thoroughly before any decision's taken.
It's the way the Indians used to do it—tribal democracy: you
talk over whether or not the idea's worthy, how it can be done,
what are the ramifications. Then everybody makes up their
mind to join or not. If there aren't enough people willing to
join—however many it takes to do the project—it fails. No one
is blamed for not joining, but once you say yes, you're in; no
backing out."
"But suppose somebody had second thoughts. Suppose somebody didn't understand fully what they were committed to and
tried to back out of something?"

The man once more gazed at some other place or time.

"Pipkin—could Pauline have been killed for backing out of something?"

Wager waited; Mallory leaned forward. "She was murdered, Mr. Pipkin. Somebody killed her in a house rented by Libeus King, and he's disappeared."

Pipkin's head wagged slowly from side to side, but he still said nothing.

"Make a guess, Pipkin," said Wager. "You're thinking something. What is it?"

Tongue licking dry lips, he grunted a few words.

"What?"

" 'No one gets hurt.' He swore that from the very beginning. 'No one gets hurt.' "

"That's what King said?"

"Yes."

"Has he changed his mind?"

Pipkin was silent.

"Did King and Tillotson fight with each other?"

"I never saw it, if they did."

"Who besides King might have killed her?"

"I don't know. I don't even know if he did it. I swear to God."

Mallory pulled a wooden chair around to sit and stare up at Pipkin hunched on the stool. "It's more than property damage now, Mr. Pipkin," he said reasonably. "More than trespassing on federal installations. It's murder." He waited, but the man said nothing. "Care to tell us why you've apparently quit your teaching job and moved here?"

His eyebrows lifted in surprise. "I haven't quit. I'm on sabbatical—the district has a sabbatical program. Half pay for the year." He waved a hand at the cabin walls. "It's cheap rent in the off-season—and peaceful." He looked past them at the shimmer of leaves. "I like to hike around. I'll be able to cross-country ski soon."

"And you've been up here for the past week?" asked Wager.

"For the past six weeks." Then he understood. "Do you mean did I go to Denver recently? The answer's no." He frowned. "When was Pauline killed? What day?"

"She was found early Monday morning."

He thought a moment. "I was here. I can't prove it—I live alone. The only place I drive to is Steamboat, to the grocery store. But I haven't been to Denver at all." He nodded toward a large poster tacked to the sloping boards of the wall; it showed a tusked elephant standing alert and tall against a background of lush trees. An inscription read WE'RE ALL ENDANGERED SPECIES. "I don't believe in killing. That's why I support Greenpeace and Earth First! pollution's a form of slow killing."

And to Wager's way of thinking, murder was a form of pollution. "Then why did Pauline Tillotson think of you as King's 'weapons expert'?"

Mallory winced, but Pipkin didn't see it. His eyes widened slightly, and he hesitated. "She said that?"

"She wrote it," lied Wager. "We found some letters that hadn't been burned in the fire." He wagged a thumb at the worktable. "You teach science at your school, and these are engineering drawings. Is it a 'project' for King?"

"It's a—ah—problem he asked me to look over. I'm not sure if it's a project."

Mallory strode quickly to the table to look. "What kind of problem?"

Pipkin rubbed a knuckle along the whiskery ridge of his jaw. "Demolitions. Of a concrete structure. Reinforced concrete."

"Where?"

"I don't know. He just asked me what if there was a reinforced concrete building—how much of what kind of explosives would it take to penetrate it."

"What kind of building? Did he describe it?"

"Not at first. He talked about half a dozen different kinds, with different variables: exposed concrete, earth-sheltered con-

crete, double walls, windows, no windows. I got the feeling he
didn't have a specific building in mind."

"What do you mean, 'at first'?"

Pipkin shifted uneasily. "Well, a little later, he brought me
a set of plans. Building plans." He nodded toward the table.

"When?"

"A while ago. A couple months, at least. It's been a while."

"When you were in California?"

"Yes."

"Did you give him the information?" asked Wager.

"I mailed it to him. Yeah."

"When?"

"Maybe three weeks ago."

Mallory stated, "From here. You finished the problem here
and mailed him the solution."

"Not a solution, exactly. What I did was point out the types
of demolitions needed and the most likely points to—ah—
incapacitate the structure. You know: different options."

"You sent that to Denver?" Wager asked.

"No. I didn't know he was in Denver then."

"To California?"

Pipkin closed his mouth, uncomfortable at admitting anything
more.

Wager sighed. "You know we had to identify Pauline by her
dental records, Mr. Pipkin? Her body was burned that badly.
She was a very pretty girl, but even her parents wouldn't have
known what they were looking at. They got her back in a rubber
bag inside a closed casket." His voice tightened. "Somebody
not only killed her; they tried to erase her from the earth." He
stared deeply into the man's wide eyes. "What you tell us might
help us find her killer. Where'd you send the plans to?"

"Boulder. Dick Simon. Libeus told me to send them to him."

"We'd like to see copies of everything you sent him, Mr.
Pipkin," said Mallory.

He shrugged. "I don't have much left." He slid off the barstool and pulled together some papers from the back of the worktable. "These are some of the rough drafts."

Mallory studied them.

Wager asked, "Is that why Pauline called you? To tell you what building they were going to blow up?"

"No. But I think she may have found out." His voice dropped. "I think that's why she was worried."

"Worried how?"

"She didn't say anything directly. Like I said, we just chatted a bit about people and things. But it was like she wanted to say something but couldn't quite find the words for it. Tell me something, maybe, or ask me."

"About King's next project?"

"That was the feeling I got."

"You think she disapproved of whatever it was?"

"I think she had doubts anyway. But why, I don't know. We—ah—we don't say much specific over the telephone." He nodded at Mallory, who was still studying the diagrams. "Security."

"Would she disapprove enough to want to quit?"

"I don't think that was the issue yet. Like I said, she would have made up her mind after a final powwow."

"But she had learned enough to be worried?"

"I'm just guessing—I really can't say for sure. It was her tone . . . her mood, more than anything she said specifically."

"If she threatened to do something to stop him, would King have killed her?"

He took a long time to answer, and when he did, it was oblique. "Did you know that developers are selling houses at Love Canal again? Change the name, make a profit. And Detroit's garbage incinerator's pumping tons of mercury into the air, and no one's stopping them because the only people being hurt are the poor? The Department of the Interior's in bed with Mobil Oil to drill the whole eastern seaboard regardless of fishing grounds or wildlife refuges. And all the time the administration claims to be pro environment, while it guts every rule and regulation that industry complains about. We're all angry!" The man's voice quieted. "But Libby's talked more and more about doing something major. Something that will really hurt the bastards." He ground the heels of his hands into his eyes. "He and Simon together. That's the scary one—Simon. That guy . . ." Pipkin shook his head. "He or Libby might have lost it. If they thought she was going to screw up a big project that they really wanted, then, yeah, Libby might have lost it."

Mallory looked up from the drawings. "Do you think King was in Denver because that's where his next project is?"

Pipkin nodded again. "That's how he does it: moves to the area and studies it, details a plan and backup alternatives, then finalizes the project."

Wager asked, "What's Simon like?"

"I only met him once, out in California. But I didn't like him."

"Why's that?"

"He thinks no one else is doing enough. That nobody else really cares enough to do what's needed—you know?"

"What did he say was needed?"

"Some kind of war. I mean, he's the one who wants to hurt people. Says we're already at war with the earth-murderers, but we just don't know it." Pipkin shrugged. "He's one of the fringe people Libby's picked up lately."

"You say he lives in Boulder?"

"Up in the hills behind town."

The FBI man watched Pipkin closely. "Did Tillotson or King or Simon ever mention the Rocky Mountain Arsenal?"

"Arsenal?" He frowned, thinking. "No . . . I don't think so." His eyes widened. "That's the biological and chemical warfare place, isn't it? The one the government claims it's closing down?"

"Yes."

And widened further. "Sweet heaven! If he blows that up

. . . It could spread . . ." He sucked in a deep, unbelieving breath. "There's supposed to be all sorts of stuff still stored out there: mustard gas, nerve gas, anthrax bombs!"

The men stared at each other, seeing not one another's faces but the vision of a flaming building that spewed smoke and anthrax and nerve gas over the northern half of Denver. Outside, in the quiet wind, the only sound was a dry, steady chatter from the aspen leaves.

They tried to get more out of Pipkin, but he said he'd told them all he knew, and neither Wager nor Mallory doubted the pale and worried man. Mallory said he would like to know if Pipkin decided to leave the Steamboat Springs area, "just in case we have questions about these diagrams"; Wager left his business card and the order for Pipkin to call at once if he heard anything from or about the homicide suspect Libeus King.

When Mallory dropped Wager off at the DPD Administration Building, he waved a hand at the bundle of drawings and plans on the seat beside him. "I'll fax these back to headquarters. Maybe someone there can make something of them."

"What about alerting the arsenal?"

"I'll take care of that."

Wager was relieved to hear it; the arsenal's officers would pay a hell of a lot more attention to a warning from the FBI than from a local Denver cop. "Was Tillotson ever afraid King suspected that she was an informant?"

"Not to my knowledge. I worked with her for almost a year. We were both very careful about contacts, and it's my guess that if King did suspect something, she wasn't aware of it." Mallory's fingers slid restlessly around the steering wheel.

"Of course, if he did suddenly learn about it—if someone told him . . ."

That was one of the possibilities. King would have felt—would have been—betrayed. And with all that anger, all that self-righteousness, he could have killed out of blind rage. "How soon before she died did she talk with you?"

Mallory acknowledged that it was a couple of weeks.

The phone call to San Diego that had led Wager to the FBI was dated sixteen days before her death. "Is that William Johnson an agent or an informant?"

"I'm not comfortable answering that one, Gabe. For security reasons. And I don't know that he has any bearing on the homicide aspect of this."

He might or he might not; that was why Wager was asking. "I'd like to know what she said to him."

"Oh—that's easy. On those calls, Johnson was just a cutout for Tillotson; she didn't talk to him at all. Johnson transferred all her calls directly to me. On that particular one, she said they were in Denver so King could work on a major project. The 'headline grabber.' " He shook his head. "That was the last time I talked to her, and she had no suspicion at all that she'd been discovered. She was to find out more about King's project—who was involved, what was targeted—and call back."

That still left sixteen days, and all it took was a thirty-second message or a scrawled note. Wager opened the car door "You don't think King's given up on that 'project'?"

The FBI agent scratched at the corner of his mouth. "I've alerted all my sources to notify me if he shows up anywhere in the country. So far, no response. So I assume he's still in this area. Besides," he added, "I can't take the chance he isn't, can I?"

No, Mallory couldn't take that chance, and Wager found himself almost hoping that King had given up. But if he had, he could be anywhere by now, in or out of the country, and Tillotson's murder would stay open for the months or maybe years it would take to find King. Still, that would be far better than Wager's vision of poison smoke drifting across half a million souls.

When they parted, Mallory had once more promised to let Wager know immediately if the national FBI alert turned up any leads, and Wager had once more told Mallory that he'd call right away if DPD came up with anything. Then he went up to his office to check his message box and to telephone Max.

Max's wife answered the phone on the second ring, her voice straining to be polite. "Oh, hello, Gabe."

"Max wanted me to call, Francine. Hope you don't mind."

"Of course not. I'll let him know. Just a moment, please."

When Max picked up the extension, Wager asked, "Meet you at Quintana's place in an hour?"

"See you there."

That gave Wager time to let Elizabeth know he was back from Steamboat and to answer the few and disappointing messages that waited in his box. One was from Stovepipe—"Please call." He did.

"Gabe, I took your advice—you know, about seeing a lawyer?"

"And?"

"It sounds like so much crap. I never heard so much pure crap. You got any idea what we have to do to have my old man declared dead?"

"No."

"Aw, man, we got to prove that he doesn't have all sorts of things. No voting record, no automobile registration, no medical records . . . You name it, we got to prove he doesn't have it. Anywhere in the goddamn country! Lawyer says it's because we're trying to deprive him of his property. Where the hell was all this protection for me, man! Swear to God, if my rights had been protected half as well, I'd've never been sent up."

"Maybe things are improving, Stovepipe."

"Yeah. And maybe I'll do better next goddamn vault I crack."

"You really want to take that chance?"

A sigh. "No. But goddamn, Gabe, I can't get the hang of doing things by all these rules! I mean, it was so simple before: I wanted something, by God, I took it. I didn't hurt nobody, I didn't take any more than I needed, nothing to worry about. But now—Christ, I try to do things the right way, and there's all these rules and laws and crap, and they all say I can't do this or I got to do that. It's like every time I turn around, there's a goddamn law! How in hell do citizens live like this?"

"They're used to it, Stovepipe."

"I don't know if I'll ever get used to it. I just don't know."

"You can make it."

A heavy sigh. "Yeah, I guess I better. For Mother's sake anyway." He added, "She really likes the place."

"What?"

"The place up in Weld County. What I did was rent it for a month, you know? Told the guy I was having trouble selling Mother's house and that we really want this place, and so could we rent it by the month. Even if we can't buy it, he makes some rent on it, and it's lived in, so the place is kept up."

"Smart move, Stovepipe."

"Yeah, it was. My case officer gave me leave to take Mother up there yesterday. It's way the hell out in the country—nothing but farmland all around, man. Just what we wanted."

"That's good."

"Yeah. Mother's getting settled in. Next leave I get, I'll go up and unpack the heavy stuff. You know, washer and dryer."

"Well, you should be able to get things settled in that time."

"I sure as hell hope so. But I'm beginning to goddamn wonder, man."

"Give me a call later, let me know how things are going."

"Yeah. Thanks."

The only other message was from Gargan, ace reporter for the *Denver Post,* who thought he was on the verge of his greatest scoop and that Wager should help him with it. He dropped that in the trash can on his way out.

Caithness was a two-block street in the Highland Park area, just west of downtown. Like its neighbors, Argyle and Dunkeld, it marked the original settlement of Scots engineers and managers hired to work in the smelters of nineteenth-century Denver. But that was a long time before, and Wager could barely remember when the neighborhood had been Italian. Now there were only a few Italian restaurants left, and most of the area was Hispanic. And even that was changing—the low cost of housing and the nearness to work in Denver had started luring the Anglos in, and property values were rising. Pretty soon it would be a neighborhood "renewed" by "urban pioneers." But, Wager reflected as he parked on the quiet street, that was better than what could happen if the arsenal went up and the wind blew this way. Even better than what had happened to his old neighborhood, the Auraria barrio. There, the people had been moved into low-income housing projects, and the hundred-year-old homes and cottages had been turned into rubble to make way for a university campus. As if the state needed another playground for a bunch of fraternity kids to drink beer.

A few minutes after Wager parked, he saw Max's Jeep Cherokee turn off Zuni and come slowly down the two blocks. This late at night, the ground-level shops were closed and only an occasional pedestrian made a shadow in the dim street lights. In the upper stories, dark windows showed where offices and commercial spaces were empty for the night. Here and there among them, lights marked clusters of apartments; Wager counted down a fourth-floor row of windows to the one or two that he guessed were Quintana's.

Max strolled up to Wager's unmarked cruiser and leaned to the window. "I appreciate this, Gabe."

"No problem."

The entrance to the apartment building was an arch of brown brick pinched between plate-glass display windows. On one side was an unpainted-furniture store, on the other an upholstery shop. A picket of iron bars protected the goods shown in each set of windows, but the building's entry door had a broken pane of glass. If you wanted to, you could reach through and open the handle from the inside. They didn't have to, because it was unlocked.

Max led the way up the steep stairway. His large shadow covered Wager and blotted out the steps. "How'd everything go in Steamboat?"

"The suspect wasn't there. We talked to a friend of his."

"Any leads?"

"Not much."

"Too bad."

The hallway was almost lit by two dim bulbs hanging naked from porcelain sockets. At the far end, an unlit sign over the window said FIRE ESCAPE. Max had to use his penlight to read the faded apartment numbers stenciled on the scarred doors.

"Place smells like a urinal," he said.

The water blisters in the baseboard paint said it might be.

"Here we are." Max loosened his revolver in its belt holster; Wager took out his pistol and moved against the wall down the hallway. Standing to one side of the door, Max knocked and waited. The muffled sound of *ranchera* music came through a wall from somewhere and mingled with the stilted voices of a loud television from somewhere else. Max knocked again.

"Yeah—who's it?" The murmur hovered just beyond the door.

Max's voice was equally discreet. "Police, Mr. Quintana. We'd like to talk to you."

A long silence. Max tilted his head. "Break it down?"

"Got a warrant?" asked Wager.

"No."

"Let him hide his stash. He can't go anywhere."

A few seconds later, a chain rattled, and a pair of dead bolts clicked back. Quintana opened the door halfway. As his mug shots pictured, the youth had long dark hair pulled back tight against his skull into a ponytail, and a sharp bend in his nose showed where it had been broken. Both shoulders, bare and heavy in the sleeveless black muscle shirt, bore tattoos. He looked a lot older than his seventeen years and already moved with the bulky stiffness of a man. "What you people want with me?"

Wager didn't like him. He didn't like the way Quintana tried to act tough, and he didn't like the way the kid sneered when he spoke. He especially didn't like the idea of wasting time to cajole scum like this when, in the back of his mind, he could still see that towering plume of poisoned smoke. "We want to talk about Ray Moralez."

"Fuck him, man. He got what he deserved."

Wager, weapon back in its holster, shoved past Quintana.

"Hey, man, I didn't say you could come in."

"You don't want to talk in the hall, Roy. Stinks worse than your apartment."

Max came in, too, and closed the door behind him. The three men crowded the small space. A sagging plaid sofa against one wall faced a portable television against the other. Littered with newspaper, a coffee table took up the center of the room. Through a doorway, Wager could see part of a rumpled bed that filled the other room. The bathroom was probably off that. There was no kitchen, but a two-burner hot plate sat on the windowsill and gave the room a lingering odor of scorched something.

"How'd you people know where I was at?"

"You have friends, Roy. People looking out for you," said Wager.

"What's that mean?"

"They know it's good you talk to us. They know it'll save you all sorts of trouble later on."

"Like what kind of trouble you think I can't handle?"

"For one thing, I don't think you can handle an accessory-to-murder charge. For another, I don't think you can handle Flaco Martínez." Wager smiled. "And I know goddamn well you can't handle me."

"Take it easy, Gabe. Mr. Quintana wants to cooperate."

Want was going to have damn little to do with it. But Wager stifled the urge to make that clear. Instead, he turned to be sure no one was hiding in the other rooms. Quintana watched suspiciously. "You people ain't showed me no warrant. There's not nothing you people can bust me for!"

"We're not here to bust you, Mr. Quintana." Max smiled. "We just want to talk with you. We'd like your cooperation in a murder investigation."

"Yeah?" Quintana turned on the television and flopped on the couch to stare at the machine. "I don't feel like cooperating."

Wager wrapped the electric cord around the toe of his shoe and yanked it from the socket. Then he propped his foot on the couch's wobbly arm. "We hear Flaco killed Ray Moralez."

Quintana shrugged, still staring at the dark TV screen.

"We hear he did it because he wants the Tapatíos' territory."

Another shrug.

"And he wants the Tapatíos' territory so he can start pushing shit he brings up from Albuquerque."

"You know so much, why don't you know where he is?"

"And this *pinche—un achichincle por los Puñales allá en Albuquerque*—he comes up here to take over the Gallos."

"What?"

"Think about it, *chingón*. First, he knocks off one of the Tapatíos so he can look like *un matacúas*. Then he gets you Gallos to take over the Tapatíos' turf—says he'll make it worth your trouble, right? Then he sets up business in your territory. You think after all that he's going to step back and let some *cagadillo* like you run things?" Wager shook his head and grinned. "You, man, you'll be on the street pushing dope; Flaco, he'll tell you how much to move, give you ten, maybe fifteen percent, and take the rest. And he'll sit on his ass and watch you *sonzos* sweat the narcs."

That scenario was a little different from the one Quintana had pictured. Wager had his full attention.

Max was a large tree bending slightly forward. "We're from Homicide, Mr. Quintana. We don't care what you people are planning unless it makes work for us. Right now, Flaco's our business—nothing else."

"We're going to get him, Roy. Along with anybody who helps him. That's what we call an accessory to the crime—*cómplice al crimen*. Murder is a class one felony, and anybody who helps Flaco could end up doing ten years, all because that *zurrón* wants to take over Los Gallos."

The sharp odor of sweaty armpits spread through the room, to swamp the charred smell from the stained hot plate. Wager wanted to open the window and let the cool night air sweep in. But too much depended on him standing over Quintana and waiting as if he had the whole night for an answer. He clamped his nose against the mingled odors and stared down at the youth. The tattoo on his left shoulder showed a spread eagle and the name Charlene. The blue letters, shaky and amateur, started large and then grew smaller as the tattooer had run out of space on the back of Quintana's arm. Like, Wager thought, the promise of Quintana's life: starting big and ending next to nothing.

"He's moved from his Thirty-eighth Avenue place," said Max quietly. "But we know he's still in town. Where is he, Mr. Quintana?"

"I don't know where he's holed up at."

"How do you get in touch with him?" Wager asked.

Quintana hesitated.

"Has he crashed with any of the Gallos?"

"No, man. Most of *mis compadres,* they live with their *familias.*" His lips twisted in a sneer as his chin included the cramped apartment. "Me, I'm fucking emancipated—my old man, he emancipated me when I was fifteen, man, and I been on my own ever since."

Wager had heard sadder stories. "So how do you talk business with him?"

Silence.

"Roy, you want to act like *un zopenco,* we're not going to waste any more time. You want that *cabrón* to take over the Gallos, you got it—it'll be your choice and your ass. Now, this is the last time I ask you, and then we're out of here, because we got things to do: How do you get in touch with Flaco when you want him?"

The thick shoulders rose and fell. "Through Sol Atilano. He lives over on Mariposa Street. Somebody needs to talk to Flaco, they go by Sol's and he makes a phone call. A couple minutes later, Flaco calls back to make sure everything's cool with Sol. You know—he calls back and if it ain't square, Sol pretends he don't know who's calling or something. If it is square, he sets up a time. Then Sol takes them to the meet." Another half sneer. "Fucker thinks he's smart—thinks he can't get set up that way."

"Atilano calls from his own phone?"

Quintana nodded.

"Can you set up a meet with Flaco?"

"Hey, man, don't use me for no *araña.*"

"Don't worry, Roy. What we do is tap Sol's phone. You ask for a meet with Flaco, Sol calls him up, we find out where he calls to and pick him up there. The only way anybody's going to know who tipped us is if you tell them."

It took a little convincing, but Quintana finally agreed to it, and Wager said he'd let the man know when the phone tap was set up. On the way back to the Admin Building, Max shook his head. "You really think we have enough for a phone tap, Gabe?"

It wouldn't be easy. The courts weren't happy about phone taps in the first place, and Flaco's rap sheet wasn't heavy. And the only link between Flaco and a felony was rumor. "If we don't, we'll tail Quintana."

"Flaco could spot us—and Quintana could end up with his butt in a sling."

Wager shrugged. "He wants to be the big boy on the block."

"He's just a kid, Gabe, and Flaco gave him a line. Quintana probably had no idea what the hell he was getting into."

"So now he'll find out." Though it was true that Flaco couldn't have pulled this scam on a gang made up mostly of adults. At best, they'd have laughed at him. At worst, he'd be chopped meat: Flaco the Taco.

As Elizabeth had promised, the light was left on for him. Wager tried to be quiet as he locked the front door and took off his shoes to move gently across the creaking floorboards of the silent house. In the refrigerator, he found a cold chicken leg sitting next to a can of beer, and he was finishing the snack when Elizabeth's voice, drowsy and husky, said behind him, "See? I think of everything."

"Guess what I'm thinking of?"

They held each other for a long moment, his hands sliding over the warm silk of her nightgown.

"I've been thinking of that too," she said.

Wager buried his face in the soft curls of her hair and breathed deeply: a scent of soap, a tinge of perfume, that cozy, fragile aroma of sleep-warmed flesh. And through those soft things, the abrasive thought of Libeus King. He held tighter to Elizabeth and tried to push away the man's name and the image of the arsenal and the things that were stored out there and the lingering vision of a charred and clenched corpse.

She leaned back, her farsightedness making her squint slightly as she looked up at him. "What's the matter, Gabe?"

"Tired." He smiled, "Glad to be here. Glad to be with you."

She studied him a moment or two more, then tugged at his arm. "Come on. I'll rub your back."

"And I'll rub your front."

Small movements settled the hollows and swells of their bodies together, and hands and lips moved with comfortable and soothing familiarity as the room's darkness became a sheltering refuge.

"That feels good."

"Mmm."

After a while she asked, "Any leads on the sniper?"

"Not that I heard about." The tension had gone out of his body, and he felt her, too, settle more heavily against him.

"It's hard to realize how much hatred and . . . cowardice would make someone do that."

The cowardice had been human nature, and the hatred had been against the police in general. The sniper had no way of knowing which patrol car would answer the summons, and it had been Markowsky's and Rosener's bad luck to get the call. It could have been anyone on duty, and that randomness increased the anger that any cop felt when the uniform was assaulted.

"So much violence." Elizabeth's voice was quiet in the dark. "It's as if people want to strike out against the things that seem to control them—to attack any authority, whether it's there to help them or not."

She assumed that the sniper attack was the reason for his worry, and Wager wasn't sure he should tell her otherwise. Mallory had labeled the information confidential. But Denver was her city. As a councilperson, Elizabeth had both a right and a responsibility to know of threats to the welfare of her city. And, to tell a deeper truth, the knowledge bore down on Wager like a stifling weight. Maybe it would be lighter if shared. But then again, maybe not. More likely, it would weigh just as heavily on Elizabeth.

But she wouldn't have been Elizabeth if she weren't bright and sensitive: "It's not just the sniper, is it?"

"Why do you say that?"

Against his chest, a shoulder lifted and fell. "It's something I feel. There's something you want to tell me but aren't. What is it?"

It was Wager's turn to shrug; she was also a very tenacious woman, who could pester like a burr in a sock, if she had a mind to. "The sniper's bad enough," he said. "Then there's that arson and homicide."

"What about it?"

He told her about Tillotson being an FBI snitch and the FBI interest in the case—hell, even Gargan knew that much.

She listened without interrupting him. When she finally spoke, the sleepiness was gone from her voice. "Has the FBI told you what the girl was doing for them?"

"Yes. But what Mallory's told me is confidential."

"So you're not going to tell me."

"I can't, Elizabeth."

The bed thumped sharply as she shifted her weight, and he could hear her stifle a hurt note in her voice with a council-person's official demand. "Does it have anything to do with the public welfare?"

"I can't tell you that, either."

"That's a yes, isn't it?"

Wager sighed. "That's a yes."

"Has the mayor been told about it?"

"I don't know."

"If so, he hasn't mentioned anything to the council."

"You don't want to talk to anyone about this yet, Liz. Like I said, it's confidential."

"That word doesn't mean one damn thing when the public welfare is involved."

"Liz, there's nothing definite. So far, it's all rumor and guesswork. Besides, if King reads in the papers what we think, he'll take off—I might never get my hands on him."

"I don't know what the possibility of that is, do I? I don't even know what kind of threat to the public welfare you're talking about, do I?"

"It's confidential," he said stubbornly.

"I heard you the first time." The note of hurt had been replaced by anger. "I know damn well you have a job to do. But so do I—and the heart and soul of my job is the welfare of this city. By God, when that welfare is threatened, I intend to know about it!"

"The mayor's responsible. It's his job."

"It's a shared responsibility, Gabe. And if I believed hizzoner could do his job, I wouldn't be worried now. But I don't, and I am. I want to know what's going on, and damn it, I intend to find out!"

"You can't tell anyone you heard it from me. I've got to work with the FBI—if they think they can't trust me, I won't get another thing out of them."

"I understand that." She flopped back on the pillow, and the anger in her voice had been replaced with cold reason. "I'll just have to find out about it from another source, won't I?"

The tension had come back into their bodies, and they lay side by side, scarcely aware of their meeting flesh. Elizabeth, angry at him despite what she had said about respecting the demands of each other's jobs, had moved into her own thoughts and was planning tomorrow's moves and contacts; Wager, too, had his mind on the coming day. And the night that had been so sheltering now seemed ominous.

• • • • • • • • •

A brand-new notice on the bulletin board said: "Markowsky passed away. Rosener's condition upgraded to Serious. No other word." Devereaux's face was gray from lack of sleep. A chalky film at the corners of his mouth hinted of Rolaids. "No leads, no tips, nothing, Gabe. Maybe we'll have to offer a reward after all."

"I heard Floyd bought drinks for everybody after Markowsky died."

"Yeah. I heard that too. Fucker." He scratched a thumb along his jaw. "It's a fact, Gabe—it's a fact: the people in that bar know something."

Wager thought a moment about the bartender at the Blue Moon and the man's flat, unyielding stare. "Maybe we should show Floyd we're thinking of him."

Devereaux's hand moved from his jaw to rub at the red flesh of his eyelids before he went heavily to his desk. "If it'll smoke out an informant, I'm all for it."

Wager grabbed the day's first mug of coffee and the slips in his box and settled at his desk to thumb through them quickly. There was nothing from Mallory, but Archy Douglas had left

a message: "Found fingerprints matching Libeus King. Call."
Wager did.

"Yeah." Archy sounded as if he had something in his mouth.
"In the bathroom." There was the sound of a slurp, and Archy's
voice came back clearer. "Four fingers of the left hand under
the lid of the toilet reservoir. Looks like he held it up to repair
it or take out his stash or something. Anyway, being in the
bathroom and protected like that, they didn't get screwed up
by the fire fighters. And being on tile, they made good impres-
sions. Definite ten-point match on all four fingers."

"Thanks, Arch. Any prints from King's known associates?"

"Not yet. There's a lot of unidentifieds, and I only got the
files yesterday. And there's only one of me. But I'm working
on it."

"Right, Archy—thanks."

King's prints would help fill in the picture by establishing his
presence, but by themselves they didn't prove him to be the
murderer. Not yet, anyway, and maybe never. And the unidentifieds would have to be screened; you never knew what
twists a case could take. One set might turn out to belong to a
witness. But it was a long, tedious job, and Wager knew that
Archy was putting his first efforts on identifying the cop-killer
from the bullets taken out of Markowsky and Rosener and from
the pile of items collected in the alley where the sniper had
waited. Wager couldn't blame him for that—Archy, like everybody else, put that case first. But the anxiety Wager had felt
the night before and that led him to tell Elizabeth about King
was even stronger in the gray light of morning. He couldn't
help the feeling that, somewhere, a clock was running and he
was one of the few people who could hear it tick. And he was
not doing enough to stop it.

Still, there was Floyd nagging like a thorn in the toe: One
less pig and let's have a round of drinks.

But that wasn't Wager's primary assignment. Nor, sore
though that issue might be, was it the most dangerous. He tried

Sheila Riggs's California number once more. This time it was answered on the fourth ring, and Wager said who he was and why he had called.

"Oh, I read about it in the paper. Pauline's obituary. It's so awful!"

"Have you talked with Mr. and Mrs. Tillotson?"

"I called them, yes. Those poor people. They're just in absolute shock!"

"Did Pauline tell you she was coming to Denver?"

"I got a letter from her a month or so ago. She said she and Libby might go there, but she didn't say for how long."

"You mean they didn't intend to stay?"

A pause. "Those weren't her words, exactly. But the way she said it, it didn't sound like a permanent move. Can you hold on a minute? Maybe I can find the letter."

"I'll wait."

The open line crackled faintly. When Sheila Riggs came back, her voice sounded slightly breathless from hurry. "Here it is: 'Libby and I might be going up to Denver in a few days—it'll be nice to have a change of scenery for a while.' "

"That's all?"

"About Denver, yes. There's some stuff here about people we both know, friends from college—"

"Was she writing to them too?"

"I think so."

"Can I have their names and addresses, Miss Riggs?"

"If you think it might help, sure." She mentioned a Debbie Powell who lived in Ventura, California, and an Alex Saunders of Lake Oswego, Oregon. He had to wait again as she located their telephone numbers from her address book. "I don't know if she saw much of them. We sort of keep in touch with each other—you know, write two or three times a year. So I don't know how much help they can be."

Wager assured her that the information might be helpful. And it might—this was the kind of plodding collection of fact and name that occasionally turned up something important. Mostly, all it turned up was a big phone bill and a sore ear, but it was something detectives got used to damn fast or they got out of the business. "Did Miss Tillotson ever mention the Rocky Mountain Arsenal?"

"The what?"

Wager repeated it.

"No. I don't think so. She and Libby are—were—into all sorts of environmental things, but they didn't say much about the army or anything like that."

"How about the San Diego submarine base? Did she say anything about that?"

"Submarines? God, no. We talked about friends and jobs and, you know, people and places we both know. But submarines . . . ?"

Wager thanked Miss Riggs and hung up, leaving the puzzled query in her voice unanswered. He dialed the Oregon number first; a woman answered, and Wager asked for Alex Saunders.

"He's not here right now. May I take a message?"

Wager told the woman his name.

"The police? In Denver?"

"Pauline Tillotson has been murdered. I'm contacting all her acquaintances for any help they might be able to give me."

The voice held no sorrow. "Well, I'm certain Alex won't be able to tell you anything about her."

"If you would ask him to call me as soon as possible, please—collect, anytime."

"Very well."

His call to Debbie Powell rang unanswered, and Wager leafed through the handful of memos, ignoring another one from Gargan that asked him to get in touch as quick as he could. He was about to call the DA's office for an interjurisdictional warrant to search Richard Simon's cabin up in Boulder County, when his phone rang. It was Mallory, voice croaky with weariness.

"I got a read on those diagrams—a kind of read anyway."

"That was quick."

"Yes. Well, I told them I wasn't sure how much time we had to work with. I'm still not. Anyway, I faxed a copy of the drawings back to headquarters and asked them to give the Corps of Army Engineers a call, tell them what we had, and tell them it was damned important. They were quite cooperative, but the diagrams don't match anything at the arsenal."

Wager felt something loosen in his chest, and he sighed deeply. "Are you trying any other agencies?"

A slight pause told Wager that the FBI agent was tempted to mention something. "I'm doing that now. So far, no matchup."

"That's good news."

"Yes, it is. I'd feel even more sanguine, though, if I knew for certain what building those plans were for."

As long as it wasn't the biochemical horror he'd envisioned, Wager could leave that worry to Mallory. He told the FBI agent about King's prints being found at the burned house.

"Well, that proves what we suspected."

But it didn't prove that King had murdered Tillotson or where the man had disappeared to. Wager asked, "When your people went up to Boulder County for that suspect—Richard Simon —did they search his cabin?"

"Not that I know of—no warrant for a search, just for an arrest. The agent only said no one was there."

"I can get a search warrant. You want to come along?"

Mallory thought twice about it. "I'd better stay with these diagrams. I'll sleep better when I find out they don't match anything around here."

Wager understood that. Despite his weariness, last night's sleep, in addition to being short, had been restless, with uneasy dreams for both him and Elizabeth. The FBI man said he'd get in touch the minute anything new came up, and Wager hung up as Max loomed in the doorway.

"I can't get a phone tap on Sol Atilano, Gabe. I tried three damn judges. Every one of them denied it."

Wager wasn't all that surprised. Like everybody else, judges bitched about the crime rate, but when it came to stretching a point of law, they sure as hell weren't willing to do much about it. "So tell Quintana the tap's in place anyway. Have him call Atilano, set up a meet, and we tail him to Flaco."

Max wasn't happy with that; tailing somebody in real life was always trickier than the movies made it seem—especially if that somebody was as nervous as Quintana.

"But, Max, we can't just sit on the kid. Doyle's not going to authorize that much overtime with the little we've got." Wager fingered the memos and notes on his desk; the gesture told Max that his partner was trying to work on other cases too.

Still, Max shook his head. "We'd be sticking the kid's neck out for him, and he wouldn't even know it."

"Let's hear your better idea."

But Max didn't have one, and the big man hunched his shoulders into his sport coat and headed out the door to lose his frustration on the street.

Wager called the duty attorney at the DA's office and had him arrange for a warrant through the Boulder County sheriff. Crossing jurisdictional lines wasn't something this deputy DA was eager to do—his reluctant voice said it meant additional paperwork for his secretary and even a few minutes of his own time. But as far as Wager was concerned, that was too damned bad. Whether the man liked it or not, providing support for the police was part of his job description. Finally, the deputy DA asked for the probable cause for the warrant, and Wager told him that the residence belonged to the known associate of a murder suspect. He added that the suspect might be hiding there.

"It'll be a little easier if we have the suspect's name on the warrant, Detective."

Wager told him, including the John Marshall alias, and

added, "I'd like to collect any evidence that might be there too."

"You'll want a search-and-seize, then. All right, Detective Wager. I'll get it signed and call it up to the Boulder SO."

Wager figured two hours before he was legal; that gave him an hour here to work and an hour to drive up to Boulder. He turned to his remaining messages and notices. A lab report had finally come in from the arson investigators that positively identified gasoline traces in the fire at the Wyandot address—no legal question, now, of arson, and Wager made a note to himself to take King's photograph around to the neighboring service stations and see if anyone remembered selling a can of gas to him.

His phone rang. Lieutenant Watterson, the department's public information officer, wanted to find out if Wager had anything more on the Tillotson homicide that he could tell the press. "I'm under an awful lot of pressure on this one, Gabe. The *Post* keeps calling to find out about the tie-in with the FBI. Can you give me anything at all for them?"

Watterson had politicked for the PIO job—wanted to see his name in the papers as a "police spokesman." Besides, the man was getting paid more than Wager. "Not a thing new, Lieutenant. Sorry."

A sigh. "You'll let me know whenever you do have something, right?"

"Sure. You bet."

Watterson's problem with Gargan wasn't high on Wager's list of priorities. That was topped by Libeus King. The man had disappeared with the completeness of a stranger who had no ties to the neighborhood, but both Wager and Mallory felt he was still in the area. Wager doubted that a check of motel and hotel registers would turn up anything—if that's where he was, it would be under still another alias and perhaps even a disguise. But Wager was tempted to ask Chief Doyle for permission to start canvassing with copies of King's photograph, just so he could feel they were at least doing something, even if it was only wasting somebody's time besides his own. King's car should have been a better lead too. Wager at least had a license plate and description to work with there. But the patrol division kept telling him they had no sightings.

Restless, he eyed the large round clock on the wall, with its tail of electric cord dangling down to an outlet near the floor. He could leave now and reach the Boulder sheriff's office in an hour. It would be a bit early, but at least it would seem as if he was doing something. And maybe the paperwork would be completed by the time he arrived.

Deputy Sheriff Lofting was the man Wager was told to see. He
was only slightly taller than Wager and had straight black hair
combed back to hide a bald spot. Like a lot of sheriffs' officers
Wager knew, the man had a mustache wide enough to droop
around the corners of his mouth. Some SOs in mountain towns
required their deputies to grow mustaches to please the tourists,
and it was one reason Wager had been tempted to shave off
his own.

"You think the suspect's up here, Detective Wager?" Their
Ford Bronco swung off the Boulder Canyon highway at the
Magnolia Road junction. The steep, rocky walls lining the two-
lane highway were marked with a cluster of houses that perched
on every near-level spot of land. Magnolia Road was narrower
than the canyon road, and steeper, and lurched up an incline
bitten into the side of the cliff.

Wager felt himself pressed against his seat back as the car
ground skyward through a series of hairpin turns. "Maybe. The
FBI didn't find him there, though."

"Special Agent Shackleton's already been out here, has he?"

"That's the Boulder FBI rep?"

"One of them. Son of a bitch thinks he's God's gift to local law enforcement."

Federal warrants didn't need local approval, and federal officers had jurisdiction everywhere. But the wise ones kept the local agencies informed when they were running a search or a bust. Wager understood the sting of resentment in Deputy Lofting's voice; nobody liked to be told they couldn't be trusted. "As I understand it, he only had a pickup; I've got a search-and-seize warrant."

"What are we searching and seizing for?"

"Anything. Everything."

This region was Lofting's patrol area. Boulder County was divided into quadrants, and usually the sheriff's officers lived in their district. Wager figured Lofting was one of those, because he showed pride of ownership and was eager to point out items of scenic interest. Of course, the interest was from his perspective: "Had a sniper up on that knob, two, three years ago. Didn't kill anybody—just drunk and dumb and shooting at tires."

Wager eyed the outcropping of gray rock that thrust like a ragged thumb above the pines. "How'd you get to him?"

"Came in from behind—off the Peak-to-Peak Highway. Scared the living fire out of me, I tell you: creeping through the goddamn bushes where I couldn't see more'n six feet ahead, and some maniac with a rifle up in front of me."

"Put up a fight?"

"Naw. Dumb shit had passed out. Had the cuffs on him before he even woke up."

A large log home set back from the road in an open field was one of the district's frequent domestic calls—"One of them's going to kill the other one of these days. Sure as the sun comes up tomorrow, one of them's going to kill the other"—and another, smaller frame home was pointed to as the site of a dope bust a couple of years back. "The SO made a little money when we auctioned off that property."

The paved road wound across a wide saddle toward a ridge that led farther up the mountain. Through a notch formed by a valley to the east, Wager could see the flat line of yellow prairie that stretched to Kansas. West, the snowy peaks of the Continental Divide were glimpsed behind a steady rise of wooded land. Here and there sat a home, usually log, silent and distant.

Finally, the deputy geared down, and they paused at a dirt road that led through a flower-studded meadow toward a stand of dark lodgepole pines. The thick grass was speckled with orange and red, yellow and white flowers. "Here we are." Lofting nodded at a fence post bearing an orange plastic tag with black figures. "That's the cabin's fire number."

"It's peaceful," said Wager.

Lofting nodded. "Too bad people have to fuck it up."

That could be said about a lot of things, Wager thought, including life itself. But somehow the foolishness and waste seemed especially sharp up here. "Let's get this done."

Simon's home was less a log house than a cabin. Small, with a tacked-on bathroom and a shed leaning against one side, the building was old, a summer vacation cabin that had been remodeled slightly for year-round use. An open porch surrounded it on three sides. In the close, hot sun of midday, Wager could see the heat radiate off its green tar-paper roof and could smell the tangy dust of pines. The squawk of a blue jay from somewhere down the steep slope on the other side of the cabin made the silence feel deeper.

No cars were parked where the grass had been worn thin by tires. A set of fresh treadmarks wrinkled the sandy earth, and Wager assumed they were from the previous day's FBI visit. But the two men went through the motions anyway, their shoes loud on the dusty porch boards, their knuckles rattling even louder against the loose screen door.

"Sounds vacant to me." Lofting eyed the door's dead-bolt lock. "Got a passkey? Or do we gotta bust in?"

Wager took out the collection of small, rippled blades that Chief Doyle would have been upset to know about. Lofting watched with close attention as he used a filed Allen wrench to give torsion to the pick and carefully lifted the tumblers in the lock's cylinder.

"You pretty good with that?"

"Out of practice." Wager would have felt better about picking the lock in a couple of minutes, but the time dragged out to almost five. Finally, the cylinder turned, and he opened the door a few inches. Lofting leaned past him. "Anybody home? Hey-o—anybody home?"

The law satisfied by the warrant, courtesy satisfied by the call, they went in. The two men made an initial quick tour of the three rooms formed by varnished plywood partitions without doors—kitchen, large living area, smaller bedroom with bath. Heavily insulated drapes framed the thick thermal glass of picture windows, and a well-used fireplace was situated to throw heat into both the living room and the bedroom. Bookshelves filled the wall over a sagging sofa that was long enough to use as a bed, and posters tacked here and there celebrated animals and forests. Framed on a wall, an ornate handwriting read: "Practicing Deep Ecology means recognizing the War on Nature. In Nazi Germany there were resistance groups who fought without the assurance that the Allies would win the war. They fought without assuming they would win. They fought because it was right to fight. We must continue that dedication to fight!" A scattering of magazines—*Earth First!*, *Greenpeace*—lay on the large table that served for work and dining. An Ansel Adams calendar with striking black-and-white mountain photographs hung beside the clattering refrigerator. A heavy red circle surrounded September 26, the next day.

"Want me to toss the bedroom?" asked Lofting.

Wager nodded. "Any papers, letters, notebooks—anything that might lead to King."

"Gotcha."

Wager took the living room table, with its stack of newspapers and its rolltop minidesk containing a variety of pigeonholes and tiny drawers. His hands moved quickly, but surely and methodically, through the drawers, pulling each one entirely free of the desk for any secret compartment or taped papers behind the wood. The desk chair had a cushion, and he folded that at his ear, listening for the crinkle of paper.

"Got some clothes and linens in here. He might be planning on coming back."

"Any papers or letters?"

"Not yet."

Wager grunted and found a locked drawer. This time, since Lofting wasn't watching him, the pick took only a few seconds. He slid the drawer open, to reveal an empty brown envelope and a scattering of tacks, paper clips, ballpoint pens, a couple of stamps.

"Here's something kinda curious, Detective Wager." Lofting's voice drew Wager to the bedroom. "I found these in the bottom drawer, under some jeans."

Wager looked at three glossy black-and-white photographs. They were eight-by-ten blowups taken from the air, looking down at an angle on a patch of scrubby and road-scarred ground. A cluster of buildings showed some kind of installation—a manufacturing site, a small military base, perhaps. It looked vaguely familiar, and Wager turned the photographs first one way, then another, to orient them.

Lofting looked over his shoulder. "Make sense to you?"

"No . . . But it looks familiar."

Lofting studied the photos for a moment, then turned one around. "Well, sure! Here's Highway 93, and this here's a corner of the Broomfield airport. And this is Highway 72—runs up Coal Creek Canyon." His slightly dirty fingernail traced a fragment of road across one corner of the glossy page. "You know that place where they make parts for the atom bombs? Just south of the Boulder county line and at the mouth of Coal Creek Canyon? That's what this is—Rocky Flats."

Wager felt the flesh along his spine crawl with a sudden chill.

Mallory's voice, too, revealed a chill. "Rocky Flats? Photo-
graphs of the Rocky Flats atomic weapons plant?"

Wager nodded over the telephone receiver. "And a date
circled on his wall calendar—the twenty-sixth. Tomorrow."

Moving through the cabin with exaggerated care to show how
quiet he could be while Wager was on the phone, Lofting began
pulling books from the shelves over the couch to riffle the pages
for any hidden notes or slips of paper.

"I'll have a search team up there as soon as possible. Don't
touch anything else. Can you bring the photos down to the
Denver office?"

"It'll take me about two hours to get there."

"I'll be waiting for you."

It took less than two hours—Lofting had run hot down Boulder
Canyon, and Wager hadn't worried about speed limits on the
turnpike leading from Boulder to Denver. The Federal Building
occupied a full downtown block between Champa and Stout,
its granite blocks and Greek pillars guarding the federal courts
as well as various agencies. Wager had never been to the FBI

offices, and it took him longer than he wanted to find his way up dimly lit stairwells and along echoing corridors that smelled of wax and the stale air of bureaucracy. But he finally found the door Mallory had told him to look for. Empty of any official sign, it bore only the room number. Wager rapped and pushed it open to show a cubicle slightly larger than a closet and almost filled with a blond oak desk of military-surplus design. Mallory sat behind it, freshly shaved; but his eyes, over puffy bags of unhealthy-looking flesh, were bloodshot. A razor nick on his chin had left a tiny red scab. On the desk, a scattering of papers, including Xerox blowups of the plans drawn by Pipkin, lay gleaming in the fluorescent glare of an industrial-size ceiling light. Behind the seated man, another door, this one with a glass panel, led deeper into the maze of offices. From behind that glass came the rustle and murmur of steady business.

Mallory didn't waste words saying hello. "Let's see them."

Wager laid the photographs on the desk, and the FBI agent stared at the glossy prints.

"Have you had a chance to check the diagrams against any of the Rocky Flats buildings?" Wager asked.

Mallory shook his head. "It's DOE, and I'm still trying to find out who has authority to produce the goddamn things. But I've alerted the security force at the plant. They're sending in the duty commander and one of their senior maintenance engineers—should be here soon."

"Think they'll recognize it?"

"I don't know whether to hope so or hope not." Mallory's shoulders rose and fell on a long breath. "And I don't know how happy they'll feel about coming here. Our agency conducted a raid at Rocky Flats a couple of years ago, and our relationship hasn't been exactly harmonious since. Especially as we found a hell of a lot of violations of safety regulations and some pretty serious security lapses."

Wager thought that over. "They've been corrected?"

Mallory shrugged. "That's what I hear. One of the big changes has been an increase in DOE oversight personnel, from sixty-five to a hundred and seventy-five."

"That includes more members of the security force?"

"Yes."

Wager, too, gazed at the photographs. "Then I don't see how anybody could break into that place. I've heard that their security people have everything from Uzis to armored personnel carriers mounting fifty-caliber machine guns."

The FBI agent agreed. "That's why I spent my time trying to fit the diagrams to other installations. I thought of Rocky Flats—it did cross my mind. But the security's been upgraded—it's been tested by agencies inside and outside DOE. . . . And I don't see how King could do anything if he did breach the perimeter." He added, "Besides, they haven't produced any plutonium triggers since 1989, and the W-88 program's been canceled. The place is scheduled to be closed, something Greenpeace has been after for years."

Wager didn't understand all of Mallory's references, but he did remember a small headline he had read lately. "The newspaper said the government was planning to store thousands of tons of plutonium there—'a plutonium Fort Knox,' they said."

Mallory rubbed the heels of his hands into his eyes. "It's already out there in the vaults. Virgin and residue plutonium. Tons of it. Nobody knows what to do with the stuff."

"What about the—what'd they call it?—the decontamination. There's talk of using the plant to decontaminate itself."

A nod. "One scenario has the plant eating itself over the years and finally disappearing. And another has the production building restarted and kept on standby in case we need more triggers in the future. It's a political question, and it's still up in the air."

"Maybe King wants to hit it while it's still news or to show that no installation's safe," said Wager.

Mallory grunted. "And maybe Simon left the photographs to throw us off the real target. But we can't take that chance, can we?"

The vague shadow of a passing figure showed against the glass panel in the door behind Mallory, and Wager heard muffled telephone bells from that busier room. The white walls of this cubicle were blank, and its single fluorescent light made a steady, high-pitched buzz. "No, we can't. But if Rocky Flats is the target, King must still be in the area."

Mallory's bloodshot eyes lifted from the photographs to Wager. "Any leads on that?"

"No."

"Me, either." A deep breath. "I've asked the search team to go over Simon's cabin with a toothbrush. They should be up there by now."

A knuckle rapped on the interoffice door behind Mallory, and the agent said, "Come!"

A woman leaned in, not glancing at Wager. "Mr. Stribling from DOE is here, sir."

"Send him in, Connie."

It wasn't one man; it was two. The first, hesitant, paused in the doorway, his light-brown eyes magnified by thick glasses as they studied first Mallory, then Wager. The second man wore a uniform of varying shades of tan and had a shoulder patch crammed with atomic energy symbols and the letters RFSF. His heavy-lidded eyes looked suspiciously at Wager before settling on Mallory.

The man with the glasses said uncertainly, "I'm Milton Stribling?"

Mallory stood to shake hands and introduce himself and Wager. The uniformed man said that his name was Lieutenant Walters and he was with the Rocky Flats Security Force. He didn't shake hands.

"Thank you both for coming in," said Mallory. He pushed

a pair of uncomfortable metal chairs up to the desk and tapped the papers on the desk. "Do either of you recognize the building portrayed by these drawings?"

Walters didn't look at the plans. "Is it a Rocky Flats installation?"

"We don't know, Lieutenant. That's what we're asking you."

Stribling ran a hand across lank blond hair that was combed to part over his left ear. "Well," he said nervously, "let's see." He was almost as tall as Mallory and had a bony face with prominent cheekbones and a cleft in the tip of his nose. That nose now bobbed up and down over the drawings as the man tilted his head to bring them into the focus of his thick lenses. Walters, too, leaned over to study the diagrams. He wasn't as tall as Stribling but had a much heavier build.

Stribling's lenses lifted toward Mallory. "Do you have any other floor plans?"

"No. Just this."

"Well, this is only the ground level. If you had other levels, I could be more definite." The lenses turned toward the uniformed man. "What do you think, Walters? Three seven one?"

"Yeah. . . . Could be." He asked Mallory, "You people pull another raid? You still trying to prove we're burning plutonium waste at night?"

"I'm not with the agency's Denver Office, Lieutenant. I didn't have a thing to do with challenging your security procedures or operations." A jabbing forefinger emphasized his words. "And let me impress upon you, I am not running a drill or an exercise. I am—we are—investigating a serious threat to national security. It has already involved one homicide, and that's why Detective Wager is here!" Mallory's voice softened. "Now, we both would appreciate your cooperation, and I'm certain neither of you wishes to impede a murder investigation. Do these diagrams fit any building at Rocky Flats?"

After a brief silence, Stribling cleared his throat. "If it's the building I think it is, most of the structure's underground." He looked at Walters for support, and the uniformed man nodded shortly.

"What building's that?" Mallory asked.

"It looks like Building 371." He oriented one of the aerial photographs to the diagram and pointed to a structure. "This one."

"What's in that building?" asked Wager as Mallory circled the spot with a red marker pen.

"It's a plutonium-recovery facility. The old chemical-process facilities—purification. It's where the americium 241 was washed out of the buttons and clean plutonium reinstalled."

"You'd better detail that for us, Mr. Stribling," said Mallory.

"Buttons are what we call the plutonium triggers. They have a field life of five or six years. After that, too much americium 241 builds up. Then they're brought back to the Flats and purified."

"You mean old plutonium triggers to hydrogen bombs are worked on in that building?"

Stribling seemed surprised that Mallory didn't know that. "Sure. Purified plutonium's too expensive just to dispose of. And difficult too."

"The triggers are stored there as well as worked on?"

"Not on this level. The storage vaults are underground."

"How big are those things?" Wager asked.

"Two and a half kilograms. About the size of a softball."

Wager blinked. "Small enough for somebody to carry, then?"

Lieutenant Walters spoke up. "If they could carry a ton of lead to wrap it in. Nobody—I mean nobody!—gets past the sensors if there's a click of radiation on them."

Stribling added, "We've drastically upgraded our personnel security procedures to guard against any inventory discrepancy."

"Goddamn right!"

Mallory asked, "What happens to the plutonium after it's cleaned?"

Stribling answered that one. "When the triggers are cleaned, the purity is tested in Building 559. Then the material is fabricated into new triggers in Building 707. The completed unit is shipped to Amarillo, to be installed in the warheads."

Wager blinked. "You have a lot of plutonium in those buildings too?"

Stribling shrugged. "What's a lot? It's enough to do our work. The main plutonium vaults are still here in Building 371: four stories underground—lead-lined walls of ten-foot-thick concrete." He explained, "Building 371 is the old purification unit. We've been working on a new one for years." His finger touched another structure in the photograph. "Building 771. But so many additional safety restrictions were added that construction got far behind, so we haven't moved into the new vaults yet. And now, with all the uncertainty about continuing operations at the plant . . ."

"You mean Building 371 is still in operation?"

The man shoved his glasses up his nose with a forefinger. "Nothing's in operation now; we've been on hold since 1989. But the vaults and glove boxes are still there, of course. We use a tunnel system to move the plutonium back and forth from the vaults in 371 to the operations in 771 and 707. But as I say, we're not doing much at all out there now."

"And all that stuff's secure?" asked Wager.

For the first time, Stribling looked uncomfortable. "We've had no incidents of security lapses or sabotage." He added bravely, "There have been a few problems in the safety sector."

Walters spoke up. "Nothing serious—nothing like the anti-nuke people want everybody to believe." He glanced at Mallory. "Or even what the FBI—the local FBI—accuses us of."

Stribling spoke quickly. "That's true. But regulations have become much more stringent." He hesitated and then went on. "There have been some . . . well, some resultant health implications. However, we now have a new primary contractor for operations, EG and G, and it looks like the problems of degraded personnel areas are being cleaned up."

" 'Degraded personnel areas'?" Wager asked.

"Areas of possible emissions hazards due to structural inadvertencies."

While Wager tried to figure out that phrase, Walters spoke up. "We've upgraded our security as well. Almost doubled our manpower, in fact."

"I read something about waste disposal problems," said Mallory.

"Well, yes, waste disposal is another factor." Stribling nodded. "That's another reason we've suspended operations."

"How's that?" asked Wager.

"The radioactive waste . . . we've been shipping it to Idaho for temporary storage, but the governor there stopped accepting it. The anti-nuke lobby's pretty strong out there. So we sort of have a backlog piled up. But the new geological disposal facility in New Mexico has just been approved, and it shouldn't take us long to move the hot waste once the GDF is in full operation."

"Where's that stuff stored?"

"In the white boxes." said Walters. "They're in a secure area."

Stribling looked at Mallory. "Oh, it's not plutonium—as I've told you, that's scrubbed and reused. At over a hundred dollars a gram, we recycle the plutonium and guard strictly against any inventory discrepancy. No, the hot waste is made up of the cleaning materials—what's left from scrubbing the plutonium. Water and other liquids: nitric acid, hydrochloric acid. But that material's no problem—it's really routine. It's just that nobody wants the waste."

"So this radioactive waste is just sitting out there?" Wager asked.

"No." Walters mimicked Wager's voice: "It's not just sitting out there. Like I just said, it's in a secure area."

"That's true," said Stribling. "And it's not really a problem once it's buried. The new GDF facilities will seal it underground for twenty-five thousand years—that's its half-life."

"It's not kept in this building, though?" Wager pointed at the diagram.

"No. With that building, the real problem is plutonium dust. That's the problem wherever any millwork is done. To control that, all plutonium-handling facilities are constructed with a series of negative air pressure zones from the vault to the glove boxes and then to the outside. That way, any draft will suck dust back into the building and into the air filtration system. Plus, every glove box has its own individual filter, and then the collective air is filtered through a four-stage system before it goes out the exhaust stacks." His finger gestured at the tall chimneys that, in the aerial photograph, threw narrow black shadows, like daggers, across the buildings' flat roofs and onto the ground.

Walters added, "That exhaust is monitored constantly by the Waste Management Division. So is any water effluent—all the water in our evaporation ponds gets checked hourly."

It was Stribling's turn. "For both radioactive and hazardous wastes, including heavy metals such as cadmium and chromium. But I have to admit, we have had occasional unscheduled events in the plenums."

"What's an 'unscheduled event'?"

Stribling eyed Wager. "Small internal fires caused by spontaneous combustion."

"What happens then?"

"The automatic sprinklers come on, and the fire's put out. The fires are in contained areas, but that's where adverse health outcomes have occurred most often. Ninety-eight percent of plutonium radiation is alpha particles, and if it gets in the lungs or in a tiny open wound in the skin, it settles in the bone marrow. However, if we get to an exposed subject right away, we can prevent terminal health outcomes. Surgical incision of any open wound is effected immediately. And of course we have a whole array of monitors, alarms, chirpers, badges, and so on to detect any airborne leaks at the earliest possible moment."

"As well," added Walters, "as two doctors on duty during the day shift and medical technicians twenty-four hours a day, trained to handle radioactive problems."

"What about the plutonium in the vaults?" Wager asked. "Isn't that a possible problem too?"

Walters snorted something, and Stribling's voice covered the sound. "They're four stories underground, encased in concrete and lead. The viewing windows for the XY retrievers are double-paned glass blocks several inches thick and filled with water. Nothing and nobody can get to them."

"But what would happen," insisted Wager, "if a bomb went off in one of those buildings or it caught fire?"

Stribling smiled. "It won't, of course. There's no possibility of an energetic disassembly in these structures. But site selection was a major consideration in locating the plant there in the fifties. The site selection team determined that the wind patterns wouldn't blow the smoke toward Denver."

"What about Broomfield? Westminster? Thornton?" Those were only a few of the Denver suburbs Wager could think of that had grown up since the fifties. They and other new bedroom communities lay directly east of the plant.

Lieutenant Walters shook his head; the possibility was highly unlikely, but since Wager asked· "In a worst-case scenario, they would of course have to be evacuated. But the chances of something like that are absolutely negative." He added, "Besides, we've recently inaugurated a Terrain Responsive Atmospheric Code computer program for predicting plume flows as part of our emergency preparedness program. We can foretell which way pollution from the plant will travel."

Foretell, Wager thought, but not forestall. The prevailing winds blew west to east—out of the mountains and across Rocky Flats toward the sprawl of homes and shopping centers that made up the northern half of the greater Denver area. In fact, the whole Front Range, and Rocky Flats especially, were famous for chinook winds, which had occasionally gone off the scale at a hundred fifty miles an hour. And despite Walters's assurance about the wind patterns, Wager remembered smelling the smoke of prairie fires that had settled over his downtown Denver neighborhood when he was a kid. Fires that had occurred in that area before it was fenced off and made secret.

A plume of radioactive smoke that might settle over one hundred thousand people? Two hundred thousand? A cluster of municipalities and unincorporated suburbs with not even a coordinated radio network, let alone a single disaster plan. There might be panic, Wager knew, but there wouldn't be evacuation. And it would certainly make headlines—bigger than Chernobyl—and last for twenty-five thousand years. "You're just sixteen miles from here, right?"

"Well, yes."

"Could someone sabotage this building?" Mallory's finger tapped 371, and Wager figured the FBI agent was thinking the same thing.

Walters was indignant. "No way! We have very elaborate physical defenses around the plant. In addition, every member of our security force is a graduate of the Department of Energy's Central Training Academy at Kirtland Air Force Base. We're trained in firearms, explosives, sniper tactics, computer security, crisis negotiations, and preemptive identification. And we're in constant readiness. I have every confidence that our security force can handle any attempt against the facility!"

Stribling gave a slightly offended smile. "We're not amateurs out there, Agent Mallory. After all, we're not unimaginative, and we do know what the risks are. More, perhaps, than anyone else. And because of that, we protect against them."

The tiny buzz from the overhead light fixture filled the silence following Stribling's speech. It was true, Wager thought. Stribling, Walters, and their fellow workers out at the Flats knew a hell of a lot more than he did about what was at stake. But Wager couldn't help thinking "what if." What if someone— Libeus King, for example—did breach the security?

Mallory pulled a manila folder from a drawer and opened it. "I understand that plans call for the plant to stay in operation until 2015, and in fact, DOE wants to expand its current operations."

Stribling peered over Mallory's arm at the papers. "Expand isn't quite the word. The plans that I've been told of are for a Plutonium Recovery Modification Project that would provide a safer place to reprocess plutonium than we have right now. When the plant's finally decommissioned, the PRMP will be able to eat the contaminated buildings as well."

"But some critics don't believe the plant will close, is that right?"

The security officer answered. "People can and will believe any damn thing they want to, Agent Mallory. I don't know what you've got there, but all we can tell you is what we've been told: Rocky Flats is closing down as a trigger-manufacturing facility. And also there are plans to consolidate the nation's nuclear weapons production facilities on one campus, possibly in South Carolina, by 2015."

"But in the meantime, plutonium storage and possible processing will continue at the plant?"

"It has to. There's no place else."

And, Wager knew, political decisions, even if they could be trusted, could also be reversed. "I read somewhere there's plutonium in the duct systems, and that's why the plant closed down the first time."

"Almost closed. But it's for a variety of reasons, including the duct system. I've mentioned some of them already: the waste disposal problem, safety modifications." Stribling shrugged. "But we have cleaned ten ducts in three buildings. The debris is less than a pound, and it's being stored in a protective glove box until we can reclaim the plutonium."

"Buildings 707 and 371 are two of those buildings?"

"Building 371 is." The man was getting tired of defending the facility. "And I know for a fact that EG and G have made quantum leaps in improving the overall safety at the plant. I wouldn't still be working there if they hadn't."

"We appreciate that, Mr. Stribling." Mallory's lips rose and fell in a tired smile. "We're just trying to view the facility as someone might who wanted to attack it."

The lieutenant cleared his throat. "That's done at least once a month, Agent Mallory. We have constant maneuvers against our defenses by aggressors made up of other members of the DOE security forces. It's part of our routine training now."

"What about someone driving in with the work force during the morning rush?"

"We have contingency plans for that, Detective Wager. As well as for terrorist activities—during the Gulf War, for example, we furloughed everyone except a carefully screened skeleton crew and made corresponding increases in our patrol routines."

Mallory nodded at Walters and started to say something else, but the rattle of the telephone cut him off. He answered with his name and listened, eyes finally settling on Wager's. Then he said, "Right. I'll get on it," and rose to shake hands with the two men and steer them to the hallway door, which was behind Wager. "Thank you for your assistance—you've been a great help."

The men could take a hint, but Walters paused in the doorway and nodded at the diagrams and photographs. "You'll inform us immediately if you have evidence of any substantial threat?"

"All we have right now are these diagrams and what I told you on the telephone. I just wish we did have more specific information to give you." Mallory shook his head. "But please don't take this warning lightly."

"Well"—the lieutenant smiled coldly—"we're ready for that

Boy Scouts

or anything else. We follow the ~~Marine Corps~~ motto: 'Be prepared!' Good day, gentlemen."

When the door closed, Mallory joined Wager in staring at the photograph with its band of red marker pencil circling one of the larger buildings. Now Wager could see the similarity between the diagrams and the aerial view of the structure. He looked again at the twin perimeter fences that enclosed the six hundred or so acres of the plant and at the pale streaks of patrol roads that followed the fencing. A thousand yards of treeless, empty prairie surrounded the plant, and Wager guessed that personnel sensors crisscrossed that space. The two roads leading into the plant had to pass reinforced and gated checkpoints, and the railroad spur, too, was blocked by a guard post. "I don't see how he could do it," Wager said.

Mallory agreed. "Pipkin said King was talking explosives. It would take a hundred pounds or more to damage the building. There's no way he could get that much onto the site without being discovered."

"What about flying it in?" asked Wager. "What if he drops a bomb on the place?"

The agent bent closer to the photograph, as if it could tell him something. "They've got air defense. They must have air defense—ground-to-air missiles. And you're talking heavy ordnance, Wager—smart bombs and combat aircraft big enough to carry and launch them." He shook his head. "Stribling said the vaults are four stories underground. They'd need at least a thousand-pound bomb to penetrate that far." He shook his head again. "I don't see it—King must plan on sneaking the explosive into the facility, possibly with help from an inside agent, probably in small lots to be assembled when they're ready to go." A deep breath. "And maybe it's already there somewhere."

"If this is the target," Wager reminded him.

"If," echoed Mallory. "I'll sleep a hell of a lot better when we have King in custody. By the way, that call was from the investigation team up at Simon's cabin. They found the impression of a telephone number on a newspaper in the trash. It belongs to a pay telephone near Pecos and Thirty-eighth. Do you know the area?"

"Yeah. Northwest side. Not far from where we found Pauline Tillotson."

"What day was that?"

"The twenty-first—the fire call came in around three A.M. on the twenty-first."

"The newspaper was dated the twentieth. The later ones were still in the newspaper box at the highway."

Which could mean that Simon and King talked sometime before Tillotson was killed, and that whatever was said made Simon leave the cabin, possibly for King's safe-house, and he hadn't been back since. And, as Wager's mother used to say, "A scared dog will bite anything to hide its fear."

Wager might worry about the Rocky Flats atomic weapons plant,
but it wasn't his to protect. It was the sphere of DOE and the
FBI, and there wasn't much a Denver homicide cop could con-
tribute to the security of the nation. His job was to investigate
a murder, and the latest lead he had, courtesy of Special Agent
Mallory, was an FBI dossier and photograph of one Richard
Simon. The photographs were surveillance shots, but Wager
could make out enough of the man's features in the grainy black
and white to stir something in his memory. He flipped back
through the pages of his little green notebook. The interview
with the owner of the newsstand: the man who had been with
King the last time the man bought a paper there—the one who
had made the comment about the Rocky Mountain Arsenal.
Wager read over the words and then looked at the photographs.
They matched: a tall, young-looking man who, as in one of the
photos, wore aviator-type sunglasses.

Wager brought Chief Doyle up to date and watched the Bulldog's eyes widen as he heard about the Rocky Flats plant.

"Does Mallory think this is a serious threat, Wager?"

"We both do. But we don't see any way the man can get that
much explosive through the security around the plant."

"And you think both of these people—King and Simon—are still in the area?"

Wager nodded and added the detail about the calendar and the date circled on it—tomorrow's.

"Well, let's have the patrol division canvass the goddamn area—knock on every door, look in every garage."

"You really want to do that, Chief?"

Doyle, hand hovering over the telephone, asked, "Why not?"

"For one thing, we made a promise to Mallory about keeping this confidential. For another, we might start a panic." Wager shook his head. "Most important, Chief, we might scare off King or push him into making his attempt sooner."

Doyle rubbed a thick forefinger across his jutting chin. "The man must know we're after him as a murder suspect."

"But he doesn't know we think he's still in the area. And he doesn't know we've linked him to Rocky Flats."

The man stared at the smoking tip of his cigar. "Well, Rocky Flats is certainly outside our jurisdiction. Still, I damn well better alert some people about this. I don't know what can be done—or if anything should be done yet—but some people upstairs better hear about what we're facing."

Wager again reminded Doyle that they'd promised Mallory to say nothing.

"Yeah, Wager. I hear you. But if by some mischance something does happen out there, I'm sure as hell not going to be the only one who knew about it ahead of time." He added, "I'll inform them the information's confidential, but my ass is going to be covered." The lower teeth jutted forward in that bulldog smile that had given Doyle his nickname. "And so will yours."

He was punching the department chief's number when Wager left.

"Gabe!" Max looked as if he had been waiting for some time. "Arnie Trujillo called. He says he might have something, but he wants to talk to you about it."

"When?"

"He wants to know if we can meet him after work. He should get off at five."

Wager glanced at the clock. "He say where?"

"Yeah. A little hole-in-the-wall bar over in Swansea—Manny's Place. Leave in about ten minutes?"

He nodded and settled at his desk to spread out the latest collection of notices and messages. Near the top of the pile was a call logged at 1215—"Henry Stover," followed by a number; Wager ignored it. Farther down, another pink message form said "Alex Saunders," with a return number whose area code was Oregon. Wager quickly dialed it, and a receptionist answered with a string of names like those of a law office or a brokerage. When Wager asked for Saunders, she wanted to know who she could say was calling.

Saunders was expecting him. "Yes—my wife told me you tried to reach me. I'm shocked. . . . Pauline and I, we were good friends. We dated in college."

"Can you tell me anything at all about her relationship with Libeus King?"

"She met him after college. We broke up . . . well, 'broke up' is a bit heavy. Pauline and I decided we wanted to date other people—it was a friendly decision. Then I met my wife-to-be and Pauline started going with someone else. But we kept in touch. She met Libeus after graduation, I remember that, but exactly when I can't say."

"Did she tell you she was in Denver?"

"No. I last heard she was in Arizona with King, and then I heard about this terrible thing." He added, "I called her parents this morning. They didn't know much except that she was murdered."

"Yes. A homicide victim."

"Who did it? How'd it happen?"

"I hope Libeus King can answer some of those questions."

"You think he did it? King?"

"I don't know, Mr. Saunders. Did she ever mention anyplace in Denver where King liked to stay?"

"In Denver? No. They had a place in the mountains near Flagstaff." He gave Wager the mailing address. "I wrote them there."

"What about Charles Pipkin or Richard Simon? Did she ever mention them?"

"Simon? Sure—he was teaching her and Libby how to fly. That was a couple of years ago, though."

"Do you know where he might be?"

"I think he lives in Colorado. I think he said near Boulder." He added helpfully, "That's close to Denver. Libby might be staying with him!"

"Do you know of any address or telephone number in Denver that Simon might have?"

". . . No."

"Do you know of any friends he might have in Denver? Anyone he might go to visit?"

"I'm afraid not. I only met him that once, when the three of them flew up here one weekend. I don't correspond with him. And Pauline never said anything about him when she wrote." He added, "As a matter of fact, I didn't like the guy all that much."

"Why's that?"

"He couldn't talk about anything except ecology stuff. I mean, it's important, sure, but this guy never had anything else on his mind!"

"Did he ever discuss any attempts at sabotage?"

"All the time. Monkey-wrenching, he called it. Or ecotage. Putting spikes in trees, sand in the gas tanks of earthmovers—that kind of thing. Absolutely no sense of humor about it at all! I remember asking Pauline how she got tied up with a nut like Simon."

"What'd she say?"

"Well, she didn't answer directly, I remember. Just said that Simon was a bore but Libeus said he was useful."

"Did Simon mention any project he was working on or thinking about?"

"No. Not that I recall. But I wouldn't be surprised to hear he'd done something. He was that way, you know? A little bit nuts on the subject. Angry and self-righteous. Said that people who didn't do anything were as guilty as those who raped the environment."

The man's tone said that Simon had placed Saunders under that guilty label too. "We're very interested in finding both of them, Mr. Saunders. If you remember anything at all that might help us, please call collect."

Max loomed at his elbow, and Wager held up a finger for "one minute." He looked up the number for the Flagstaff Police Department, identified himself, and asked to talk to one of their homicide detectives. Max sighed and settled on the corner of Wager's desk, making the metal frame creak.

It usually worked better to ask favors of fellow detectives rather than uniformed cops; chances were greater that they'd need a favor in return someday, and in fact, Wager had worked with the Flagstaff plainclothes division before.

"You want to spell that name for me, Detective Wager?" The voice at the other end of the line repeated the letters as Wager spelled out Libeus. "We get some far-out names, but I never heard of that one before. OK, what's the address again?" Wager told him, and the detective said he'd check it out himself and call as soon as possible. Wager thanked him and shoved back from his desk.

Max was already moving toward the door. "Rosener's out of the ICU, I hear."

Wager's mind was on a vision of Rocky Flats, and at first he didn't hear Max's comment. "What?"

"Rosener. He's making it OK."

"That's good—fine." It had been a while since Wager had thought of Floyd or the Blue Moon, and the rage he'd felt earlier at the shooting of two officers was now just a cold disgust and a settled understanding that something would be done.

Max tried again. "Are you getting close to your suspect?"

The elevator doors opened to the chill, exhaust-tainted air of the underground garage, and Wager followed his partner to the car. "Not as close as I'd like to. There's a chance he might be holed up somewhere in District One."

"You put out a notice to the patrol division?"

"Yes." But if King and Simon were there, they wouldn't be walking the streets. They'd go out only when necessary, probably at night, and—to judge from the lack of reports on King's car—probably on foot. MVD had listed a Chevrolet Blazer belonging to Simon, but in the few hours since Wager had put out an alert, no one had spotted that vehicle, either.

Max grunted. "If he's around, he'll turn up sooner or later."

Sooner, Wager thought. It better be sooner.

The address where Arnie wanted to meet them turned out to be one of the dumpy little bars scattered around the industrial and trucking area of Denver's north edge. A grimy cloth sign was tacked on the blank outside wall under a row of high, cramped windows: FRESH MENUDO EVERY NOON. Wager had passed the small, warehouse-like building dozens of times but never stopped. Never wanted to, either, and, from what he saw as they entered the dark and stale-smelling place, was glad he hadn't. Old-fashioned wooden booths lined one wall, and a long bar lined the other. The bartender looked up, toothpick at the corner of his mouth, and nodded hello, then went back to his paper. A vacant pool table filled the space in the center of the room, but no one was playing. Not many were drinking, either. Two men wearing denim jackets and perched on barstools stopped talking to each other and looked up suspiciously;

the first five booths were empty, and the last held only Arnie. He nodded and sucked at a glass of beer as Wager sat beside him. Max filled the facing bench. The heavy bartender, breathing loudly through half-open and thick lips, folded the paper and came over to take their orders.

"Beer," said Wager. Max nodded.

"Bottle or glass?"

Bottles were safer than glasses. A few minutes later, the man thumped down a pair of Coors and collected his money. Arnie sat silent until all the preliminaries were over. The two men in denim began talking again, head-to-head, in a low murmur.

"All right, Arnie. What do you have?"

"I got a line on Flaco, but this person who tipped me, they can't get, you know, involved when you people pick him up."

"No problem," said Max. "We don't have to tell him who tipped us."

"Yeah, well, it ain't that easy. What I hear is, Flaco's living in this person's house who didn't know anything about him. Took him in, you know? Do the *cabrón* a favor. Now this person can't get rid of him. He don't go nowhere. People want to see him, they come there. Flaco's *compadre,* this Sol Atilano, he takes them there. They talk, then they leave. But Flaco don't come outside."

Max nodded. "That explains why we haven't had a sighting of him.

And the information fit what they'd learned from Roy Quintana. "But this person's willing to have us pick up Flaco?" Wager asked.

"Only if she don't get in trouble—not with the police, with Flaco. He's *un tipo,* you know? *Loco.* She's afraid if he finds out, he'll do something to her to get even. And she's afraid the cops'll bust her for taking the fucker in."

"Does she know anything about Ray Moralez getting shot?" Arnie shook his head. "No. Nothing about none of it." He hunched lower over his glass and glanced at the two men sitting at the bar. "Look, she's one of my cousins, you know? Second cousin or third cousin, but still *familia,* you know?"

"Your cousin? And she's shacked up with a Gallo?"

"Hey, I told you she don't know shit about the gangs. This *pendejo* Flaco, he give her some line of shit about hiding from *la migra*—tells her he's *un espalda mojada,* you know?"

Wager knew: a wetback. Most of the Chicano community saw no crime in sheltering illegals. In fact, many of the illegals were relatives of one kind or another and had claim to family hospitality and protection. "So what happened?"

"*Carajo!* First couple days he's smooth, you know? Polite. Then he starts getting mean—wants this, wants that. My cousin tells him to get the fuck out, and he shoves a gun under her nose. Tells her she does what he says or he blows her away, man. *Un chiflado,* man."

Max caught Wager's eye. "Think it's the same pistol he used on Ray?"

"I don't know, man. She don't, neither." Arnie's head wagged in disgust. "She called her mother late last night—whispering, you know? Scared the shit out of her, so her mother called mine. Thinks maybe I can do something. But fuck, man, I can't figure how to get in that place without a lot of shooting!"

"When was this?"

"This afternoon. *Mi madre* called me at work."

It could be the same weapon. Flaco seemed dumb enough and arrogant enough not to get rid of the murder weapon. If they could get the man and the gun, they might have a good case. Wager asked, "You think he'd use her as a hostage?"

Arnie's frown clenched dark eyebrows above a nose that had been flattened at one time or another. "Yeah. Crazy fucker'd do something like that. Especially he finds out she got a cousin who's a Tapatío. Hell, he might waste her just for that!"

"What's the house like?"

He described his cousin's home and said no, she didn't have a dog.

"All right. Give us the address. We'll work it out so Flaco won't know how we got to him."

The man pushed a slip of paper across the table. It held a street address on the city's west side, in an area Wager wasn't too familiar with. He slipped it into his jacket pocket and pulled out a pair of photographs and shoved them across the table toward Trujillo. "We're looking for these people too—they might be over in Sunnyside or Chaffee Park. Maybe Zuni Park."

Trujillo glanced at the pictures and shrugged as he flicked them back with his fingertips. "I don't know them."

"I know you don't know them, Arnie. I want you to look for them."

"Come on, man—I'm no goddamn snitch. I give you Flaco, OK—that's one thing. But don't make me into no goddamn snitch!"

"And don't give me shit, Arnie. You want Flaco out of your cousin's house and you don't want to do it yourself. That's why you dropped the dime. Fine, we'll get him. But these people are important too. What you do is get the word out to all the Tapatíos, tell them to look everywhere. Ask everybody in the barrio if they've seen these people." He turned the photographs over to show some writing, "Or these license plates. I want them, and I want them yesterday."

Trujillo looked up from the numbers to study Wager. "What they do?"

"They're homicide suspects."

Trujillo's shoulders rose and dropped. "They didn't kill nobody I know." He shook his head. "It ain't worth the rap, man. I mean, I want you to help my cousin and all, but like you keep reminding me, I got a daughter now. I don't want her to be no snitch's orphan."

Wager nodded. "There's something else, Arnie, and I'm thinking of your daughter. Yours and everybody else's."

"What's that mean?"

"You know Rocky Flats?"

"That atomic bomb plant up north?"

Wager had been thinking of that circled date on Simon's calendar, and of some way to get help without tipping the fugitives. "These people—and don't go yelling this around, Arnie—these people might try to blow it up."

Max stopped swallowing his beer. "Holy shit!"

And Trujillo stared at Wager, jaw loose.

"If they do, it'll take half of Denver with it," said Wager.

His eyes rounded. "No shit, man?"

"No shit, Arnie." Wager smiled. "Your cousin won't have to worry about getting rid of Flaco if that happens. And if your daughter does grow up, she might have two-headed babies."

Slowly, the man's tattooed hand reached out for the photographs. He studied them. "These guys Anglos?"

"Yeah. This one made a call to a pay phone near Thirty-eighth and Pecos a few days ago. We think he was calling this one. That's the last we heard of them."

"Jesus. What they want to blow up the atomic bomb plant for? What kind of crazy fucks are they?"

Wager couldn't answer either question. "We need to find them as soon as possible, Arnie. We need them now."

The man rubbed a chipped and grimy thumbnail in the sparse hairs of his black mustache. "Tell you what, man—some of those *babosos* in the gang, they wouldn't give a shit if Rocky Flats did blow up. Just be a big show for them, you know?"

"What are you telling me, Arnie?"

A shrug. "Vickie Salazar's been shooting off her mouth about the Tapatíos not doing nothing about Ray Moralez."

"You mean we've got to get Flaco before they'll look for these guys?"

Another shrug. "*Peor es nada.* Flaco's big on their mind. If I can bring them some good news about that *cagón*, they'll feel better about looking for these *locos*. They'll, you know, owe us, man."

"All right. Tell them we'll get Flaco tonight, Arnie. And you tell the Tapatíos we need these people tonight too."

"Yeah. OK." He drained his beer and started to stand. "And my cousin?"

It was Wager's turn to shrug. "All we want is Flaco."

"Can I have these pictures?"

Max drove, but his mind wasn't on the rush hour traffic that clogged the bumpy, truck-damaged streets. "Gabe, that Rocky Flats story . . . I mean, that's all it was, right? A story to get Arnie's cooperation?"

Wager glanced at his partner. "You think I'd lie about something like that?"

Max chewed on his lower lip. "You mean it's true?"

"It's true."

"But there's no way . . . That place is like a fort. Nobody could get into it!"

"You know it and I know it. That doesn't mean they know it."

"Yeah." Then, "The people who ought to hear about it have been told, right?"

"The FBI's on it."

Max whistled a brief little tune. "Why don't I feel overjoyed at that news?"

"There's not much I can do except go after King, Max. The FBI knows, Rocky Flats security knows. They've been alerted."

"Yeah. I hear what you're saying. But it's our asses too— we live here. Us, our families . . ."

So did Arnie and the Gallos and the Tapatíos. All the names and faces Wager had run across in the last couple of days. All going about their business, with no idea how fast the clock was running. Even Flaco and Floyd the bartender, though Wager didn't think they would be missed by anyone.

They rode for a while in silence, the magnitude of what could happen capturing both their minds. Finally, Max said, "We better go after this King, Gabe. To hell with Flaco. I mean, we should have the whole damn department going door-to-door for King!"

"If they did, it'd probably start a goddamn panic."

"But you just told Arnie about it—and he's going to pass the word to all the Tapatíos!"

"But they're not going to talk about it all over the city, Max. And even when the word does get around, it'll just be a rumor, a whisper. If we came in knocking on doors, it would be official, and Christ only knows what would happen." He added, "Besides, if King and Simon are in the area, we could scare them off or push them into doing it sooner. But a bunch of street punks wandering up and down don't mean a thing to them."

Max thought it over. "Yeah—I guess that makes sense. About as much as anything else anyway." He added, "Some of that district is Gallos turf. Maybe that's another thing we should talk to Roy Quintana about."

Wager agreed. "Let's see if maybe the scum bags can do something useful for a change."

Roy Quintana wasn't happy to open his door to them. He wore the same muscle shirt, and the same sharp odor of unwashed body filled the small apartment. The hot plate had been moved from the windowsill to the stained coffee table in front of the television, and a can of chili, lid tilted back for a handle, sat warming on it.

"You a pretty good cook, Roy?"

The youth stirred the can with a plastic spoon. "Why—you hungry?"

Wager grinned. "Not anymore. Eat up—we got things to do."

"What things?"

"Things like picking up Flaco."

He licked the spoon and pointed it at Max. "This one, he told me you couldn't get no tap planted on Sol's telephone, and I sure ain't going to let you follow me to wherever the hell Flaco's holed up. Fucker'd kill me quicker'n he'd kill you."

"We know where he is."

The black eyes stared at Wager. "Then you don't need me!"

"Yeah, we do. We need Sol for one thing, and we need you for something else."

The spoon paused in its scraping. "Like what?"

Wager told him what they had in mind for Flaco.

"You want me to call Sol and tell him you people know where Flaco is?"

"Tell him we're on our way to pick Flaco up. Tell Sol one of your *compadres* heard some people talking while he was being booked down at Cherokee Street. Tell him this *compadre* made his one phone call to you, and you're doing Flaco a favor."

Roy scratched his tattooed shoulder and studied the problem from all sides. "I guess I can do that. I don't see how Flaco could blame me for telling Sol you people are coming after him. I mean, man, that's what you'll be doing, right?"

"You got it," said Max.

Wager took copies of the two photographs from his jacket pocket. "Here's what else you do." He told Quintana he wanted the Gallos to look for Simon and King.

The youth gazed at the photographs. "Yeah, *por supuesto*— we can find them if they're around the barrio. But why should we, man?"

Max leaned forward. "If you don't, you might not have a barrio."

"What's that mean?"

Wager told him, and the young man's black eyes widened until they were ringed with white. Wager added, "The Tapatíos are looking too."

"Those *cagadillos?* They in this?"

"We're all in it," said Max.

"Shit, man, those fuckers can't find their asses with both hands! Why you want to ask them?"

"Because I got to find these two. Fast. You think the Gallos can find them before Tapatíos do?"

"Aw, man . . . ! That's our turf—we know those streets, man. We own them!"

"So show me," said Wager,

The plan was for Wager and Max to be in position before Roy made the call to Sol Atilano. They told Roy what time to dial and exactly what to say and how to say it—"Remember, you're excited, Roy. You just heard from your *compadre.* You can't wait to get the word to Sol"—then they drove across west Denver to the address Arnie Trujillo had given them.

It was in the Westwood neighborhood, where the diagonal artery of Morrison Road cut through the grid of north-south streets and made intersections of odd-size triangles. Jouncing across the dips that served as both rain gutters and speed bumps, they raced through residential streets until they neared Dakota.

"Should be the next block," warned Max.

Wager slowed and turned onto Osceola at the beginning of the block. He pulled to the curb near the intersection. The two men got out and crossed the quiet street to the south side of Dakota, eyeing the homes that sat back behind shallow lawns. Most of the boxy structures were one-story and sheathed in that kind of Masonite siding that was used so much in the fifties.

"There it is. Arnie said it has blue shutters."

It was almost halfway down the block, and they walked past casually in the failing light of dusk. From behind a pulled blind, a single window showed the dim glow of a lamp and the irregular colored flickers of a television.

"Somebody's inside," said Wager.

"Yeah." Max glanced at his watch. "Seven-ten. Roy should call in five minutes."

Wager nodded, and they turned at the corner of Perry. The weedy gravel of an alley, marked by telephone poles, garbage cans, and garage doors, ran between a variety of backyard fences. "I'll take the back. Click me when you're set to go."

"Will do."

Max turned back up Dakota; Wager headed down the alley.

He'd counted the houses and, at the eighth, gingerly lifted the rusty latch that fastened the yard's gate. Despite Arnie's assurance, Wager waited for the frantic rush and snarl of a dog, but the only barking came from across the lane and down a couple of garages—something big and nervous and excited to hear a stranger's footsteps in the gravel. The back of the house, too, had blue shutters; but the windows on this side were dark, and it was hard to tell if anyone was looking out into the unkempt backyard, where a clothesline sagged between metal poles and a large ash tree made the gloom darker. A pitted and narrow strip of old sidewalk ran from the gate and through the browning spikes of an iris bed; it touched the door of the garage and then angled to the porch stairs. The porch was a screened addition tacked on a long time ago and beginning to sag now. The rusty screen blocked any view of the house's back door. Wager's watch told him that Roy would be dialing any second, and Wager tried to spot a place where he could crouch out of sight. The radio pack on his belt clicked three times; Max was ready. The only place in the yard itself was behind the tree, and he sprinted to it, pistol drawn, and answered with two jabs on the transmit button.

The barking dog down the alley had finally quieted, and in the silence Wager heard a telephone bell jangle inside the house. It rang once, twice. The third ring was broken as someone picked up the receiver. Then more silence. Then, down the strip of yard leading around the side of the house, came the loud rap of heavy knuckles on the front door.

The thud of heels pounded somewhere inside, and a moment later Wager heard the back door rattle. The porch's screen door slapped open, and a dim figure sprinted down the steps two at a time: their little ruse had worked. The man cut across the yard toward the back gate, a figure about Wager's size, his head tucked low as if he was trying to hide even while he ran. Both hands seemed to be empty of weapons, but in the dim light it was hard to tell, and the man's dark jacket covered the waistband of his pants.

Wager leaned out from the tree, arm level and Star PD tracking the running figure. "Hold it, Flaco—Denver police—you're under arrest!"

Shocked eyes and mouth made dark circles in a blur of pale flesh as Flaco's head jerked toward Wager. But the man didn't stop. He didn't slow. Instead, his legs stretched longer and he hunkered even lower. An arm disappeared inside the dark coat, and then the shape became dim in the dusk. Wager called once more, and the answer was an explosion and the hot flash of a weapon as the blurry figure sprinted for the gate and started to roll over it. Wager squeezed off a round, the flash of his own weapon blinding him, then a second round, lower, at the vague shadow of movement near the ground. The dog down the alley was barking again, frantically now, joined by animals in the surrounding blocks, and Wager's ears rang with the smack of his own pistol and the even louder report of Flaco's weapon. Blinking the glare from his eyes, he peeked around the tree trunk and saw a jerking tangle of darkness collapsed at the base of the fence.

"Throw the weapon over here, Flaco! Throw it out where I can see it!"

"Goddamn!" The word was a grunting cough, scarcely audible.

"Gabe—you OK?" Max's voice called from two places: behind the corner of the house and through Wager's holstered radio pack. "Where's Flaco?"

"He's down. Stay there. He's still got a weapon."

"You hit?" The voice came quieter now and solely through the radio, and Wager could see the dark line of a pistol barrel angled up against the pale corner of the house.

Wager, too, used the radio. "No, but he is. I don't know how bad." He called again to the grunting man. "Throw it out, Flaco—the pistol. Throw it where I can see it."

"Goddamn . . ."

"You're going to bleed to death, you dumb son of a bitch. Throw it out!"

Lights flicked on in neighboring houses and made the dusk turn to black, and now Wager could see nothing of the crumpled figure against the dark ground.

"Max—go back to the car and get a flashlight."

"Will do. You stay put, partner."

He did, listening to the rhythmic grunts from the dark. The dogs kept up their mindless yapping, and from the distance came the first wail of a siren. Patrols out of District Four, Wager guessed, cutting through the evening traffic as they came from the station at Federal and West Florida. He switched his radio to the district channel and called his code number. The dispatcher answered immediately, her voice calm, almost bored: "Go ahead."

"Suspect down on an arrest. Need an ambulance." Wager gave her the street number and added, "Come down the alley, but do not approach until I give permission. Suspect is still armed."

"Shots were fired?"

"That's affirmative." And it meant the department shooting investigation team would be coming to survey the scene and then interview Wager and Max. In his mind's eye he could see the official forms and reports beginning to stack up mountain high. You fired a round in one second, and then you spent the next week explaining why you did it. Damn Flaco anyway.

"Do you need backup, sir?"

"Just whoever's in the neighborhood."

Another voice eagerly broke into the net with its call numbers. "I'll take it—I'm about five blocks away."

"Right," said Wager. "Come into the backyard from the street side of the house."

Another voice broke in without identifying itself: "Gabe, did you get him?"

It sounded like Sergeant Davis, but all Wager said was: "He's down. I don't know how bad. He still has his weapon."

A second unidentified voice said happily, "All right—that's one for us! Let the fucker bleed to death!"

"Keep the net clear, people," said Wager. But he could understand the savage joy that came when a fellow cop nailed one of the bastards who'd tried to shoot a policeman. It was a joy intensified by the lingering soreness of the sniper attack behind the Blue Moon Bar. And with that thought, Wager remembered to pull his badge from its case and clip it to the vest pocket of his dark sport coat. Regulations said he should wear the badge conspicuously whenever an arrest was to be made. And of course he would tell the shooting investigation team that the badge had been dangling there the whole time, like a shiny target over his heart.

"Flaco—an ambulance is on the way. Throw the pistol out!"

Feet pounded the earth behind Wager, and a moment later, Max's huge shadow loomed through the dark and his voice whispered hoarsely, "He still there?"

"Yeah. Keep behind the tree, Max." Wager held the long flashlight an arm's length away from his body and aimed the bright beam toward sounds whose rhythm had become shorter and more intense. In the circle of white light, Martínez lay half on his side, legs tangled beneath him and an arm twisted under his torso. The tangled black hair of his head jerked a time or two as the light played over him. His other arm, hand spread wide to show it was empty, wagged in the glare.

"Keep the light on him," said Max. He swung in a wide arc through the darkness toward the man.

Wager aimed the silhouette of his pistol's sights against the figure. From somewhere behind them in the house, a woman's voice called out, "Is he dead? Officer—is he dead?" A siren shrilled loudly and then began to die to a growl as the squeal of tires sounded from the street in front.

Max's voice spoke from the blackness surrounding the flashlight glare. "Put your other hand out, Flaco. Let's see it."

"Goddamn—I can't. I can't move it."

"Roll over, then."

"I can't, man!" It sounded to Wager as if Flaco was crying now. "I can't—it hurts like shit, man!"

Max's figure came into the edge of the light, crouched, intent on the man on the ground. One large hand made his cocked pistol look like a toy, the other reached for the grunting man's hidden arm. "Don't move, Flaco. Not one fucking move, or you're buzzard meat." A moment later, Max stood and stepped back, the glint of something in his other hand. "I got it, Gabe."

Wager sighed, surprised to become aware he had been holding his breath. Behind him, he heard another sigh. A uniformed officer added his flashlight to the scene and half-laughed. "Jesus. I think I'd've pumped another round into him before I tried that!"

Wager was right about the paperwork. A formal hearing would be held in a few days, and there were forms to fill out immediately, diagrams to draw, indicating where each round went, statements of justification to be worded in the safest way. He sat at his desk in the deserted homicide office and half-heard the scratch of his ballpoint pen and the distant squawk of a television down by the duty clerk's desk. Flaco's weapon, a chrome-plated .45, was upstairs in the ballistics laboratory, waiting for proof of recent firing. Then they would test a slug against the one found in Ray Moralez. Wager put money on its being the same pistol—it wasn't a Saturday-night throwaway but a trophy weapon, something shiny and impressive, to wave around in front of people and brag about. It was also a pistol that fired a bullet a hell of a lot heavier than that allowed the Denver police. They were authorized to use .38 caliber or 9-mm bullets no heavier than 147 grains; the bad guys, of course, could use .45s or magnum loads or even bazookas if they had them. When bazookas were licensed, only the criminals would have bazookas. Public safety versus firepower was an unending argument—you wanted a bullet that wouldn't go through a wall or a perp and hit an innocent bystander, but you also wanted one that would do the job with a single round. Just last week, an officer trying to serve a no-knock warrant had to use six bullets to stop a Doberman. Six, just for a damned dog; they had been the official size. Wager rubbed his eyes and stretched back against the creak of his chair before turning to the next section of this form: Describe Options Other Than Confrontation Available to Officer at the Time.

Flaco had still been alive when the ambulance carried him away to Denver General. One of the uniformed officers had gone inside the house to take a long statement from Arnie's cousin. The other man had interviewed the neighbors to record what they heard and saw. The duty homicide officer had arrived, called out by the shooting; it was Ross, and Wager heard him tell Max that if he and Wager were members of the police union, the union's lawyer would be out here right now, setting up their defense. Max had said he would think about joining; Wager hadn't bothered saying anything.

"Well, partner, got that finished up?" Max, drained of energy, came in with a clutch of papers in one hand and a tepid cup of coffee in the other.

Wager thought about noting, under "Options," Use of Sweet Reason, but instead wrote "None," signed the last page, and clamped the pile of sheets together with a spring clip. He, too, had felt the adrenaline ebb from his body and mind as the tension of the shooting faded and the routine of paperwork replaced it. "Why don't you call it a day? Francine must think you've started another shift."

"I phoned her a while ago—she knows where I am. What about you?"

Wager dug the heels of his hands into the dry and crinkly flesh of tired eyes. Elizabeth wasn't home, but Wager had left a message on her telephone answerer, saying he was hung up on a case. "I thought I'd cruise the barrio. Flash some pictures of King and Simon, see what Arnie and Ray have come up with."

Max nodded. "That's what I told Francine we'd be doing. I told her I owed you."

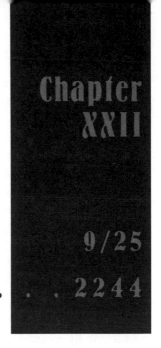

● ● ● ● ● ● ● . . .

Afterward, they'd argue over who got the credit for coming up with the idea. Wager guessed they'd both thought of it at the same time, and probably for the same reasons: the need for comic relief from the Flaco bust, the lack of luck with King and Simon, the chance to get around the bureaucratic rules that let Floyd attack cops. What they would later both agree on was that the results were a hell of a lot more spectacular than either of them expected.

They were heading from the Admin Building to the northwest side of town, armed with another pocketful of photographs of Simon and King. The idea was to canvass clerks who served the late-night businesses in the area—grocery stores, gas stations, convenience stores—to see if either man had been noticed. Since neither King nor Simon nor their cars had been spotted yet, there was a chance they did their shopping late at night and on foot.

They were heading up Lawrence toward the Thirty-eighth Street bridge when Wager heard something loose rattle under the seat of the unmarked cruiser. He reached down, to find the gray canister of a smoke grenade, and he held it up for Max to see. Their eyes met. "The Blue Moon's just around the corner," said Max. "Not two minutes away."

"Yeah," said Wager. "Ain't it, though."

Max swung the car in a sharp turn. At this time of night, the traffic on upper Larimer was light and the sidewalks almost vacant. The neon sign for the Blue Moon Bar splashed a pale glare against the neighboring storefronts. Max let the vehicle coast while Wager scrambled into the back seat and pulled the safety pin of the smoke grenade.

"Ready?"

"Let's do it."

Max aimed the cruiser across the street lanes toward the bar. The blue of neon made the pavement look steely and cold, and a man leaning against the wall lifted a cigarette off his lip and stared with his mouth hanging open as the car lurched up across the curb toward him and slowed in front of the open door. Wager quickly opened the door and leaned out to lob the canister into the bar. Still unmoving, the leaning man turned his head as he watched the thing arc past him. Then Wager slammed the car door and Max stepped on the gas, tires squealing on the smooth concrete of the sidewalk. The noise seemed to wake up the openmouthed man, and he turned to sprint for safety up the empty street, cigarette left behind to bounce on the pavement in a spray of sparks.

Wager watched out the back window while the car careened into Larimer. A dim flash lit up the doorway, and just as Max heeled over in a turn toward Wyandot, a handful of figures came tumbling onto the sidewalk. Then the bar was lost to sight.

"Let old Floyd put that in his pipe." Max grinned.

Wager slid into the front seat. A smoke grenade wasn't all Wager would have liked to do to Floyd and the Blue Moon, but it sure made a good start.

They had reached Thirty-eighth when the district's channel picked up the first calls: Possible bomb explosion at the Blue

Moon Bar. The dispatcher asked for any available officer to report to the scene. There was a long silence.

"Any units available, please respond."

More silence.

Max laughed. "I think everybody's on coffee break, Gabe."

"Two twelve, are you in the vicinity of the Blue Moon? Check in, please."

A laconic "Two twelve . . . go ahead."

The dispatcher gave the information. The responding officer, voice breaking with suddenly discovered static, asked her to repeat it—he was having radio difficulty. By the time Max and Wager reached the first 7-Eleven on West Thirty-eighth, the dispatcher had finally made herself understood and two twelve said he would get there as soon as he finished working up the traffic stop he'd made.

The clerk at the cash register in the 7-Eleven looked at the two photographs and shook her head. Wager had the feeling that it was just the first of a long series of negatives. The feeling proved right. He and Max stopped at every store and market still open along that section of Thirty-eighth. Finally, they pulled into an aging neighborhood Safeway, which, Wager had been told, stocked more Mexican foods and condiments than any other store in the city. A large sign in the window said OPEN 24 HOURS, and even this late, the store's narrow aisles were dotted with shopping carts. The cash registers made a steady rustle as lines of tired-looking people fed through. Max started with the cashiers; Wager started with the butcher shop. It was closed for the evening, but the seafood counter had a sign that said PLEASE RING FOR SERVICE. He did, and after a while a woman whose bleached hair puffed from under a flat cap came from somewhere in the back of the store. Wager identified himself and showed her the two photographs. She frowned and held one at an angle, then used the side of her hand to block off the lower half of the face.

"This one—but he had a beard. A scrubby-looking thing,

you know? Maybe four or five days old. I remember thinking he must be just growing it and wondered if it didn't itch." She handed back the photograph of Simon. "Made my face itch anyway. What'd he do?"

"He's wanted for questioning. Can you remember when he came in?"

"Yesterday. Had to be night—I work the evening shift. Maybe ten or so, when it was pretty slow." She gestured toward the PLEASE RING button. "He had to ring me out of the back; I was setting up for the morning shift. Half pound of halibut and a quarter pound of crab flakes, jar of Bookbinder's sauce, two pounds of boiled shrimp—I remember the order. We don't sell much seafood. I asked him if he was giving a party. He said he was going to pig out on seafood for a change."

"Was he by himself?"

Her pale and bloodshot blue eyes lifted to the ceiling as she thought back. "He took everything in his hands and walked off toward aisle fourteen. He maybe left his cart over there, or maybe somebody else was pushing it, I didn't see."

Wager left the two photographs and gave her a business card. He asked her to call immediately if either man showed up again. At the front of the store, Max met him with a headshake. "Nothing."

"Lady back in seafood saw Simon around this time last night. Positive ID."

"By golly!"

It gave them a squirt of adrenaline that lasted through the final dozen or so fruitless stops and a careful tour of the neighborhood's side streets and alleys. Occasionally, their slowly moving headlights would pick out groups of three or four figures walking on the sidewalks or crossing the dimly lit streets: kids in jackets of matching color and cut, or wearing their colors tied in a band around head or thigh: the Tapatíos or the Gallos, sifting through the neighborhood.

"They've got to be holed up around here. What'd the woman

tell you he said? He wanted to pig out on seafood 'for a change'?"

Wager, peering at parked cars and license plates in the dim light, nodded. It sounded that way to him too: the two men waiting for something to happen. Or working on something. They were here in Denver as of last night anyway.

"We could saturate the area, Gabe. Knock on every door, look in every garage."

That's what the Tapatíos and Gallos were doing right now, and the argument against having the cops do it hadn't changed.

Which Max realized. "But they probably expect that. They probably have a plan for something like that."

Their cruise through alleys and quiet streets was accompanied by increasingly busy radio traffic from District Two. The fire department had responded to the Blue Moon call, and the dispatcher called for more officers to handle traffic control, but many were tied up with other contacts.

"Jesus, Gabe. All that for a little bit of smoke."

It was more than a little, Wager knew. But it would be clearing by now, and Floyd would see the canister and might even get the point. "I'd like to use a flash-bang next time."

Max let his imagination run. "How about a grenade launcher? Make that place into a downtown firing range!"

"Let's try this gas station up here."

It was another wasted effort. They were turning toward a small block of stores on Tejon Street when Wager's call number came over the radio: "That information you wanted from PD Flagstaff just arrived."

"Right. I'm coming in."

"Think it's anything?" asked Max.

His guess was as good as Wager's. The most they could do was hope. As they entered the CAP offices, the duty clerk handed him a scrolled fax sheet.

"You hear about the Blue Moon?" The woman's round face grinned at them.

"What about it?"

"Three-alarm fire—somebody threw a grenade or a bomb in it, and the whole place went up."

Wager and Max looked at each other. "Anybody hurt?"

"No. They all got out. But the whole place is gone. It was a firetrap anyway. And no loss to anybody, I say."

Wager nodded. "Those things happen."

"Sure do," said Max. He muttered as they went down the hall to the homicide office. "I didn't think we'd burn the place down."

"Must have set that wooden floor on fire—spread from there," said Wager. "Let's hope Floyd didn't have any insurance."

He flattened the fax sheet and began reading.

The glossy paper held only a few lines, but Wager read them twice before he picked up the telephone and dialed Flagstaff.

"No, Detective Wager. Detective Wood's off duty now. He'll be on in the morning after eight."

"Can you give me his home number? It's very important."

"We're not allowed to give out that information, Detective."

Wager tried not to sound irritated, but the Spanish lilt crept into his voice. "Can you call him at home, then? Here's my number. Tell him to call me collect right away. Like I said, it's very important, miss. I would wait until tomorrow if it wasn't so important."

A pause. "I'll ask him, sir."

Wager read over the fax sheet one more time: King's residence had been vacant, but armed with a search warrant requested by the FBI, Detective Wood had searched the premises. A brief list of the items secured named clothes, correspondence, books, computer and printer with disks, and, in the garage, a disassembled practice round from a rocket launcher. The telephone rang; Detective Wood asked for Wager.

"Can you tell me if the papers or computer disks held any diagrams?" Wager asked the man.

"I didn't go through them, Detective Wager. I don't know shit about working computers."

"Do you have them in your evidence locker?"

"Yeah. We took the whole setup back for the FBI to look at. One of our officers said the computer had a hard disk or something like that. He said there would be all sorts of stuff inside it that wasn't on the floppies."

"Thanks."

Wager hung up and quickly dialed the number Mallory had given him. The measured voice of an operator answered and said thank you, Mr. Mallory will get right back to you. A couple of minutes later, Wager's phone rang.

But it wasn't Mallory. "Gabe, thank God!" Elizabeth's usually husky voice had a rough, strained note in it, and she took a deep breath before speaking more calmly. "I've heard something—I've heard something horrible!"

"Like what?"

"About some terrorist planning to blow up Rocky Flats! Is it true?"

"Where'd you hear that, Liz?"

"The mayor's office—I can't tell you who. After last night, I started asking around today. One of the people I talked to called me a little while ago and said they're having an emergency meeting. The mayor and the chief of police and the emergency response directors. For God's sake, Gabe, is it really true?"

"I didn't know last night that it was Rocky Flats, Liz."

"But you knew it was something like this."

"And it was confidential. I promised the FBI."

"Well, it's not confidential now. The person who told me said she lives out in Arvada, near the Flats. She's on her way home now to grab her children and run, Gabe!"

The person wasn't wrong to do that. "They have a lot of defenses out there, Liz. And we're combing the area for the people involved."

"So it is true."

"Yeah. But I'm just a small wheel in this. The FBI, the chief, I guess the mayor too, it sounds like—they're on it now. All I'm trying to do is find the guy for a murder."

She finally asked, "I heard there was a shooting too. You were in a shooting?"

"Yeah. But that one had nothing to do with Rocky Flats. It was Max's case."

"You're all right, aren't you?"

"Oh, sure!" He blinked and saw again the spurt of yellow light spearing toward him and knew that, in coming moments on the threshold of sleep, the scene would come back, teasing him in its dreamy slowness and starting a scream from his throat as the bullet grew out of the flame toward his frozen eyes. That's what fear did: ambushed you when your guard was down. "Guy was a marshmallow. The paperwork is tougher than he was."

"Thank God. I figured if you . . . if an officer had been hurt, the news would be broadcast, as it was for those two poor policemen. But still . . ."

He tried not to let impatience slip into his voice; being shot at was something he didn't want to talk about or magnify with war stories. And the fear that had been ignored in the heat and action of the moment wasn't something he wanted to admit to, even to Elizabeth. Especially to her. "I'm all right, Liz. Not a scratch."

But she heard it, and an ironic note came into her own voice. "All right, tough guy. I won't congratulate you anymore on still being alive. But what about this other thing, Gabe—the terrorist? What can I do? Who should I talk to?"

Wager didn't think talk would do much for anybody now, but maybe it would be therapeutic for Liz. After all, she was a politician, even though Wager didn't often describe her that way to himself. "Maybe the mayor. I don't know what to tell you, Liz. I'm looking for the guy. I'm working with the FBI, and we're doing all we can to locate him without spooking him into doing something stupid. That's all I know right now."

A long silence, and Wager could picture Elizabeth nibbling at the outside edge of her little finger, as she did when she was puzzled or thinking deeply. "Gabe—I love you."

Where the hell did that fit in? But he said, "I love you too, Liz." And he realized that he did.

As soon as he hung up, the phone rang again. This time it was Mallory. "What's up?"

Wager told him what the Flagstaff police had reported.

Mallory was silent a moment. In the background, a jingle of telephones and the occasional murmur of voices told Wager that Mallory had set up some kind of crisis center. "We just had the information from those disks come in from our agent in Flagstaff, Gabe. I haven't had time to look at all of it yet."

"How'd he get it to you so fast?"

"Modem. Anything on computer disks can be telephoned via a modem."

"Does it have any information to help me find King?"

"Nothing I'm able to tell you about, Gabe."

Which meant that Mallory was ahead of Wager now and didn't need him. The FBI knew enough to make them urgently marshal their agents and specialists into teams to defend Rocky Flats whether King was captured or not. It was what they should be doing, Wager knew, but a deal was a deal. "We're supposed to be working on this together."

"And we are! Anything I judge to be of help for your end of the case, Gabe, I'll certainly provide you with."

Even the man's tone, falsely sincere, told Wager of the widening gap between Mallory and himself. "Why can't I be the one to look at it and decide if it'll help?"

Mallory's next phrase was like a door closing; it left no room for argument: "It's a question of national security."

It was clear that the man wasn't going to share what information was on the disks. "I see." Wager kept his voice pleasant. "But you will call me if you do turn up something, right?"

"Sure! You bet."

Mallory didn't bother to ask if Wager had anything new. Perhaps he didn't need to because he had it all. Instead, the line clicked dead, and despite knowing that the Rocky Flats threat was a hell of a lot more important than the Tillotson murder, Wager had the feeling he was being shoved out of his own case.

Elizabeth was waiting up for him when he dragged himself to her house. Waiting up wasn't quite right—she'd left a dozen lights on and curled up asleep on the couch wearing a flannel nightgown and quilt. The television set was showing a stoic Indian face that Wager vaguely recognized. Someone out of Hollywood from decades past . . . Jeff Chandler—that was the guy. Looked like an Ivy League professor dressed up as an Indian. He was making noises about sacrificing himself for his woman and his tribe.

The soft click of the "off" switch startled her out of sleep. "Gabe?"

"Yeah."

Standing, she stumbled drowsily toward him to hold and be held. "I'm glad you're here."

He pressed the small, intense body close to him and felt her warmth penetrate beneath his weariness and into that icy knot that had formed and been ignored when Flaco Martínez shot at him. "I am too."

"I have some fish in the refrigerator. Hungry?"

Food was something else he'd shoved to the back of his mind

during the last few hours. Now the thought of it suddenly filled his mouth with a spurt of saliva. "Starved."

"You make the salad; I'll warm up the fish."

His food disappeared in seconds, and Wager sighed as he leaned back from the kitchen table, a half-empty beer mug in his hand and a wad of half-chewed food in his belly. "That was good."

"How would you know!"

"It really was good." He watched her pick a cucumber out of lettuce leaves. "Have you talked to anybody yet?"

She nodded, mouth full. "A couple of people. The mayor— I managed to get him on the telephone. He verified a lot of what you told me."

"Did he want to know where you found out?"

"No. A lot of people are whispering about it now. It's not something you can keep secret."

"What are they doing about it?"

"From what I could gather, pretty much leaving it up to the FBI. Any metro emergency evacuation plans dealing with something as massive as that don't even exist, Gabe. Some of the municipalities have their own disaster plans, but not all of them do, and nothing's coordinated. There's no metro-wide plan at all." She finished her salad and stacked the plates on the table while she talked. "Most of the people I spoke with weren't sure that, with a catastrophe of that magnitude, anything could be done anyway." A clatter of dishes. "Have you had any luck?"

"Plenty. All bad." He drained the beer mug. "Could you call the mayor first thing in the morning and tell him the FBI's not keeping the city police informed?"

"What?"

Wager explained. "We had an agreement—Mallory and me—to work together. Now he's taken off on his own, and I don't know what information he has. I don't know his plans for stopping an attack on the Flats, I don't know what he has that might help me locate the people I'm looking for."

A red area appeared high on her cheeks, a sign of her quick temper, and she glanced at the electric clock on the kitchen wall. It was shaped like a large green apple, and each number was a different kind of fruit. A gift, she had explained once, from a West Slope fruit grower who had been gathering support for a bill to defend Colorado produce against malicious slander. "He has a breakfast meeting at seven-thirty. I'll call him then."

"Think he'll help?"

"For a change, yes. He's very worried about this, as he damn well should be." They carried the dishes to the sink, and she began setting them in the washer. "I also talked to a man who's active in a local peace movement. He's not a wild-eyed type, Gabe, and I trust what he says." Her dark eyes, puffy from the late hour, gazed at him—serious, upset, but more determined than fearful. "His biggest fear is the plutonium that's still in the ductwork."

"I was told they're cleaning out the ducts. That they've already removed something like eight pounds of the crap."

"He told me they plan on removing a total of thirteen pounds of dust. They say that will ensure against criticality. But, Gabe, the estimated total amount of plutonium scattered through the ducts is sixty-two pounds. That's enough for seven nuclear bombs!"

Wager rubbed a hand across the weary flesh of his stubbly jaw. "What do you mean, 'criticality'?"

"Concentration of plutonium. If too much is concentrated together, you can have a spontaneous nuclear chain reaction."

"Jesus—like a bomb?"

"More a radioactive burst and fire, as I understand it." She added, "And I don't understand all of it. That's what makes it even scarier. Anyway, it would be fatal to anyone in the immediate vicinity."

"A local explosion, then—kept in the building."

"Except that a major explosion would probably blow out the

filters—they're only paper—as well as the monitoring system. That would leave the other fifty-four pounds of plutonium dust free to escape into the atmosphere."

Wager visualized the architectural drawings they'd got from Pipkin. He remembered watching Stribling's finger trace the channel of ductwork through the maze of rectangles and symbols as he earnestly told them about the cleanup project. The channels converged at a final filtration center on the ground floor just before the air was drawn into the tall stacks. If the filter system blew and the building pressure equalized, the contaminated air could be pulled by the rising warm currents out of the bowels of the building and up those stacks like water through a straw.

"There have been two major incidents with the filter system already, in 1957 and 1969. Fires that breached filters and destroyed monitors. No one knows how much burned plutonium escaped each time."

"It came over Denver?"

"No one knows. The tracking system and ground-level sample boxes weren't in place then. But it had to go somewhere."

Wager dug his thumbs into burning eyes and tried to fight back a yawn. It wasn't boredom, it wasn't the company, and it certainly wasn't the subject; he was just exhausted. Elizabeth turned out the light over the stove and, as Wager pushed himself up on weary legs, once more held him tightly. "Somebody, Gabe—my God, somebody somewhere has to know how to protect us from it!"

If there was a somebody, Wager hadn't heard of him. The only somebody he knew of was people like Milton Stribling and Lieutenant Walters, who thought they had everything under control. Or Mallory, who had started playing games with DPD. Or Wager himself, whose efforts were futile and whose flesh was aching with exhaustion. And along with his weariness, he felt the vast weight of death—the emptiness of space, and light years of nothingness surrounding this small drop of life, this tiny spark that could be snuffed out so easily by us alone. The street. It was the morning of the twenty-sixth, and he should get back on the street. But his eyes wouldn't stay open any longer, and the surging pull of sleep rose higher and higher like waves he could hear and feel. Even as he stood holding Elizabeth, they sucked at his consciousness like an onrushing darkness.

Elizabeth's voice woke him, and through the lingering fog of slowly ebbing numbness, he half-heard what she was saying.

"Councilwoman Voss, and it's more than important. It's an emergency. Yes—right now. No. I don't want him to return my call, god damn it—I said this is an emergency. Now!" She was propped against a pillow to hold the receiver to her ear. The figures on the clock radio flipped to 7:32, and Wager stifled a grunt as he began to struggle fully awake. Elizabeth smiled down at him, then turned her attention back to the telephone. "Yes, Frank, thank you for interrupting your meeting. I found out last night that the FBI is no longer working with our police liaison on the Rocky Flats case. . . . No, I'm not at liberty to say, but the information is accurate. An Agent Mallory . . . I know what their primary responsibility is, Frank; I also know what our responsibility is to our citizens and that we need information to carry out that responsibility. . . . Yes, apparently they know about the terrorist's plans and they've suddenly clammed up. . . . No, I don't—but by God, we should, and we should right now. . . . Yes, you and the governor, both—a phone call's not too much to ask in a situation like this. . . . Yes, that's a good idea! All right, Frank, thank you."

Wager was pulling on his clothes as Elizabeth hung up the telephone. "What'd he say?"

"He and the governor are going to call the local FBI office immediately and demand to know why the liaison's been broken. And he's going to call Senator Brown and have him demand full cooperation from FBI headquarters in Washington." She added thoughtfully, "I didn't think Frank had the guts to make waves—he's even more worried than I believed."

Wager glanced at the clock again. "He's right to be worried; if the voters are killed off, he'll have a hell of a time being reelected." Getting close to eight A.M. Five minutes for a shave and a cup of coffee. He could check in at the office early enough to be over in District One by the time stores started to open. And while he was showing photographs, the wheels—big and little—started by Elizabeth's phone call should be turning. Mallory would probably guess that the complaint originated with Wager, but that was something Wager didn't give one small damn about; the FBI agent had broken his word. "Thank you, Councilwoman. You've got my vote next election."

"Didn't you vote for me last time?"

Using the sound of the hot water splashing into the sink, he garbled his answer.

Morning traffic was worse than usual, and an accident had clogged Speer Boulevard at the University intersection. Wager, half-listening to the news, worked his way through the back streets. But a lot of other people were listening to the morning traffic report, too, and had the same idea. He finally reached the office only a few minutes ahead of the rest of the shift and was disappointed there too: the only messages in his pigeonhole were one from Stovepipe—"Gabe, please call"—and another from Lieutenant Watterson: "Denver Post reporter Gargan requests interview re Pauline Tillotson and the FBI involvement. Be a good idea to accommodate ASAP. Chief wants to ensure success of I-PREP program."

He tore yesterday's leaf off his desk calendar and stared at the new numbers: 26. Then he quickly shuffled through the latest notices and alerts as he dialed Mallory's number. It was busy. Disgusted, he dialed the one Stovepipe gave him. An elderly woman's suspicious voice answered. "Detective Wager? Oh. Yes, just a minute—he's here now."

"Gabe—thanks for calling, man. Listen, I found an outfit that'll lend me the money if I can get a cosigner."

"That's fine, Stovepipe."

"You mean you'll help me? That's great, Gabe!"

"Whup—you mean you want me to cosign the loan?"

"Hey, who would be better than a cop—I mean a policeman?" He answered his own question. "Maybe a banker. I know a few of them. But we're not on what you'd call speaking terms."

"Stovepipe, I don't have enough collateral to cosign a loan that size. I can't do you any good."

"Gabe, I talked to the lawyer and all. Remember you told me to go see a lawyer? He says with the house's value, all I need is a—what'd he call it?—'unimpeachable' cosigner. Man, I'm not asking you to take any risk. The house is worth a hell of a lot more than I'm borrowing. It's just my old man's name's on it as an owner, and it's taking for fucking ever to call the bastard dead."

"Why doesn't the lawyer cosign?" Wager glanced up at a hand waving urgently at him from the doorway; the duty clerk's wide eyes said it was important.

"Well, I didn't really ask him. He seems all right, you know? But truth is, Gabe, I don't trust him too much. After all, he is a lawyer. I mean, he gets his hand on a piece of property, he's going to start acting like a lawyer. He can't help it."

"Look, Stovepipe, this is going to take some time—"

"No, Gabe, no time at all. All you got to do is sign it, man. I've already told Mother about it, and she's really happy, Gabe. She's really grateful, man. I tell you how much she likes it out there in the country?"

"Yeah, but look, Stovepipe, I've got—"

"Gabe, I swear to God, it's no risk to you. I'll get the papers ready and everything. All you got to do is drop by the bank and sign, man. Anytime in the next couple days. If anything goes wrong—and nothing will, man, I swear—the bank gets mother's house. That's it—nothing from you. And that house is worth a lot more than the loan, man. I got the—what do you call it?—the appraisal I can show you!"

The clerk's silent lips mouthed "Chief Doyle wants you right now" and Wager nodded. "Stovepipe—"

"Jesus, Gabe, please. I'm begging you, man! This means so much to Mother and me. And it's our only chance at it. I'm not shitting you, Gabe—you know me. I wouldn't do that. I know how much you helped out before and all."

"All right, Stovepipe, all right. I got to go."

"Thanks, Gabe! I'll bring the papers by your office—"

Wager hung up on the man's happy voice, a tiny nagging laughter at the back of his mind telling him that he'd just made a big mistake. But there was no time to worry about it now. He found the Bulldog mashing a cigar between his teeth and staring hotly as Wager entered.

"You know anything about that fire at the Blue Moon Bar, Wager?" Doyle leaned across his desk, challenging the detective to say that he did.

Wager, disappointed at the topic, shrugged. "I heard they had one."

"Yeah." The cigar's wet end pulled off Doyle's lips, dragging a glistening thread of spit. "And Floyd Chavez is screaming police brutality. Claims the fire was started by a smoke grenade and claims somebody told him it was thrown by a plainclothes cop driving an unmarked car." The cigar end waved in a circle. "I hear you and Axton had a car out last night."

Along with two dozen or so other plainclothes dicks. "What's the arson report say?"

Doyle's other hand picked a shred of tobacco off his tongue and flicked it to the floor beside his swivel chair. "Nothing. It's gone down as unknown origin."

Wager, managing to mask his relief, made a mental note to

give a generous, if anonymous, donation to the fire department party fund. "Floyd claims a lot of things. For instance, he claims he doesn't know anything about the sniper."

The chief's shoulders rose and fell, and the cigar jabbed back between his teeth. "We'll get that bastard. At least something good's come out of that fire: Ross has a lead. Somebody who thinks the police bombed the Blue Moon is scared shitless now. Says he wants to talk before he gets killed. By a cop." Doyle's head wagged once. "But I tell you this: if anybody in this department was involved in that fire, he's through. Finished! I'm not going to have an epidemic of police brutality start in my department. Is that understood?"

Wager shrugged again. "Fine with me."

"Yeah." Doyle's hard blue eyes studied Wager's face for a long minute. Then, with a puff of breath, the clench went out of the man's face, and his voice almost held a note of pleading. "I've—we've worked for years to make this one of the best goddamned police departments in the country, Wager. And we are. Self-discipline is one of the things that's got us where we are, and I'd hate to see it all out the window because of some scum bag like Floyd Chavez."

Wager had learned to distrust the gold badges when they started to talk buddy-buddy. There was a line between administrators and street cops; Wager didn't step over it their way; he didn't expect them to cross it his way. Doyle gazed at him again, and Wager noted with some surprise the number of lines that had become etched in the man's face and how, in the silence, Doyle seemed older and slightly smaller. But what the hell, nobody was getting any younger, Wager among them. "Chavez wouldn't have a damn thing to worry about if he came clean about Markowsky and Rosener."

The softness went out of the man's voice. "Be that as it may, I better not find out one of my people started that fire, because I don't think there's a damned bit of difference between that and this nut who's trying to blow up Rocky Flats." The cigar plugged back into Doyle's teeth. "Second item: I got a call from Chief Sullivan very early this morning, asking about our relationship with the FBI on this terrorist thing. Apparently the mayor called him with a complaint about a lack of cooperation. What the hell's going on?"

Wager told him about his telephone conversation with Mallory the night before.

"And you think he's hiding something?"

"I know damn well he's not sharing all his information."

Doyle had a clear target for his anger now. He picked up the telephone and jabbed a stiff finger at the number pad. "Angie? This is Chief Doyle. Chief Sullivan available? Thanks." The man's thrusting lower jaw chewed once or twice at the cigar end. "Yessir—I got Wager here. He tells me the FBI man's not being forthcoming. Yessir, sounds like the sons of bitches are about to pull the rug out. Yessir, I will." The chief set the phone back on its cradle. "Sullivan's going to make some phone calls. He wants you to go over right now to the FBI offices and camp there. Anybody gives you any shit, you call me. Hear?"

Wager heard and obeyed.

There was enough truth in Doyle's remark equating the Blue Moon fire with Rocky Flats to rankle. Wager told himself there was a lot of lie in it, too: they hadn't meant to burn the damn place down. But that sounded like Father Schiller's instruction on sin being in the intent and not in the result of an act, and Wager never had agreed with that, either. All of which thinking left him feeling defensive and surly as he knocked on Mallory's door. It didn't help that Wager's DPD badge didn't carry much weight, and it took the agent's nod to get him past security. The small operations room wasn't much different from the first office, except in size. There was room for two desks, which filled the floor space, and a series of blowups, aerial photos of Rocky Flats, covered one wall. Two agents shuffled papers at one desk and answered the telephone that kept ringing; Mallory had a desk to himself. Its surface was covered with papers. Despite its dark color, the tall man's face looked gray and unhealthy from lack of sleep, and the smile he forced across dry lips wasn't a friendly one. But it was officially polite. "Someone somewhere seems to have gotten a wrong impression, Gabe. Goddamn phone's been jumping off the desk for the last hour—people calling and wanting to know why we're not cooperating with you." He added, "I even had a call from Washington."

Wager, too, smiled. "I don't know anybody in Washington."

"Sure. Funny how rumors start." The polite smile went away. "I didn't think you'd pull something like that."

"You mean you didn't think I had the clout to pull something like that." Wager's smile didn't go away. "What's that saying about politics and bedfellows?"

Mallory understood half of Wager's allusion. "Right. And the politics have put us in bed together whether I like it or not. And I don't."

That was too damn bad. Wager nodded at the papers spread over the desk. "This is stuff from King's house in Flagstaff?"

Mallory glanced down. "Yeah. Designs."

Wager turned one of them so he could see it more clearly. A long, narrow rectangle was divided into three uneven sections. The first held a V-shaped line that cut into the interior of the rectangle from a narrow side. The center section, the largest of the three, was crosshatched. The third and smallest segment had a different crosshatch pattern and a little rectangle halfway up the narrow side.

"What is it?"

Mallory's breath whistled in his nose in a long sigh. He was a pro; he'd been ordered to cooperate; he'd cooperate. "King was drafting shape charges. He used the practice bazooka round as a model and was drawing variations on the basic design."

"A shape charge?" Wager remembered from his days in the Corps that low-velocity antitank weapons made use of shape charges to penetrate the hardened steel hulls of the vehicles. The V was a hollow cone that collapsed against the steel skin of the tank. The explosive, usually plastic, would then spread around the V in a mounded pancake, and the detonator, coming last, would ignite the plastic. The result was a focused explosion that punched through twelve or eighteen inches of hardened steel, turning the tank's own metal into a weapon by scattering the hot and spalled fragments through the crew as shrapnel. "This is what you didn't want to tell me last night?"

Mallory looked at him coldly. "All you had to do was ask!"

"I did."

The taller man's thin lips clamped over what he wanted to say. Then he smiled again, a tense stretch of lipless flesh. "Call it water under the bridge, Gabe." It was as close to an apology as the man was going to offer, which was all right with Wager—he didn't want to kiss and make up; he just wanted information. But Mallory couldn't help adding, "Just remember, this involves national security, and national security is the primary responsibility of the FBI."

If national security didn't serve the lives and welfare of the nation's citizens, including those in Denver, then Wager didn't know what it meant. But like Mallory said, it was water under the bridge. Until next time anyway. Wager nodded at the diagram. "What's King going to do with this?"

"That's the question, isn't it? We haven't figured that out yet. I don't see how he could get close enough to any of the buildings to use a launcher. And even if by some chance he did, he would only have time to get one round off." Mallory thought a moment. "Maybe that's all he wants, though—a symbolic act."

Wager disagreed. "I don't see him killing Tillotson for that."

"Yeah. You're right. Whatever the plan is, it's worth killing to protect." He looked up. "Anything on her death?"

Wager told him about the clerk recognizing the photograph.

"Christ! I had a team go all through that area yesterday.

They didn't turn up a thing." Mallory called to one of the men. "Ted, give Bunting a call—tell him the Denver police have a lead on Simon." He glanced at Wager. "You—ah—don't mind if we help you develop that lead, Detective Wager?"

They wouldn't get any more out of it than Wager already had. "Provided we're kept informed." He smiled.

Mallory didn't smile. "Of course."

Wager's news caused a flurry of telephoning and gave him a chance to study the aerial photographs tacked to the wall. They looked familiar, and he recognized one as a magnification of the print they'd found at Simon's cabin. The others seemed familiar too, but he couldn't remember where he'd seen them. It wasn't too long ago. . . . . He was close to recalling the image, when his beeper went off, the tweedling sound almost drowned by the office's telephones. Wager stepped out into the gloomy and antiseptic-smelling hallway to use his radio pack. The dispatcher told him that Detective Axton was trying to reach him, and in a few moments, Wager heard the big man's voice. "Some Tapatíos found the Toyota, Gabe—I just heard from Arnie Trujillo. They located it in a garage over on Shoshone, just north of Forty-seventh."

"Don't go near it—don't let them get near it!"

"They didn't. He said they spotted it and backed off, just like we told them to. They're watching the garage and house now."

"I'll meet you there." Wager hesitated before going back into the office. He was tempted to hold the information, but not to tell Mallory would let the agent off the hook. He leaned in the doorway and beckoned. "Located King's vehicle."

The bloodshot dark eyes widened with surprise. "No shit! Where?"

"West side. I'm on my way. Want to come?"

The agent did, carrying on a cryptic conversation over his own radio as Wager sped through downtown traffic for Twenty-third Street and the underpass under the barrier of I-25.

"I hope you're not calling in any people," said Wager. "I don't want your agents and our cops tripping over each other."

"I alerted a team to stand by, Gabe. Just in case you need some backup. They won't get in the way."

"I don't want any evidence screwed up, Mallory."

"We agreed to work together, right? Coordinate our efforts and share information, just like I've been hearing about all goddamn morning, right? Anything to do with the homicide is all yours." He stared through the windshield. "Anything on Rocky Flats is mine."

Wager stepped on the gas.

He spotted Max's car at the corner of Forty-seventh and pulled in behind it. The big man leaned down to Wager's window. Dark glasses shielded his eyes against the glare of a hot midmorning sun. "It's in a garage about halfway up the block. East side."

"On private property?" Mallory asked. "Did you go on private property to locate it?"

Max's glasses tilted toward the agent. "The tip came from a previously reliable informant."

Wager introduced the two men, who nodded to each other. "Anybody spot King or Simon?"

"Nothing yet," said Max.

Except for their two unmarked cars, the street seemed empty of official interest. Wager couldn't see any gang members hanging out, either. "Any of the Tapatíos still around?"

"A couple across the street from the house—somebody's cousin or something lives there. They're keeping watch out the front window."

"Who's got the back?"

"Arnie and a couple more kids. In a car parked down the alley."

Mallory had been busy with his radio again. He said, "That's affirmative," and checked out of the net. "We're legal—I have a warrant."

"You mean you're legal. It's a federal warrant, right?"

"Well, yes. It covers federal officers and"—he smiled—"local agencies under my command."

A warrant was a warrant, and it had been obtained a hell of a lot faster than Wager could have done it. "All right—let's go."

Max took the street side, Mallory and Wager the alley. Parked in a wide spot between garbage cans sat a metallic-purple Chevrolet with tasseled fringes across the top of the rear window. A voice hissed as Wager went by. "Hey, man—Wager—come here." Arnie Trujillo, sitting low against the seat so that he could just see over the hood, beckoned.

Wager crossed the alley and leaned against the driver's window. "Where's the car?"

"That green garage down there. Hey, I hear you almost blew Flaco away, man. Good going!" His head jerked to include the three younger faces slouched in the car. "Me and *mis compañeros,* we appreciate it, you know?"

Wager glanced at all of them, automatically registering the new faces for the next and less companionable time. "If we get witnesses to Ray's shooting, Flaco's gone for a long time. We'll both appreciate that.

Arnie glanced at the youth sitting beside him before he answered. "Yeah, well, I'll ask *los broders.* See what they want to do. What's his name—your *respaldo,* there?"

Wager gestured for Mallory. "Meet the FBI, Arnie: Special Agent Mallory."

"Yeah, I thought he looked like *un federal.*"

Mallory flashed his badge case, and Arnie tried to keep his cool in front of the younger gang members. "What I tell you people, hey? Something real important going down here, and you in on it." He turned to Wager. "You want some more help with this *loco?*"

"Not right now, Arnie." Wager nodded to them all. "You people did good. But we'll have to take it from here."

The youth sitting in the rider's seat scratched at the silky hairs of a mustache beginning to darken his upper lip. "You need us, man, we be here."

"Thanks."

Wager and Mallory walked slowly down the alley, their shoes loud against the gravel. The sun drew out the odor of rotting garbage from the cans.

"Nice bunch of citizens," said Mallory.

"They're not so bad."

"You have a lot of gang activity in Denver?"

"Some. Nothing like L.A." Wager had to admit, "It's coming in, though."

Mallory grunted. "Tell me where it's not."

But whatever crap the gangs pulled, at least Arnie and *sus broders* weren't trying to blow up an atomic bomb plant. At the green garage, Wager peeked in through the dusty window. The dark Toyota sat jammed into the dim space. Mallory verified the location to somebody on the other end of his frequency. Across the yard between the back porch and the garage, the house was silent. From a neighboring home down the block, a radio or stereo blared the monotonous and self-righteous chant of a rap song. Wager keyed his radio, and Max answered.

"We're in place."

"All right. I'm going up."

They listened for the sound of footsteps on the front porch, the ring of a doorbell, the thump of heels in the house. But there was only silence. A couple of minutes later, Max's voice said, "No answer, Gabe."

"We'll go in through the back."

"Ten four."

They sprinted across the lawn, weapons in hand, and pulled to a stop at the small landing that served as a porch. No sound from inside. Only the distant rap song and a high-pitched buzz from some insect bouncing the purple-and-white flare of a hollyhock bloom. The wooden four-by-fours holding up the small porch smelled hot and dusty from the sun on the old paint.

"You ready?" whispered Mallory.

Wager nodded.

The agent had the warrant; he muttered something into his radio and went first. Both hands gripping his pistol, Mallory slammed his heel against the door near the handle. The frame split, but the door held. Another heavy kick, and then Mallory's shoulder drove it open with a splintering rip. Wager darted in behind the man, stepping to the opposite side of the doorframe.

"We're in, Max."

"Right."

In the silence, they moved cautiously toward the front door, where Max waited, listening for any sound. The rooms had the sparse furniture of a rental unit, as well as the closed-up feeling and stale odors of an unaired house. Wager opened the door to Max, who was standing out of the line of fire with his weapon half-hidden at his side. Across the street, on the porch of a brick bungalow, a youth had come out to stare their way.

"Nobody?"

Wager shook his head, and Max closed the door quietly behind him. Quickly, they scanned the rooms downstairs: kitchen, living room, a small bedroom with its half-bath off the living room. Above their heads, the upstairs floor creaked with Mallory's weight as the man moved rapidly.

"I'll check the basement," said Wager.

From the kitchen a stairway led down to a large and undivided concrete room with a washer and a dryer near the bottom step. A line of window wells let dusty light into the space. A small worktable next to the appliances was covered with grime and a few dead beetles, legs pointing stiffly to the floor joists and cobwebs above. In the center of the room, a larger table, almost six feet long, stood. It was dustless, and its surface was littered with shreds of gleaming metal, tin shears, and, on one end, a jumble of metalworking tools: a hand riveter, molding blocks, wooden mallets, and steel hammers. At the table's far end stood the twin cylinders of a gas welding set, mounted on a dolly. Welding rods sprouted from a quiver, and a pair of goggles dangled from a brass control knob. On the grimy concrete floor, sheets of brown paper had been kicked around by busy feet. Wager unfolded a large sheet; it was a full-scale diagram for another cylinder, complete with measurements for hollow nose, payload compartment, and base detonator. Against a wall and catching the light from the basement window leaned a square of unused aluminum plate. The rest of the basement, except for a hot-water heater and a dusty furnace, was empty. Wager went back up, to find Max glancing through the kitchen drawers with quick efficiency. Mallory was in the living room, delving behind the cushions of the weary-looking furniture.

"No telephone," the agent said. "They didn't plan on being here long enough to need one, apparently. You find anything?"

He showed Mallory the diagram.

The FBI agent spread it out and studied the drawing and figures. "They'd never get something this big past the security out there." Then he went to his radio and described the diagram to someone on the other end. "Yeah—seven feet, eight and a quarter inches long; diameter, sixteen inches. . . . Right—as soon as you can."

Wager told him, "The workroom's in the basement. It's where they made their rocket or whatever the hell it is."

"Show me."

Max looked up as Wager and Mallory came into the kitchen. "Nothing here. My guess is they rented furnished. A little crap in the refrigerator, and that's it."

Mallory said, "Wager's found something in the basement." He led them down the stairs, and they stood a moment surveying the table and equipment. "Looks like they finished up here," he said. "I think—"

Whatever he was going to say was silenced by a faint scrape from somewhere in the upper part of the house. The three men looked at each other and then moved quickly and silently up the basement stairs. Max headed for the back door. Mallory took the stairs leading up to the bedrooms, and Wager darted through the front door to the porch and down the front steps, to look along the side of the house.

The blur of a figure falling from one of the second-story windows caught his eye, and he shouted for it to halt. The man crashed feet-first through the low shrubbery lining the house's foundation, and a frightened face flashed Wager's way. Then the man sprinted for the back. Above, Mallory leaned through the open window to shout "FBI—halt!" and then speak quickly into his radio.

Wager ran after the figure and heard the thud of heavy feet as Max came down the back porch stairs. The fleeing man dashed for the alley fence and, ignoring the gate, sprawled over the sun-warped boards. Wager had the eerie feeling of watching himself run after Flaco Martínez and for a tingling instant expected the hot flash of a round fired in his direction. Pistol in hand, he sprinted for the alley and tried to deny the image of the gun flash jabbing at his face. Somewhere up the alley, a car engine raced, and after a moment, Arnie's Chevrolet sped past, a blur of motion and screaming rubber and scorched oil. A second later, from out of sight beyond the corner of the garage, came the wet crump of a body hit by something solid and then a shocked silence.

Rounding the garage, Wager saw the car angled across the alley and, in the weedy gravel under the front bumper, a pair of sprawled legs. Arnie was already out of the car to lean over the front fender and stare down; the other youths were piling out of the back, their excited voices a garble of Spanish and English.

"Here he is, man! Fucker tried to get away, man—we stopped him!"

Wager holstered his weapon and pulled to a halt beside Arnie. On the ground at the nose of the car, a young man lay unmoving. His cheek was claw-marked by gravel scrapes, and a slow welt of blood started to rise up through the dirt. It wasn't King or Simon.

Wager checked the man's pulse. It was strong, but his breath came in quick, shuddering gasps.

"Fucker alive, man?"

"Yeah." Wager glanced up. "You people better clear out of here."

"Hey, man—he was getting away. We helped you out, right? He was a—what you say?— excaping felon, right?"

"Right. But there's going to be a lot of paperwork on him, Arnie, and a lot of cops here in a few minutes. Believe me, you don't want to get caught up in it. Take off now, before they start getting here and you can't take off."

Arnie nodded. "OK, man. You don't forget me and the Tapatíos helped you out, right?"

"Believe me, Arnie, you're forever in my memory."

He and Max watched the car back rapidly down the alley and swing out of sight. Mallory, puffing, trotted up. "Where're those people going?"

"I told them to get the hell out of here. Fewer complications that way."

"You nuts, Wager? You want to get blamed for assaulting this man?"

"Call it a hit-and-run, Mallory. The guy did run out in front of a car, right?"

The agent shook his head. "It's your town." He knelt by the man, who was beginning to make noises.

"Recognize him?" Wager asked.

Mallory nodded. "Wayne McGonagle. One of King's hangers-on from San Diego." He spoke to the grunting man. "McGonagle—you hear me?"

The man's eyes blinked open and then winced shut again. "My head!"

Max was bending over the man, hands running lightly along his legs and torso. "No weapons. Want me to call an ambulance?" The nose of a plain brown sedan skidded across the alley's mouth, and three men in suits tumbled out and ran toward them.

"Wait a minute, Max." Wager, too, leaned over the man. "Where's King and Simon?"

"I don't know. . . ."

Mallory snorted. "Wayne, you're in big trouble. You won't be riding a bicycle for a long time." The agent explained to Wager, "He runs a mountain-bike shop in El Cajon."

"What's he doing here?"

"You heard the man, Wayne."

"My head—it really hurts!"

Wager leaned into the man's vision. "Can you hear me?" He waited until McGonagle nodded. "You're under arrest on suspicion of murder. You got a right to remain silent . . ." Wager gave the youth the Miranda, as Mallory talked quietly to the three men and then came back to listen. "You understand everything I told you?"

The youth stared up at Wager. "I didn't kill her."

"You were there? You were in the house?"

"Not when she was killed, no. I was out getting some stuff. I got back, and . . ."

"Who did it?"

"I don't know. I came back, and they said we had to get out right away. They said she was a spy."

"Who said she was?" asked Mallory.

"Libby. He said Dick had been suspicious of her, and then Libby caught her trying to make a phone call. They said she had found out about what was going on. Libby said she tried to call the FBI or somebody and tell them. She admitted it, they said."

"Simon and King were the last ones to see her alive?" Wager asked.

McGonagle's head nodded, and he winced. "My head hurts. It's starting to hurt bad."

Mallory rocked back on his heels, his shadow a wedge of black across the sweating man's torso. The sun beat full in McGonagle's clenched face. "We want King and Simon, and we want them now."

"They're gone."

"Where?"

Beneath the pain and the mud and the blood on his face, McGonagle stiffened against saying anything else.

"Where?" Wager asked.

No answer.

Wager reached out and grabbed the man's matted hair and jerked his head.

"Ah—!"

"Where?"

The answer was muffled with gasps. "Don't know! Swear to God—don't know. They didn't tell me!"

"Let's get him back in the house, Gabe." Max glanced around at the silent alley. The three federal agents went back to their car, and Max's large hands lifted the young man up onto wobbly legs. He and Wager walked McGonagle slowly down the graveled lane and up the back steps. They sat him at the small breakfast table in the kitchen, and Max handed him a wet dish towel to wipe his face.

"Why are you here?" asked Mallory. "What's your part in it?"

"Tubes . . ."

"What tubes? What are you talking about?"

"A metal tube—a cylinder. I'm a metalsmith. They used aluminum—it's hard to work with. You got to know what you're doing to weld aluminum." He groaned again. "God, my head hurts. I think I got a concussion. Can you please call an ambulance?"

"You do us a favor, we do you a favor," said Wager. "Did you make explosives out of the tube? A shape charge?"

The wet, red face squinted painfully at Wager. "You know about it?"

"A shape charge to attack a building—that right?"

"They didn't tell me what it was for. I just fabricated the metal. They took it disassembled, but I don't know where."

Wager made certain. "They took it in Simon's car—they drove away with it this morning. What time?"

"A couple hours . . . two, maybe three hours ago. But they didn't tell me what they were going to use it for. I swear it!"

Wager stared back at McGonagle. But it wasn't the twisted, scraped face he saw. "You knew it was going to be used for explosives."

The man's Adam's apple bobbed. Finally, he admitted, "Yeah. I figured that much."

"And you finished it in time for use today."

"After it's filled, reassembled, and armed, yeah."

"How long will that take?"

McGonagle started to shake his head and then winced as Wager leaned toward him. "I'm not sure! A couple hours, at least. Maybe more."

Mallory looked at Wager. "There's no way they can sneak something that big into the security area."

"They won't bother to sneak it." What Wager saw in his mind's eye were the aerial photographs on the wall of Mallory's office. They had reminded him of something when he first saw them, but now he knew that something wasn't another photograph—it was the real thing. They reminded Wager of how the Rocky Flats plant looked when they flew over it on the way to Steamboat Springs. And that was the answer to Mallory's question. "Air," said Wager. "A bomb."

"We considered that already—they can't get past the air defenses!"

Wager focused on McGonagle again. "They're going to try, aren't they? They're going to try to bomb a target from the air, aren't they?"

The man swallowed. "Libby didn't say outright. But from the way they talked—impact . . . wind resistance . . . worried about keeping the weight down—yeah. They didn't want me to put fins on the tube, but yeah, I think that's what they're going to do."

Mallory muttered, "Oh, goddamn," and spoke rapidly into his radio, the words "airport," "security," "leasing agents" repeated. He looked up to catch Wager's eye. "I'm having all the airplane rental agencies in the area canvassed. There can't be that many."

"If they've already taken off, it's too late. Better get the word out to Rocky Flats. Warn them about airplanes."

The agent nodded and spoke again into his radio.

While Mallory talked, Wager settled closer to McGonagle. "Did King ever say anything about an airport? Or an airplane? Anything at all?"

"No. Nothing that I remember."

"McGonagle, do you understand what they're planning to do?"

He gingerly shook his head. "All I know is what they told me to do—build the tube." He added, "This other stuff—you know, the bomb—I guess I kind of guessed. . . ."

"Did they say what the target is?"

"No. Just a building. They just talked about a building."

"Why were you still here?"

"I was supposed to leave tonight. Take Libby's car and drive it back to California."

"Tonight? You were supposed to wait until tonight?"

"That's what Libby said. Load up all the tools and stuff out of the basement, clean the house and wipe down everything. Then stay out of sight and leave here after dark." He took a deep breath and held the wet cloth to his stinging cheek. "You got here too soon. I hid under the bed when I heard you guys, but—"

"McGonagle, do you know anything about Rocky Flats?"

"Sure. It's the nuclear bomb plant. Libby hates that place."

Mallory asked, "Doesn't the damned fool know the government's closing that plant?"

"He said they're not really closing it, just moving it. Libby said the government can't be trusted, anyway. They're still testing bombs in Nevada, he said, and—"

Wager slammed his fist on the table. "He's going to bomb the Flats—now—today! And when he does, he's going to spread plutonium dust over half of Denver."

The man stared at Wager's angry face. "No. Libby wouldn't ever do something like that!"

"Yeah. Right—tell that to Pauline Tillotson. Why in hell do you think they killed her?"

McGonagle said nothing, bloodshot eyes staring at Wager.

"That's what that tube's for, McGonagle. That's what you helped build—a bomb to blow up Rocky Flats. There's no way in hell to control the radioactive dust that's going to come out of there when that bomb goes off."

Mallory was on the radio again, but he glanced at McGonagle long enough to tell him, "He's right."

"Schools—kids outside on the playground—they're all around the plant, McGonagle. Pregnant women. They'll all be poisoned. The ones who don't die of radiation poisoning are going to have their genes screwed up for generations." Wager angrily returned the man's stare. Behind him, he heard Max clear his throat in cautious warning. "God damn you, McGonagle, what did they say?"

McGonagle flinched as the heel of Wager's hand thudded

against his shoulder. "They didn't say anything to me—I swear it! But Simon has a plane. He has his own plane."

"Where does he park the damn thing?"

"Boulder airport. I heard him tell Libby that one time. He keeps it at the airport in Boulder."

• • • • • • •

Mallory was busy on both his radio and Wager's office telephone.
McGonagle was booked on every possible charge Wager could
think of, including conspiracy, criminal complicity, criminal
attempt to commit a class one felony, first-degree assault,
second-degree assault, reckless endangerment, first-degree
arson, first-degree criminal tampering, obstructing a police
officer, concealing a death, three counts of accessory to a crime
(arson, assault, murder), membership in anarchistic and sedi-
tious associations, suspicion of murder, and littering. The last
charge was based on the probability that if the bomb went off,
it would scatter bits of aluminum all over hell and gone, and
the littering statute was one of the few that applied to both
public and private property. Wager hoped they'd have King
and Simon in custody by the time a lawyer finished reading up
on all the charges, and that the youth would be willing to testify
in return for a hundred years or so knocked off his sentence.

"The airplane's not there." Mallory's weary voice said more
than the words. "The airport manager showed them the empty
parking space; Simon's plane wasn't there."

"Any guess when he left?"

"No. The manager thinks Simon flew out a couple days ago.

Pilots are supposed to file flight plans, but they don't always, he says, and there's no tower at the field."

From the west side of the Police Administration Building, visitors had a sweeping view of the Front Range and the prairie leading up to the abrupt foothills. That wall of mountains, tilted slabs of rock cut by canyons and gullies dark with pines, formed a line as far as the eye could reach. Glittering with snow, Longs Peak anchored the northern range, and seventy miles south, Pikes Peak loomed just above the horizon like a pale-blue shadow. Toward the north, at the foot of the line of jutting mountains, Boulder was hidden behind a rise of brown prairie dotted with scattered housing developments and industrial parks. If you knew where to look, you could even make out the distant silver wink of the water tower that served the Rocky Flats installation. Above, the cloudless blue sky seemed empty.

"He could be coming in from the west," said Wager. "He'd pop up from the other side of the mountains and be on top of the Flats before anyone spotted him."

"I don't think so—the air's too thin." Mallory shook his head. "The lab in Washington estimated a shape charge that size to weigh almost a thousand pounds. And the airport manager described Simon's plane as a Beechcraft Turbo Bonanza—single wing, single engine. I happen to know that model can barely carry a thousand pounds at sea level. Unless he had to, King wouldn't take a chance on not clearing those mountains."

"Can the bomb blow up a building?"

Mallory nodded. "They said a shape charge that size could cut through a reinforced-concrete structure four or five stories high."

"The plutonium vaults are only four stories down."

"Yeah. And the explosion and fire would suck that stuff straight up. The burning building would turn into one big chimney and pull out everything caught in the ducts as well."

Wager rubbed at eyes tired from filling in the last blanks on the charge sheets for the DA to play with. "What kind of air defenses do they have out there?"

"New-generation Redeye missiles. Hand held. Their primary defense is against ground attack." The agent paused. "Unfortunately, there's so much nearby traffic out of the Broomfield airport that they usually curtail the air defense to prevent any accidents."

"Close the goddamn airport!"

"I've already requested that, Wager." He added, "And I've got men searching it for Simon's plane. No luck so far."

"King and Simon aren't going to give up now even if they find out we've got McGonagle."

Mallory, too, rubbed at the puffy flesh beneath his eyes and nodded. "But they wanted him to leave as soon as it got dark." He sipped at a cup of office coffee, mouth pursing at its bitterness. "If I was trying to bomb the place, I might do it just before dark so I could still see the target. No running lights, come in low, be over the target before they could locate me."

McGonagle had told them that he finished the tube late the night before and that King and Simon had carried the parts off in Simon's car that morning. "Does the Flats have radar?"

"No. It wouldn't do any good anyway—the Broomfield flight pattern goes right out to the property line. There's no way to tell a hostile out of all that traffic."

"They can black out the buildings, can't they?" At night, the installation was a glare of orange sodium light. Rows of security lamps illuminated the periphery fencing against infiltrators, and each building had its own spotlights shining on walls and doors. The gleam could be seen for miles across the prairie.

"They can. They probably will." He tilted his watch so Wager could see its large dial and smaller windows. "But tonight's a three-quarter moon." He glanced out the window. "And not a cloud in the sky."

Wager's telephone rang again, and a crisp voice asked for

Special Agent Mallory. Wager handed him the receiver, half-hearing one side of the conversation as his mind went over what McGonagle had told them. King and Simon would have to fill the main tube with explosives, assemble the parts, and arm its detonator. Then load it on the plane. They'd need some kind of rig to carry it and then to drop it, and that meant someplace to park the plane while they worked on it. And, Wager knew, that's what they were doing right now, if they weren't already through.

Mallory hung up the telephone and showed Wager what he'd noted down from this latest call. "One of our engineers did some estimates from McGonagle's drawings. The main charge probably weighs eight hundred pounds. The explosive could be several things: black powder, composition B, whatever. But for the most effective shape charge, it's probably pentolite—it's more powerful than TNT and more sensitive. A forty-pound, concave charge of pentolite can penetrate five feet of concrete or twenty inches of armor plate. Eight hundred pounds will do a hell of a lot more. It can be detonated by a pressure-type fuse or a nonelectric blasting cap in the base of the main charge. Detonation is always the trick, but probably the shock of impact would set off the cap, and the cap would fire the pentolite. If dropped from, say, two hundred feet, and if the nose hit the target squarely, it would work. The harder the impact, the more likely the detonation, of course."

"He thinks that contraption will really work?"

"He's scared shitless."

Wager nodded. He knew the feeling. "We'd better let Doyle know."

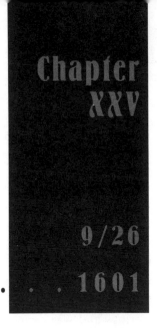

· · · · · · · · ·

Doyle was the first to hear, but he wasn't the last. The Bulldog
listened to Mallory's report without once removing his cigar to
play with it. When the agent finished, the chief slowly placed
the dead stogie in his oversize ashtray and muttered, "God,
Jesus." Then he started punching buttons on his telephone con-
sole. By midafternoon, McGonagle was being interrogated for
the fifth or sixth time by yet another team of experts, this one
flown in from a Department of Defense regional office in St.
Louis. Like the FBI interrogators, they wanted to take the man
back to their own territory, but Wager's stack of charges had
anchored him in Denver, so the interrogation took place in one
of DPD's mirrored rooms. Each team took over with an un-
spoken air of succeeding where the previous interrogations had
failed, and Wager had spent some time behind the glass, listening to the youth wearily repeat what he had already said.
But nothing new came up.

Mallory telephoned to tell Wager that he'd assigned airport
searches to Agent Bunting of the Denver office and was receiving periodic reports on airplane rentals, tie-down spaces,
aircraft mechanics' shops, high-octane fuel sources, and navi-
gational equipment and electronics outlets. Agent Wilmore had

taken the office's leased plane to fly around and touch down on every private strip in the vicinity of Rocky Flats—including stretches of packed dirt in farmers' fields—where a small plane could sit while the bomb was being attached to it. He said that the plane wouldn't be noticed if it was hidden among other planes, so he was checking flight lines and maintenance areas as well as sales lots. But if King had parked it in some unlikely place, they could only wait for a call from a citizen puzzled or upset at seeing an airplane where it shouldn't be. How long that would take, God only knew; so far, no one had reported anything.

A small flurry of telephone activity told Wager that Pipkin had been brought to the Denver FBI office from Steamboat Springs and was being questioned there, and Deputy Sheriff Lofting from Boulder called to ask what in God's name was going on—he'd just seen a bunch of people in FBI jumpsuits taking apart Simon's cabin log by log and stacking the damn thing up like a Tinkertoy. "They came in a helicopter, Wager! The neighbors thought it was a goddamn invasion—had half the SO coming out with riot guns!"

An excited Gargan had called once, and Wager told him to talk to the public relations officer, and when Lieutenant Watterson called to find out what to tell Gargan, Wager referred him to Chief Doyle: "I don't know how much he wants classified, Lieutenant—better check with him."

Even Elizabeth called. "Is it true? You have definite evidence of a planned attempt on Rocky Flats?"

"How'd you hear that?"

"My contact in the mayor's office. She said a message came in this morning and the mayor's been calling the FBI every half hour to find out what's happening."

"Well, it's true, Liz. And the mayor probably knows a lot more about it than I do now. FBI, Department of Defense, the National Security Agency, even the Alcohol, Tobacco, and

Firearms people are around. I'm out on the edge of things now. It's like watching a damn circus."

And in the middle of it all, Max gave Wager another message: "Goddamn riot on the west side, Gabe—Tapatíos and Gallos. Every uniform on duty's being called out, and the reserves are being brought in!"

"Oh, Christ! I thought that was settled when we got Flaco."

"Arnie called me. Said some of the Tapatíos started hitting on some Gallos about evening things up for Raimundo. He said it was a bunch of the younger pepperheads, but one thing led to another. Now they're scattered all over the west side, and some of them are using guns."

"They need us?"

"Not you. Chief Sullivan said you stick with this case. And Doyle wants me with you in case something happens—says you won't be able to call on any uniformed support tonight."

Wager's road to hell was paved with the good intentions of others. "All I'm doing is watching things happen. And answering the damned phone."

One of the day's last calls was from Stover. "Gabe, you know that place we're buying?"

"Stovepipe, I don't have time right now—"

"I understand, Gabe. But I don't like to call you at home, you know? And, man, you ain't been home much anyway. You're a hard man to find, so I mean, where else can I talk to you, you know?"

"Stovepipe—"

"I wouldn't bother you about this, but it's my mother. You know we got that place in the country for her so she could have some peace and quiet."

"I know. Believe me, I know. But I don't have time to sign a goddamn paper right now, Stovepipe! I'm—"

"It ain't that, man. There's no rush on that—you know we got that month's lease. This is something else. And believe me,

I tried to think how I could take care of it by myself. But there's no way. They gave me leave a couple days ago to take Mother up there, and they're not about to give me leave again so soon."

"Stovepipe, just tell me what the hell the problem is. Maybe I can get to it later." If there was a later.

"That's what I'm trying to tell you, man. Mother says there's these people next door running a goddamn engine, making all kinds of racket. Says it sounds worse than Stapleton, man— noise hour after hour! My mother's getting old, and she can't take that kind of shit. She even called the sheriff, and he says there's nothing he can do. The noise is on private property, he says, and there's no county ordinance against noise, and if somebody wants to build goddamn airplanes on their property they can do it."

"If somebody what?"

"Airplanes. Mother says yesterday one landed on the county road right down from her house—came so low over the front porch it scared the living hell out of her. And now they been working on the goddamn thing all day, running the engine, rattling the whole house."

"Stovepipe—"

"She's about ready to break down crying, Gabe! And I can't do nothing about it, man. First place, they won't give me another leave so soon. Second, if I go up there and start kicking butt, I'm off parole. I'm back in the can."

"Stovepipe!"

"But that sheriff's not doing nothing, and she really likes the place except for all the goddamn noise, and now it looks like what we planned and hoped for is turning to shit, man! I mean, we moved way the hell out on the prairie to get away from noise and shit, and now here it is right next door. You got to help her, Gabe—mother's a really sensitive person, and this has got her really upset!"

"Goddamn it, Stovepipe, where is the place?"

Stovepipe stopped thanking Wager long enough to give him directions to his mother's new home: out in Weld County, north of Denver and, Wager determined, northeast by only twenty-five or thirty miles from Rocky Flats. It might not be King and Simon, but then again, it might be; and that was reason enough to check out the possibility. And to do it fast: the sun was dropping toward the shadowed mountains west of town, and it wouldn't be long before dusk.

No one else from the department was free to go; Wager tried to get through to Mallory, but the agent was tied up in his command center at the Federal Building and couldn't come to the phone. Wager didn't want to take time to explain his hunch to the flunky who answered. More important, Mallory—anchored to the command center—might want to detail some agents to go with them, and calling them in from the field would take even more time. And if Wager's hunch turned out to be wrong, those agents would have lost precious time from their own leads. If it turned out to be right, there was always the radio. One squawk on the radio that King and Simon had been located, and the whole alphabet army would converge. He left a terse message for Mallory and grabbed his jacket. "Come on, Max—we can do something besides sit here!"

I-25 was choked with the remnants of rush hour traffic. But it was the fastest route north, and as they cleared the high ridges that held the suburbs of Federal Heights and Northglenn, the traffic thinned enough to let Wager weave from lane to lane and pass vehicles doing less than eighty-five. Steering with one hand and using the other to radio the state patrol, he cleared his passage for an emergency run. The shallow valley of the South Platte River and the widely spaced clusters of high-rises that made up the sprawling metro area were caught momentarily in the rearview mirror. Then the tilt of earth shut it out. Wager swung into the right lane to zip past a speeding semitrailer, then pulled back onto the open fast lane and pressed even harder on the gas.

Max looked up from the sketch that Wager had made as Stovepipe gave him directions. "It's about ten miles more to the State 7 turnoff."

Wager pressed harder.

To the west, the sun hung a couple of fingers over the black raggedness of mountains. A small airplane crossed the northern horizon just above the farthest hump of twin concrete ribbons. It flew from the east, headed toward the low sun. The two men watched in silence as it neared the black mountains and then angled down slightly, gliding closer to earth.

"That's the Broomfield airport over there, right?" asked Wager.

Max nodded. "Rocky Flats is just beyond it. Can't see it from here, though."

The small dot of airplane banked, wings making a tiny flash in the sun, and turned in a slow approach to the distant landing field that was supposed to be closed to air traffic.

"Christ," said Max. "It could be just that easy."

"Yeah."

"They'd think it was just another plane coming into Broomfield."

That, Wager figured, was the idea. Plus being close enough to the target so the fuel tanks wouldn't have to be filled with a heavy load of gasoline. In another twenty minutes or half hour, dusk would spread like a rising tide coming up over the prairie's eastern horizon. The shadows of the mountains would reach out to meet it as the edges of the sky turned that soft purple color and the outlines of farms and trees and houses began to blur. Simon and King could take off then—still light enough to see the pale dirt of the section road, lift into the last glow of sunset, be just another homeward-bound airplane trying to land at Broomfield before it grew too dark. Circle a bit wide over Rocky Flats in their approach to the landing field . . .

A green highway sign warned Exit 223, and Max said, "Six miles."

Wager lifted his foot from the gas pedal as they approached warnings for the Lafayette-Brighton exit. The smell of scorched oil and hot rubber filled the cab, and Wager figured the people in the police garage would have some valves to replace tomorrow. If anybody was worried about valves tomorrow. He coasted along the exit ramp and up to the stop sign and turned right.

"OK, Gabe—we angle off here." Max pointed at a narrow secondary road that soon branched away from State 7. "Five section roads down." Max squinted at the drawing. "Didn't he know the road's name?"

"Not for certain. Thought it was VV or TT, maybe. He said it was definitely five road crossings."

Five section roads, five miles. The narrow blacktop bounced the speeding car. In the flat, treeless fields on either side, black oil pumps nodded slowly as they sucked at the earth, and occasional clusters of trees rose like small, ragged islands to mark ranch and farm houses.

"This looks like the first reservoir."

They passed a high berm topped by cottonwood trees, whose leaves were bright yellow in the setting sun.

"OK—this should be the fifth crossing up here. Road runs along this high ridge up here."

Wager swung onto the section road, loose gravel kicking loudly under the car.

"Stovepipe wanted country living—goddamn, he's got plenty of it."

"How far?" asked Wager.

"Second crossing."

They dipped down a long decline before starting up the next ridge. The next turn was the second section line, and Wager saw the dark streak of high grass and tumbleweeds caught in the fencing that ran beside the road. He slowed further, letting the dust cloud behind his car thin out.

"One of those over there must be Stovepipe's place." Max

pointed to three clumps of dark evergreens and taller locust trees that offered shelter from wind and sun to houses set back from the road. The nearest was a two-story farmhouse surrounded by trees. Behind it was a large unpainted barn and silo. The middle cluster held a small white house that seemed dwarfed by its trees. A quarter mile beyond and across the road was another ranch house and silo, masked by its enclosure of greenery. A long way down the road, they could see a cluster of treetops that marked still another prairie farm.

Wager slowed, and Max leaned forward intently. "He say which one?"

"Second on the right."

They swung into the dirt driveway of the small white house. The grass was brown and dying from lack of water, but it had recently been cut, and a pile of lawn rakings sat under one of the tall locusts. "There's a car in the garage out back," said Max.

"Come on." Wager parked and Max followed him to the slab of concrete that made a front porch for the cottage's entry. It looked like the kind of dwelling leased to a farm manager as part of his pay—while there had been a farm to manage. Then, when the farm stopped operating, it had been left vacant to wait for the possible buyer. Lately, it had been freshly painted, and in the lowering sunlight, Wager could see the brighter green of a scattering of new asphalt shingles on the roof. Wager rapped on the door, and a moment later a key turned.

The woman who opened the door didn't remind Wager much of the gaunt and stooped Stovepipe. She had a square jaw, square shoulders, and stood squarely in the doorway. Her hair was lifted up from underneath into an eruption of iron-gray sprouts above gray eyes that stared without warmth through heavy lenses. "Yes?"

"Mrs. Stover?"

"You're that cop, right? Wager?"

"Yes, ma'am. Can you tell us—"

"Henry called a little while ago and said you'd be coming out. I don't like cops, and I got good reason not to. Not the way cops have treated Henry. But he says you're going to sign so we can get this place, right?"

"Ma'am, it's really important—"

"Damn right it is! But with all that noise, I don't know if I want anything to do with this place anymore."

"Yes, ma'am. That's why we're here—to look into that. If you can just tell us—"

"Here. I got the papers right here."

"What's that?"

"The loan papers. So you can cosign. We'll go ahead and get that taken care of. Then I can make up my mind whether or not I want to stay here. And that depends on whether or not you can shut them people up. I don't want to live next to no damn airport."

"Ma'am, I want to know where that airplane is!"

"And I'll tell you where it is. Soon's you sign right here!" A finger thumped the paper where a red X had been marked. The line was labeled "Co-Signer." "I want you to talk to them people like you promised Henry. But you best sign while you're here—save you from having to come back afterwards, right?"

"Lady—"

"Right here. It says, 'Co-Signer.' "

"Christ!" Wager grabbed the paper and inked his name. "Where's the airplane, Mrs. Stover?"

"Place across the road. Noisier'n hell's own bells. Came in to land on the road, of all things! Swung down just over my porch and like to took off the top of my head. Swear to God, I thought the world was ending. It's so quiet and peaceful out here, and then all of a sudden—"

"Has it taken off again?"

"Taken off? No—it's quiet now, but for the longest them people been running that damn engine as loud as they could. Wake the dead!"

"Yes, ma'am." Wager turned and sprinted back for the car, understanding why Stovepipe's father had left but not exactly why Stovepipe felt he had to look after the woman.

There was no way to approach the ranch house or its barn without being seen, and Wager was grateful that he hadn't alerted Mallory and his army—a platoon of vehicles converging across the empty prairie in this silence would be like sound effects for *Sands of Iwo Jima*. On all sides, fallow fields stretched level and treeless, and the only concealment was a line of lilac hedge at the side of the house. Already there was a yellow light in one back window—kitchen, probably—and to the east the coming night thickened into a dark band just above the curve of earth.

Wager stopped the car, leaving it on the gravel road. He and Max got out. A wide dirt driveway ran down one side of the house in the lane between wall and hedge line. It led toward the backyard and the barn beyond, standing as isolated as a tombstone. From here, they could see a corner of the barn and a slice of the open door. In its blackness, Wager made out the faint gleam of a wing's leading edge.

"If it's Simon's plane, it's still here."

"If," said Max. "Let's hope to God it is."

The two men walked cautiously across the wide lawn toward the dark front windows. The long, unmown grass deadened their steps. The evening wind made a faint sigh in the emptiness and weeds of the neighboring field. From the drainage ditch beside the road came a single cautious croak.

"Gabe—" Max's finger pointed to a track of mashed grass that ran from the driveway across the front lawn toward the thick growth of another lilac hedge. Under the sheltering trees and behind freshly broken shrubbery, a Chevrolet Blazer glinted. Wager squinted to read the license. "It's the car—it's Simon's car!"

Max whispered, "What do we do? Take them?"

Wager shook his head. "Not just two of us—can't take a

chance." Glancing at the empty-looking front windows of the square house, he quickly led Max back to their car and quietly pulled it as far into the weedy ditch as he could hide it. Then he tried his radio.

It took half a dozen channels, and the only police frequency he could reach was for the highway patrol. He quickly identified himself and gave the voice Mallory's number and told it to get an emergency message to the man as soon as possible. Then he told about the car, the airplane, and gave the voice their location.

"You want this Agent Mallory to call you, Detective Wager?"

"He can't—no phone. Just tell him to get people out here as soon as possible. Tell him the car has been positively identified, and the plane hasn't yet taken off."

" 'The plane hasn't yet taken off.' OK—I got it."

Max had been looking toward the house while Wager talked. "Gabe, you stay out of sight here with the car. I'm going down behind that tree line so I can see the barn. If they start to bring out the plane, I'll signal. You pull the car in the driveway and block it."

It sounded like as good a plan as any. "Keep where I can see you."

"Will do."

The big man run half-crouched across the road, his shadow a long black streak on the dusty gravel. Then he went down and up as he crossed the other ditch and began limping from tree to tree at the edge of the plowed field.

Wager watched him and the house and the glimpses of yard and barn that he could see through the branches. His radio made the hollow hissing of empty channels and covered the sound of the evening wind. The eastern horizon was darker now; night's shadow rose higher against the cloudless sky, and in the rearview mirror Wager could see a mountain's silhouette begin to eat into the lower rim of the sun. Five minutes. Eight. Fifteen. Nothing on the radio, nothing at the house. The sun was completely down now, and the sky over the black mountains red with the dying fire of day. Max, a squatting and increasingly dim figure at the distant, graying edge of the plowed field, stayed motionless, his eyes on something that Wager couldn't see.

Then suddenly the figure stood.

Wager popped out of the car to squint through the gloom at Max.

The man turned a pale blur of face his way and made two wide sweeps with his arm, then he plunged into the tree line. Wager started the car and pulled it rapidly for the driveway, slewing it across the dirt tracks to block as wide a path as he could. Then he grabbed the keys and jumped out, running for the far side of the house in case the plane came that way.

He had just reached the porch when he heard the shout of Max's voice and an odd whining sound and the sudden, explosive pop of cylinders that ruptured the silence. The engine noise revved to an angry snarl and almost buried the cracking sound of a weapon.

Wager turned the corner and sprinted down the far side of the house. A weedy lawn stretched in shady gloom between the house and the tree line, and he could see the barn past the screen porch at the rear of the home. The deafening roar came from the black mouth of the gaping doors and then, wobbling and bobbing on the uneven ground, the cone of a whirling propeller, followed by the plane's long nose. The wingtips barely cleared the doorframe, and Wager, pistol in hand, dropped to one knee to steady his Star PD in the palm of one hand while he squeezed the trigger with the other. Before he could fire, a rifle cracked from the corner of the house, and Wager felt the whip of hot air as a round sizzled just off his ear. Rolling, he fired blindly, the tail of the plane disappearing and the noise roaring slowly down the drive on the other side of the house. Another spurt of yellow slapped a second shot at

him, and Wager rolled again, coming up on his feet and sprint-
ing hard for the shelter of the house's wall.

He yanked his radio and keyed the highway patrol channel,
half-shouting over the racket that stopped moving up the
drive. "Emergency—police officer—anybody: come back!" A
humped silhouette leaned away from the black bulk of the house
to fire another shot. Wager crouched in the weedy darkness at
the foot of the wall. "Emergency—officer needs assistance—
come back!"

An unhurried voice replied with its number as Wager crawled
toward the corner of the house. "Who's this and what kind of
assistance you want?"

Wager told him as little as he needed to as fast as he could:
Officers being shot at by fugitives, call FBI Agent Mallory immediately and tell him the airplane was on its way.

The rifle boomed again, its muzzle blast a slap of heat across
his face as Wager fired twice in return. The first round straightened the figure and sent it diving for the stone foundation of
the house. The second round went somewhere, and with a tiny
corner of his mind Wager noted a miss and where it might land
for the shooting forms that he'd have to fill out sometime. His
ears heard the airplane's engine roar, then back off to an idle,
and then roar again, apparently in an awkward and cramped
turn around Wager's car. Then it fell to an idle again, and
another corner of his mind sought some sound from Max—the
pop of the man's Smith and Wesson, a shout, something that
would mean he had stopped the aircraft.

Then Wager was on top of the writhing, grunting figure at
the corner of the house. Slapping at the man's arms, Wager
pulled his hands free and visible from his body and shoved his
pistol against King's wobbling head. "That's Simon in the
plane? He has the bomb?"

A cough and gasp of pain as Wager turned the man over and
ran a fast hand down his body. "You gut-shot me—stomach."

"Max—Max!"

No answer. At the front of the house, the engine idled, then it roared again, and the sound began to move slowly.

"The bastard's going after Rocky Flats, isn't he? He's going to drop it on Rocky Flats!"

King, his lean and tanned face made even tauter by pain, shook his head and grunted something.

"What?"

"Not drop. Dive. Kamikaze. Dive into the place."

"Jesus . . . Max!"

Wager saw a dark, lightless blur lumber past the front of the house and flicker between the trees. He fired two more rounds, cursing as the plane's engine pulled it clumsily down the gravel road. It moved slowly and heavily out of range, a cloud of dust barely visible in the dusk, then it began to pick up speed.

"Max!"

"Shot."

"What?"

"Your buddy," King gasped. "Over there." He bobbed his head toward the driveway. "Shot."

Wager slapped handcuffs on King and ran for the blacker shadow huddled in the darkness of lilac bushes. It made a shape much smaller than Max, but it was his partner, clenched and still. Wager jammed a thumb against the man's warm neck. "Max—Max!" He felt a weak pulse, but the big man made no sound.

The airplane engine was a distant, straining scream, and it seemed to pull with every decibel against the tug of earth as the sound slowly lifted. Wager, radio at his mouth as he called the highway patrol for a Flight for Life helicopter, saw the craft, a distant black silhouette against the smoky dark of the eastern sky. It struggled upward, visibly laboring in its gentle incline until it was clearly outlined against the cooler blue of the evening sky. Then its engine softened, and it turned in a wide arc to sail back over the farmhouse. In the clearer light of altitude,

Wager could see a long silver canister tucked beneath the fuselage. The airplane's wings wagged once in salute as it passed overhead and then aimed toward the fading red of sunset.

Wager's radio popped with a tense voice. "Wager—this is Mallory. Came up on channel five."

He switched the dial. "Mallory—the plane just took off. It's headed for the Flats now. It just passed overhead. I saw the bomb—a long tube under the fuselage. He's going to crash the bomb on the target. Read me? He's going to crash the bomb on the target!"

". . . All right. We're on our way and Flats security's been alerted. They'll be looking for it."

"Get a Flight for Life out here, quick. Officer wounded."

The band was silent.

"Mallory—you hear me? Flight for Life chopper! My partner's down!"

"First things first, Wager."

Another long silence. From the lighter sky in the west Wager heard the plane's motor fade slowly as it labored with the awkward and heavy cyclinder. From the yard behind him, he heard King make quicker, more rhythmic groans. From Max he heard nothing, not even a labored breath.

Then he heard something else; the pat-pat-pat of a helicopter rotor driven by an engine straining to push it faster. Low on the western horizon he saw a cluster of quickly moving lights —red, white, green—that marked the flight of something.

"It's on its way, Max. The chopper—hang in there, partner. They're coming now."

But it wasn't the Flight for Life. It was the sculpted and deadly silhouette of a combat helicopter, and there were three of them, which sped just above the dark earth toward the sound of the droning airplane. They crossed the last remnant of sunburst, a close, intent formation whose sound faded rapidly.

At the green edge of night, Wager saw the tiny black dot of Simon's airplane holding steady for the Flats, which, by now, must be coming up under its nose. Then the three thicker-looking dots strung out in a line and swung toward the plane. They hung against the sky for a moment, seemingly motionless and silent, then Wager saw a spurt of flame, followed by a soundless red-orange flash that billowed out and sprayed streaks of glowing fragments. A puff of thick smoke spread and hung like a ball of dirty cotton against the final glow of day, and the three dots began to circle the air where the plane had been.

• • • • • • •

The hospital corridor had that exhausted silence that marks the
late-night shift. Max and King had both been flown in by the
Flight for Life. Both were still alive, both critically injured, and
both went into surgery immediately. But Wager cared only
about one; as far as he was concerned, the other could die on
the table and save the state money.

He'd done the paperwork to charge King with both murder
and accessory. The man insisted, on the flight back, that Simon
had killed Pauline Tillotson. Enraged—almost incoherent with
anger—Simon had confronted her with being an informant and
shoved her so hard she cracked her skull against the kitchen
table. Then, to cover the murder and gain time for the attack
on Rocky Flats, Simon had dragged her into the closet and set
the house on fire.

"Why attack the Flats now?" asked Wager. "They're closing the damn place—the government said they're shutting it
down."

King grunted a short, painful laugh. "The government? You
believe those bastards? . . . Five years, ten years . . . start it
up again . . . Read their lips . . . Politicians!"

No, Wager had to admit he didn't believe them. But he didn't fully believe King, either. Of course, Simon wasn't around to give his version of how Tillotson died. But it wouldn't make any difference—shouldn't make any difference. King was part of it, at least an accessory to Tillotson's murder, participated in the attempt on Rocky Flats, shot a police officer. He wouldn't go to the death room, maybe, but he'd be in jail. Where Gargan or somebody like him could make Simon and King heroes, one dead and the other jailed in the attempt to save the earth by killing its inhabitants.

The rest of the paperwork—a thick stack of documents—could wait until tomorrow.

Wager had tried to make Mallory wait too, but the agent wouldn't be put off. He wanted to interview Wager even as he followed his partner's gurney into the emergency room.

"You should have told me about that farm, Wager. You two people shouldn't have gone out there alone!"

"I left a message, Mallory. I told you where I was going."

"Some message: 'Going after a lead to King. Will check in'!"

"As soon as we knew it was him, I called you."

"Yeah. Well, I hope for your partner's sake he makes it. For his sake and for his family's. Now excuse me—I've got a news conference to attend."

For Max's sake, for his family's sake, and for Wager's.

He sighed and hauled himself off the waiting room couch one more time, walking nervously along the line of tiles that he'd paced a hundred times already. The sound of a well-oiled door hinge turned him quickly around. Max's wife, Francine, was coming out of the intensive care unit. Her face was white and drawn and without makeup as she stared over a long, long distance at Wager. Then she nodded and smiled.